Acts of Forgiveness

Acts of Forgiveness

A NOVEL

Maura Cheeks

BALLANTINE BOOKS

New York

Published in the United States by Ballantine Books, an imprint of Random House, a division of Penguin Random House LLC, New York.

BALLANTINE is a registered trademark and the colophon is a trademark of Penguin Random House LLC.

LIBRARY OF CONGRESS CATALOGING-IN-PUBLICATION DATA
Names: Cheeks, Maura, author.
Title: Acts of forgiveness: a novel / Maura Cheeks.
Description: First edition. | New York: Ballantine Books, [2024]
Identifiers: LCCN 2023024306 (print) | LCCN 2023024307 (ebook) |
ISBN 9780593598290 (hardcover; acid-free paper) | ISBN 9780593598306 (ebook)
Subjects: LCGFT: Novels.
Classification: LCC PS3603.H4453 A63 2024 (print) | LCC PS3603.H4453 (ebook) |
DDC 813/.6—dc23/eng/20230523
LC record available at https://lccn.loc.gov/2023024306
LC ebook record available at https://lccn.loc.gov/2023024307

Printed in the United States of America on acid-free paper

randomhousebooks.com

1st Printing

First Edition

Book design by Debbie Glasserman

For my grandmothers,
Elizabeth Parker and Marjorie Cheeks

Williams Family. *Mrs. Louisa Wade, 113 Williams Street, Hopkins, Kentucky, wants to locate her family, separated during slavery. She lost them at Little Rock, Arkansas. During slavery, they belonged to Joe Williams, whose wife's name was Sarah. There were eight children, including Mrs. Wade, Mattie and Narcissus, sisters; Henry, Moses, Bob, Tommie and Isaac, brothers; mother's name was Millie; father Flanas. If any of them live, write their sister, Mrs. Wade at above address (May 24, 1924).*

—Lori Husband, *Lost Kinsmen*,
featured in *Finding a Place Called Home*
by Dee Parmer Woodtor, PhD

Acts of Forgiveness

Marcus Revel was willing to trade the illusion of his sanity to keep his home. The day before, neighbors found signs taped lopsidedly to telephone poles, slid under their front doors, and swirling around the playground:

Last Chance Yard Sale, 237 Hortter Street

Saturday, 6 am–??

Come for the food, stay for the history you make

Beautiful antiques, funky knickknacks

Help me get my house back

The signs had appeared overnight, scribbled in what appeared to be red crayon on the backs of paper bags, but that wasn't what startled the neighbors. No, the signs were confusing because everyone knew Marcus Revel didn't own his house. Like most of them, he had traded his life savings and his John Hancock for a promise. So, Marcus Revel drew a large crowd in part because his neighbors wanted to see what the signs really meant and in part because the signs were wholly out of character for the quiet, respectable man they knew Marcus Revel to be. The Marcus Revel they knew hid signs of indignity beneath clean clothes and a well-maintained beard. Not tacked onto public spaces.

By ten A.M., the small audience in front of Marcus's house looked like the type of crowd one might see when firemen talk a man off a ledge. The old folks gripped coffee mugs while staring wide-eyed at the lawn, the melodrama adding color to their cheeks. Mrs. Solomon squeezed the hand of the five-year-old daughter she had just adopted from Macon, Georgia. A follower of Father Divine offered to lead a prayer session. Marcus's best friend, Al, tried to get people off the sidewalk and into the yard to make a purchase or two, while Marcus's eight-year-old son, Max, strutted around the yard, fingering old toys like an underpaid store clerk. The entire scene was buttressed by the smell of Marcus's piquant barbecue, wafting under the noses of his neighbors, as Marcus focused his attention on the baby back ribs that needed slathering. As much slathering as it would take for him to forget how low he had sunk.

Mrs. Solomon clicked her tongue. "Imagine, ribs at this hour. What could Marcus be thinking?" But still, she didn't move, and neither did anyone else.

Al attempted to persuade Marcus to abandon the grill and say something to the crowd.

"They want to know why they are here, Marcus. They want to know what the hell is going on."

Marcus hated public speaking, but he hated the idea of being homeless more. He walked from the grill to the edge of his manicured lawn and wiped his hands on his apron.

"I want to thank you all for coming out here so early and spending your Saturday morning with me," he said, looking at no one in particular. Marcus paused. "I am behind on my payment to Mr. Friedrich," he said, touching his short black beard and clearing his throat. "I owe him three hundred dollars, and he said he will take my house from me if I don't get it to him by Monday. Please understand I am a proud man, and this is not easy. But all I want is to provide a home for my son, and so here I am, offering what I can."

Mrs. Solomon cast her eyes downward. Others felt cherry pits in their throats. The old folks shook their heads. They didn't want to see Marcus Revel pleading on his front lawn to keep a house that wasn't even his.

"Who is that?" Lourdes Solomon whispered, pointing at Marcus during his speech.

"That is Mr. Marcus Revel," Mrs. Solomon answered her new daughter. "And please don't point," she admonished, folding Lourdes's finger back into her palm.

"Is he crazy?"

"No, baby. Just sad and desperate is all."

Marcus had been the olive branch on the stunted Revel family tree. While the other boys drank the fear of war away with cheap beer, Marcus handed out see-you-laters instead of goodbyes, talking about how great his life would be when he got back.

"I'm going to be a doctor, and I'll open up a family clinic right over there," he used to say, nodding toward the abandoned blue row home on the corner.

And the war didn't break him, but the way the country treated him afterward did.

After the war, he went to a bar once a week to drink beers with two friends from the army. One evening his friend Ron, a stout bald man with translucent skin whose life Marcus had once saved in the Serchio River Valley, handed the bartender a ball of crumpled dollars. "I'm buying the first round," he said, beaming. He told them the government was paying for his engineering degree and had backed his mortgage on a house in South Philly.

The next week, Curtis appeared with his own bold headline. The local Veterans Affairs office had backed his mortgage on a house in Wayne. Curtis's monthly payment would be cheaper than Marcus's parents' rent.

Early one morning, feeling hopeful and not without proof of concept, Marcus put on his best suit, kissed his wife and toddler goodbye, and caught the trolley into the city to meet with the local officer in charge of benefits.

He arrived at a nondescript office building on Chestnut Street, walking up to the third floor, skipping every other step. There were ten men ahead of him. Marcus sat down in the last folding chair, spreading his legs apart and bending at forty-five degrees to rest his elbows on his kneecaps. He was a tall man, and the chairs seemed built for short men too squirrelly to put up a fight. When a plump secretary in a red skirt called, "Next," and no one else remained, Marcus walked into the office, his suit jacket swung over his right arm to stanch the sweat dancing down his spine.

The officer gestured reluctantly at a chair and then looked back down at his yellow Rite in the Rain notebook.

Marcus sat wide-kneed in the black leather chair across from the officer's desk. "Good morning, sir," he said. "My name is Marcus Revel. I fought in the Ninety-second Infantry Division." The man didn't look up. Marcus spoke louder. "I'm looking for information on tuition reimbursement and mortgage-loan guarantees."

"Only get one or the other. Can't get both."

"Well. I'd like to learn more about getting the VA to cosign a mortgage. I'm looking to buy a house."

"What area you looking in?"

"East Germantown, sir. Hoping to stay close to family."

"I can tell you now, we won't be able to guarantee a loan there."

The officer was sketching what appeared to be his name in large block letters. SCOTT. A smiley face filled the O and he had shaded around the T's to make them look three-dimensional. Marcus wondered whether it was the officer's first or last name.

"I can be flexible," Marcus said. "Where can you guarantee a loan, then?"

SCOTT glanced up, looking through Marcus, as if trying to see if it were possible for a suit without a face to speak. "I'm going to be honest with you," SCOTT said, placing his pen down slowly.

"The VA is not going to guarantee your loan. I suggest you investigate alternative methods."

"Excuse me." Marcus cleared his throat. "I don't want to overstep, but I know a few people who have received these benefits."

SCOTT stared at him for what felt like minutes but must have only been moments. "No, you excuse me. I've got some other business to attend to."

Marcus looked at the officer and the stack of paper on the man's desk. He thought about the papers' sharp edges and their ability to slice a thin, clean cut into his fingertips. How even the most innocent objects can be used to draw blood.

Back home, his wife was agitated. "Why didn't you push him, Marcus? Tell him you have friends who have gotten the benefits?" Sweat glistened on Dorothy's hairline as she flipped sausages. Max, balanced on her hip, started to cry, reaching for her headscarf. "I can't live with your parents anymore, Marcus."

When Mr. Friedrich drove through town, promising affordable houses on a layaway system, Marcus forked over all he had for 237 Hortter Street, to keep his wife happy. With a house he couldn't afford and the inability to secure steady work, Marcus began to feel like he was drowning, and to keep himself afloat he started cooking. He cooked chitlins and fried chicken and cornbread biscuits. He made anything he could think of with the groceries he could afford. The old folks, smelling the fruits of his labor, shook their heads. It smelled like someone who cooked because of a bad taste in their mouth.

An incessant, unemployed cook was also not what Marcus's wife signed up for, and one day he came home to find a note taped to the kitchen table, informing Marcus she had gone out to find herself a life.

A few years had passed since then, and now, Marcus Revel turned slowly back to the grill and didn't turn around again until the streetlights flickered on one by one. The old folks had wandered home to eat dinner. Mrs. Solomon had left to get better acquainted with her new daughter. Al handed him the old coffee tin set out in the sun to collect money. Its insides were lined with $305.75.

Marcus and Max went inside their house, the draft from the front door causing the American flag on the front porch to swirl softly upward. Inside, father and son were wrapped in an echo, most of the rooms now empty. Marcus sighed a brief release of relief. But Max. Max looked up at his dad and learned a lesson his eight-year-old brain never forgot: You can beg for what you want, but once you get it, you could still be left empty-handed.

"The results of the study confirm what we have long known to be true. That the tentacles of slavery are far-reaching. They have ripped our moral fabric, morphed our systems, and distorted our laws. But let me be clear: Slavery is only an animate, living thing because of what human beings did to other human beings. Moreover, the harm perpetrated on African Americans by the United States government goes beyond slavery. It includes a compounding list of harms directly aimed at destroying the wealth and freedom of Black citizens. When I was elected, I vowed to make sweeping changes to move our great nation forward. As president, I intend to chart the course that my ancestor, Andrew Johnson, regrettably reversed. I intend to support the Forgiveness Act."

—PRESIDENT ELIZABETH JOHNSON,
September State of the Union Address

Chapter 1

The diner was full of people who wanted to be around others the day the Forgiveness Act passed the House. The proximity to precedent felt good. There was no danger, no history yet, per se, no need to stop routine completely, so it was enough to sit in the old diner at the blue-speckled tables with scrambled eggs and large steaming mugs of coffee. Enough to ask the person next to you to pass the ketchup and also whether they thought this would go anywhere. "Not in my day" was often the answer. Enough monotony rubbed off of a dreary fall day for neighbors to linger and comment that Forgiveness would never pass the Senate, as the anchor announced the House's intention to vote on it in the evening. The country, the city, the diner—connected by the same wavering thread of expectation.

As Willie hurried in, she took up her usual stool beneath the television and tried to look optimistic, but she had imagined when a moment like this one came she would be sharing the news not watching it. Writing about representatives wrangling last-minute votes, what families needed to do to prepare for its passage—not sitting, as she was now, thirty-four years old in the same town where she was raised. Most days she successfully calmed the disquiet, but today she couldn't help it and picked silently at her life choices like they were scabs.

Vice president . . . at her father's construction company.

Mother to a precocious daughter . . . from a one-night stand.

Loving parents . . . whom she lives with.

The second half of those ellipses ruined the mirage.

For a long time, she was buoyed by the belief that change was around the corner, and now that it was here, she realized she should have been more specific in her faith. The Forgiveness Act, for many reasons, threw this into sharp relief.

A waitress arched her back against the counter and pointed the remote at the television, inching the president's voice up several decibels. Everyone in the diner talked over one another, and it was possible to hear both the din of the restaurant as one throbbing sound and the individual pieces of conversation. The men next to Willie threw their voices at the screen as though President Johnson stood ready to take their orders from behind the bar.

"Fifty bucks she's on here tomorrow saying the House delayed the vote."

"It doesn't work like that."

"How do you know how it works?"

"At least she's not using war as an excuse."

The man to Willie's right, whose bald head glistened underneath the harsh fluorescent lights, jabbed his knife at the screen. "She's alright. I'd let her forgive me."

"What are you even talking about?"

"I'm talking about her priorities and how they're on straight. They keep killing us, and while everyone else wants to pause and look abroad, she's trying to start fixing what's broken."

Willie squirmed in her chair, sighing, and they turned to look in her direction. "Well, what do you think?"

"I think Johnson's alright." She took a sip of coffee and contin-ued staring at the television, unable to tell them that she'd ex-pected to feel a sense of release, or excitement, that hadn't yet arrived.

The men shook their heads and exchanged glances that man-aged to lament the state of all young people of Willie's genera-tion.

Suffice it to say that it is not whether we, as a country, should make amends, President Johnson continued. *It is that despite the fact noth-ing can ever atone for the injustices, we should still try. With approxi-mately forty million Black Americans in the United States today, the amount owed to each African American with an enslaved ancestor is $175,000 per person. This amount will help us begin to close the racial wealth gap in our country.*

An angry grunt escaped from the gray-haired man to Willie's left. "Doris, can you turn this down? Not all of us want to listen to this Forgiveness shit."

The mood shifted as the men at the other end of the counter looked at one another, now lamenting certain white people of their own generation. A young mother who had been watching the screen expectantly turned back to her toddler.

Doris ignored him and looked at Willie. "When is your mother coming in? I need to talk to her."

For a moment Willie stared at Doris, whose eyes reflected the concern of someone who still saw her only as a child. "I'm not sure," she replied, shifting again on her stool.

"Tell her I want to talk to her. See, there's this—"

Willie, clipping a ten-dollar bill on top of her check, cut Doris off by saying she had to get to work. Waving goodbye, she stepped out into the thick September air to begin her short walk to the office. The sky was devoid of clouds, stamped instead with the faded color of worn-out leaves. The familiarity of her surroundings made her a stranger to herself. Rather than Forgiveness allowing her to put a name to her anxiety, as national events tended to do, it instead confused her senses.

Years ago, she had been told that the point of a family business was to be in control of your own destiny. For Willie, it had meant the opposite. The business that her father created out of dust and broken promises slowly rose to suffocate her even as it gave her life, gave her family certain freedoms.

Her father made her mother believe it. And then her mother made her believe. The business became bigger than itself even as it was their lifeblood. And there was nothing to do with outsize false hope except continue to believe. So believe she did, because there was no other choice. What right did she have to help white people write about art and politics and books when her family needed her? It was one thing to feel like your sacrifices were worth it but another to feel like you sacrificed for nothing. Was it possible to be a good person if you were always resenting the sacrifices you made to be good? Maybe part of her never lost the belief that Max's work was more than a paycheck. She had wanted to believe it was true.

At work, as she stared out of a window in her office, she saw not the trees outside or the train station across the street but the man on the other end of the phone line, his thumb hooked through his belt loop, impatient to end the conversation, and wondered if he could hear the anxious rattle in her voice. She did her best to sound resolute, knowing the key to making someone think they had to pay was making them think she'd never give in.

"Patrick. Patrick," she repeated. "The payment was due a month ago."

"I can't give you a better answer than the one I already gave you."

"Which wasn't an answer."

"It's the best I can do until I know more on my end."

She walked over to sit at her desk, fingering the professional symbolism of her small diamond studs, and bit her tongue—if not the best journalism technique Alfie Cane ever taught her, at least the most useful.

"Look," Patrick finally sighed. "There's a holdup with the FTC, okay? There are some concerns that our latest acquisition is going to be blocked."

Willie raised her head and looked out the window. "And what happens if they block the acquisition?"

"We pause construction. Probably try to find a buyer for the lot."

"The kill fee is $175,000." The irony of the amount made a bitter laugh whisper through her throat.

"Ms. Revel. Willie. We wouldn't be killing the project; the

government would be. Either way, we should know more next week."

Her chest constricted unceremoniously. They were never going to get this money.

"Your late fees are still accruing, whether you pay the kill fee or not. Let me know where things stand as soon as you can." Before she could catch herself, she told him to have a good weekend.

She watched as a train pulled slowly into the station across the street. It opened its doors as if yawning, not letting anyone but the ticket agents off. At this time of day, people were preparing to go into the city, not return from it. She watched the commuters on the platform playing Friday's rhythm, their bodies relaxed with the weekend's promise of respite ahead. A man waiting to board the train patted his jacket pocket and then jogged back to his car. Two women wearing pencil skirts and sneakers gripped large tote bags on their shoulders like workplace Barbies. Commuters coming from comfortable lives who would return to houses filled with children, fridges filled with food. Houses similar to 512 Lewaro Street in their outward façade and dissimilar in the ways all houses are dissimilar because of the people inside them. The train filled slowly with passengers, and Willie kept her eyes on the ticket agents, who laughed at something on their phones. She was embarrassed by the quick flash of jealousy that pierced her.

Willie flicked off her left sneaker and rolled her ankle on the carpet. She tossed a little rubber earth in the air a few times and caught it, dipping her head back between her shoulder blades to look at the popcorn ceiling. She was methodical and circular in her worrying. If they paused work, they wouldn't get paid. But the more they worked, the more the costs added up. She ran through the company's projects in her head. If she dropped down to a skeleton crew with Patrick, she might buy some time. Then she could reallocate the most effective guys to their jobsite at Drexel. She nudged her computer awake to look at the same page she had been staring at for the last month: At this point the company was $150,000 in debt because the union had raised rates, their projects weren't meeting the timelines, and certain clients had chosen to voice their opposition to Forgiveness by punishing Black-owned businesses. The irony, once again, was not lost on her—that despite how much she had wanted the Forgiveness Act, despite her family eschewing handouts, they were now in need of the money.

When she saw the headline SOTERIA WINS CITY RECYCLING CON-TRACT, she tossed the rubber earth in the air once more, watching the blue of the oceans rotate. Soteria, one of the largest employers in Pennsylvania, was run by a man named Hank Lasure and would need a company like MRA to fulfill his obligations to the city. When she was a journalist, a man like Hank would have occupied her mind for reasons opposite than he did now. Hank believed that Forgiveness was unnecessary, dangerous, too expensive, would cause inflation. His company, Soteria, he wrote, was doing much more to create equity than a piece of legislation serving as a handout to unqualified takers. His work in Philadelphia was the way forward. Anyone who took the Forgiveness money, he claimed, was weak. She reread the memo he had sent her father: *Soteria is buying a lot on Columbus Boulevard, and I'd like to work with MRA on the development. It would start with this one com-*

plex, and my hope is to then form wider partnerships with the city on different municipal projects. If all goes well on the initial contract, I would like to continue working with MRA for the long run. Now she was supposed to see him as an opportunity, not a problem or a story.

She dropped the earth and sat at her desk, thinking on what to do.

The place where she'd spent nearly every day of the past eleven years made her feel unmoored. There was the table she and Lourdes had recovered from an estate sale on the Main Line, covered on one side with papers, the other half branded with permanent marker from when her daughter had accidentally colored through an assignment and damaged the wood. Paloma was inconsolable afterward, crying and apologizing, unable to catch her breath despite Willie telling her it was fine, the table was old. Her sensitive daughter nearly came undone at her small mistake. There was the bookshelf in the corner, filled halfway with an awkward mix of construction management books, historical fiction, and essay collections. A framed journalism award from college bookended one side of the shelf. Below that sat a framed photo of her with her best friends, Nell and Celine, laughing at some inside joke they have all long forgotten. A stack of issues of *The Village Voice*, where she once worked, took up a corner of the bottom shelf.

The train platform outside her window was now empty. Her phone vibrated, startling her out of her stupor, and as she answered quickly, the woman announced herself as Fern Jacobs, Paloma's history teacher.

The gravelly voice asked if it was possible for Willie to come by the office. "There was a small disagreement in my class this morning."

Out of reflex, Willie checked the calendar on her phone. "Anything I should be concerned about?"

"It's the beginning of the school year. I find it best to discuss these things in person so we can start with a clean slate."

Willie hung up and thought about texting Paloma but decided against it; birds must learn how to fly and all of that. She plowed through the rest of the day, and though in a few hours they would be staring at each other over dinner, she poked her head into her father's office, savoring the unnecessary formality of telling the boss she was leaving.

Twenty-two

Years

Earlier

Chapter 2

Wilhelmina Revel stood panting in the kitchen holding glasses of ice water as guests mingled on the other side of a pair of swinging doors. She steadied her breathing, wanting desperately to reach into a glass and trace an ice cube along her forehead. Instead, swiftly stoic, she took a deep breath and walked into the room on the balls of her feet, despite this causing the ice water to dance in the glasses. She hoped it made her seem older—fifteen or sixteen, instead of twelve. She scanned the room for Andrew, her father's employee, the reason she was out of breath and late. There were, she guessed, roughly forty people in the dining room, the women's high heels sinking into the rug like index fingers poking into dough. The room was both long and wide, with a mahogany table in the center decorated with her mother's white and yellow orchids. It smelled faintly of the women's perfume and grease from her mother's black-eyed pea fritters. Council member Graves, a short man with tufts of black hair at his temples and small, welcoming eyes, stood talking in a corner with her father. Professor Cornelius and Sadie Washington stood by the windows, looking out at the Japanese maple. Sonny, one of Max and Lourdes's oldest friends, sipped a scotch and glanced around for a group to align himself with. Reggie, a former Panther, stood talking to her mother, who wore a black silk dress with orange fringe at the wrists and a gold cross, her brown hair pinned on one side behind her ear, the most beautiful woman in the room.

Since the parties began in her family's new home, she and Andrew had been placing bets on how many neighbors would draw their blinds. Once her best friend, Nell, distracted Lourdes, Willie would mount her bike and pedal up the gravel driveway, snaking between all of the cars, racing around the cul-de-sac, counting how many families had closed off their houses as if preparing for a tornado, a few eyes always visible around a bend in the shades as they peered out at the elegantly dressed guests. The escapade took Willie less than seven minutes but, even so, Lourdes threatened to not let her help with the parties if she caught her performing the stunt one more time. Willie considered the threat incredibly unfair because Willie, unlike her brother, understood that her parents' salons were more than parties. They signified something important, something changing in her city and in her family, and she didn't want to miss being a part of it. Her bet with Andrew was *her* way of seeing how much had changed and how fast. She couldn't understand her older brother, Seb, hiding away upstairs with his old radios without any interest in seeing the guests, her mother allowing it for fear he might cause a scene.

Anyway, this party was different from the others. Last week, the day after Mother's Day, a boy at an elementary school not far from Willie's school had died of lead poisoning. A lot of parents thought it was the school's fault, but no one in the government was listening to them.

Her mother had stood frozen in the middle of the room with her oval fingernails digging into her hips as the news announced the boy's death and played interviews with the parents who for a year had complained about the school's conditions.

"What makes them think it happened at the school?" Willie asked.

"Because his parents tested their house, so they know it wasn't there," Max explained.

Her grandfather Marcus grunted. "Lead poisoning. An acceptable way for Black children to die apparently."

Willie stared at the TV, recognizing the school's playground, which she passed every day, and wondered how so many angry, beautiful parents could be so easily ignored.

"If there was even a question of this shit going on at a school somewhere else it would be evacuated before I could finish this beer." Marcus drank down his Heineken and sat back in his chair, yelling for Seb to bring him another.

"We have to do something," her mother said. Willie looked around and felt ashamed at their neat cleanliness, the fresh grass gleaming neon on the other side of the sunroom windows. What could they do?

But her mother was a woman who saw problems like a two-way mirror, and it was often her reflection that presented itself as the solution. So she organized a party—this party—to raise money for the boy's funeral and to get people to sign a petition urging an investigation into lead paint in the neighborhood's schools.

Her mother was a woman who prized the illusion of perfection and order. Up until the first guest arrived, Lourdes adjusted refreshments on the sideboard, trying to appear casual as the start of the party approached, as though someone else helped prepare the sweet potato pie and mustard chicken and she was merely applying the finishing touches. Instead, Willie knew, her mother had spent two days cooking and cleaning the house from top to bottom. If the party was on a Saturday, by Wednesday Willie would have ironed the tablecloth and linens. Each Revel had assigned tasks: Max and Seb cleaned out leaves and bugs from the pool. Willie, in addition to the ironing, hand-washed the Wedgwood china. All in all, it took them three days to prepare for one of her parents' salons, but her mother wanted it to look effortless, as though in addition to trading up zip codes six months ago, they had also traded up in other luxuries as well, like household help. Her mother wanted it to seem as if they hadn't changed at all since moving to 512 Lewaro but also as though they had always lived there.

A Macon orphan raised in Philadelphia, Lourdes had found her home with the boy across the street. When she and Max were kids, Lourdes liked to remind anyone who would listen that Solomon was only her adopted name. "I could be a princess, or I could have the blood of a madman in my veins," she would say, baring her teeth like a vampire. This was the rationale for Max's proposal. "If you don't like your last name, how come you don't take mine, then?" He asked her four times to marry him and she refused. The fifth time she said yes. A week after their high school graduation, they were married in the Solomons' backyard, with white Christmas lights strung across the bushes. Since Lourdes didn't know where she came from, Max promised to give her roots from which to grow.

The house at 512 Lewaro Street meant more to Lourdes than she dared to admit. It was like a phantom limb. Surely there were leaking pipes in the basement, corners she forgot to clean, or parts of the ceiling buckling from moisture. But it felt as though she knew every last inch of it, felt as though the house told her what it needed and vice versa. It wasn't so much a vain obsession as it was a map on which she had charted her identity; 512 Lewaro Street was the first thing she owned that other people wanted. And the journey from a house to a home? There was no other journey worth taking.

Lourdes knew her greatest superpower was to help others see theirs. She made space for others. She appreciated the way pine needles fell onto bushes on a windy fall day, creating a lattice. She knew what looked good and how to design beautiful and elegant rooms that still felt lived-in, welcoming. She made soulful meals from scratch and from memory. She read voraciously. Lourdes was smart enough to know she could have been more than Max Revel's wife.

On this unseasonably chilly Saturday in May, like every Saturday of a party, 512 Lewaro Street was not just a place but a destination. The nearest train station was a thirty-minute walk, and no one wanted to risk scuffing their shoes or breaking into an unseemly sweat, so people drove from downtown Philadelphia and various suburbs. Since so many people drove, the driveway was lined with cars, which spilled into the street like dominoes. When Willie stared at all the cars, she felt famous and important, knowing each car meant at least one person had traveled all the way to their home just for them. Every now and then, a guest would be too drunk to drive home. Lourdes kept the spare bed on the third floor made up with fresh cotton sheets. A few people tried to secure the third-floor bed on purpose, but her mother had a way of knowing who was truly inebriated and who only wanted to stay over to snoop. "What if you make someone drive who's too drunk?" Willie asked.

Her mother winked at her. "The snoopers always carry a larger purse."

Willie spotted Andrew by the hallway and started toward him, asking along the way if she could offer anyone water. The party had an air of forced somberness. People would be laughing and joking one minute and then would lower their voices and look down into their glasses the next. "So sad what happened to that boy." "They wouldn't handle a school in a white neighborhood like this." "We will make sure they look out for our babies. Trust me."

As she waited for Andrew to finish his conversation, she watched her mother collect empty wineglasses and disappear into the kitchen to refill them, always striking the careful balance between host and participant. Guests would wait for her mother to come back into the dining room and would touch the small of her back when she reentered, speaking closely in her ear. The women always pointed out something about the design of the room—the green settee in the corner or the Fabergé egg in the glass case on the far wall—using it as a springboard to compliment Lourdes on how well she had decorated the entire house. But the men would ask her opinion about politics, about organizing a fundraiser or what she thought about the police commissioner's recent handling of a case. Willie was never sure if they were flirting with her mother or genuinely interested in her responses. When Max's company began winning jobs with the city, he often met with officials in the sunroom of the new house. Lourdes would greet them at the door, so that by the time they met Max, their bodies and minds were relaxed and supple.

When Andrew was alone, Willie hurried over to relay her report: The McGuinnesses, Urlachers, and Smiths had all closed their blinds by the time she was on her bike.

"I even heard Calvin McGuinness yell to his wife to turn the lights off!" Willie whispered, giggling.

Andrew shook his head and handed her a dollar. "I was really hoping we'd get it down to at least two."

"I still saw them looking." Willie fanned herself like a socialite. "They can't help but stare."

Andrew laughed, placing his finger over his lips. "You're going to get me in trouble."

"What are you two snickering about over here?"

"Your neighbors," Andrew told Max, who had appeared next to them and wrapped his arm around Willie's shoulder.

Max smirked. "You hate the neighbors. But you don't mind using our pool, do you? Anyway, keep it down. There are neighbors here."

"Neighbors from the old neighborhood don't count, Daddy," Willie said, causing Max to raise his eyebrows. "Sorry, sir."

"Just don't let Lourdes see you two betting."

Willie exhaled, relieved at this pacified reaction. Ever since Max had moved the family into their new home, he was more measured in his responses, as though the increased square footage brought with it a certain license to be subdued. It had taken them several tries to get a house. Every time her parents came home excited about a new one, the realtor called later to say the sellers had reconsidered. When they finally got 512 Lewaro Street, she was grateful for how much more at ease her dad seemed. They were the first Black family to move in on the block, and it felt to Willie as though there were twenty eyeballs peering out behind curtains, wanting to ask what they were doing there. Two days after they moved in, she came home early from school and there was a small burning cross on the lawn and a noose hanging from their mailbox. She looked around her, but the street was deserted. Her mother was out, and Max was at work, so she gripped the straps of her backpack and sprinted past the emblems, opening the door to an empty house, the fear mostly dissipating once she was inside. Despite knowing the cross and the noose were meant as warnings, she felt safe behind her family's closed doors, as though no one could break what they were building.

The entire Revel family philosophy rotated on the axis of visibility: to resist the space between others' perceptions and your own perception of yourself. The visibility that made it necessary to succeed also made it feel impossible. When they discovered who the unimaginative soul was that planted the cross and noose (a pimply, brooding teenager a few houses down), Lourdes and Max declined to press charges. Instead, they made the house beautiful and brought the sounds of Lena Horne, Ella Fitzgerald, and Bill Withers to the street. Willie tried to show how grateful she was by helping Max at the business after school, anticipating what he might need, answering phones, making copies when he asked.

Out of high school, Max had gotten a job driving for the owner of a large construction company, a white man named Francis Deed. Every morning Max picked Mr. Deed up in front of his four-story stone mansion, waiting around the corner so he would be on time without making Mr. Deed feel rushed. Every morning Max was polite and deferential, and every morning Mr. Deed acted as though he was driven by a driverless car, calling him "boy" if he called him anything at all. But Max listened as Mr. Deed gave orders to his crew. He took notes religiously on what Mr. Deed did at the jobsites, how often he went and how he organized his day. After a few years of driving for him, Max swallowed his pride and asked Mr. Deed to help him get into the union. Seven years later he opened Max Revel Associates. Once her father's construction company had partnered with a larger firm to work on a job at the university downtown, it grew quickly. As her dad's business became more successful, more important people arrived at her parents' parties. Congressmen and council members sought out her parents for advice—as though Max and Lourdes held some universal knowledge they could use to their advantage. In their old neighborhood, everyone crammed into the kitchen and living room. Here at 512 Lewaro Street, it was as though the new ideas had multiplied. Max invited more businessmen. Lourdes invited artists and musicians and professors. At first, only their friends from the old neighborhood came—Nell's parents, Sonny, Roy, and Eva—but as word spread about the beauty of the house, about the ambition of her parents, more people came, people Willie sometimes heard about on the radio. When Willie was younger, Max had told her that *HVAC* stood for *Heaven's Vaults and Closets,* and she loved imagining her father following God's blueprints, constructing worlds bigger than all of them, bigger than Earth itself.

Now her father tapped a spoon against his wineglass several times. "Can I get everyone's attention?" Lourdes switched off the music, and as Max thanked everyone for coming, Willie looked around the room. All eyes were trained on her father. She wished she could stay in that room forever.

"Last week, a family lost a bright young life. My wife had the idea to raise money for the young man's family. You can find the petition urging a more thorough investigation on the table by the door and Andrew or I can tell you who to make a check out to. We appreciate any money you can give, and we appreciate, as always, your willingness to come out and support the community." He raised his glass and people applauded.

Lourdes gestured for Willie to take plates back into the kitchen, and at the sink, Willie and Nell traded stories about what they overheard.

"I think Mr. Graves is going to have to testify."

"He will not!" Nell gasped, rinsing congealed gravy out of a saucer.

Willie nodded while twisting a plate back and forth. "They think he knows something about tests they ran at the school."

Nell, whose parents had started dropping her off without coming inside, spent most of the parties dashing in and out of the room, nervous to spend too much time around the guests. Now Willie flicked soap in Nell's direction, and Nell tossed a discarded pie crust at Willie's shoulder. The girls laughed like they were in a pillow fight.

When Willie learned the Revels were moving, she'd sprinted to Nell's house and cried at her kitchen table.

"You're only moving ten minutes away," Nell reminded her. "And you're not switching schools."

"But what if I hate the new neighborhood?"

Nell thought for a moment. "Do you have a suitcase you can fit in?" she finally asked.

"I don't know. Why?"

"If you have a suitcase that's big enough for you to fit in, I'll come to your house and smuggle you out and you can live here."

They embraced, but Willie's heart felt like it might burst through her denim jumper. She had driven by the new house with her parents, and, though it had been brief, she could tell the neighborhood was different. The few neighbors who were in their driveways all stared instead of waving. It smelled like nothing. Not onions or garlic or meat grilling. The streetlights were so bright they looked synthetic. The closest stores were on a cobblestone road with trolley tracks down the middle, and all the stores were already closed by the time the Revels drove past at seven o'clock. All of life seemed to be indoors, instead of among neighbors and friends. "This place sucks," her brother had whispered, his forehead leaving a greasy spot against the car window.

Willie tiptoed back to the dining room door and cracked it open, peering at the guests. The home and all it represented had grown on her, even if the neighbors had not. Usually, change didn't bother her (of course, until then, nothing much significant had ever changed in her life, though she liked to imagine she was flexible), but something still felt forced here, and she was skeptical of how differently people treated them. So, there was another game she played at every party (by herself, not with Andrew), which was to interview a guest so she could write about it in her journal afterward. It was a way for her to make the parties distinct in her mind so she could remember them later. She saw a woman standing by herself and pulled out the small notebook and pen that she kept stuffed in her pocket.

When her mom wasn't looking, she approached, and the woman turned and smiled, adjusting her stance to hear Willie better. Willie asked why she had come tonight and how she had heard about her parents' parties.

"I love what your parents are doing," the woman said, twisting the stem of the cherry submerged in her drink. "I love being here. It makes me feel like I'm making a difference, like I'm part of something."

Later, while Max entertained stragglers in the sunroom, Willie wrapped herself in a blanket and climbed into her parents' bed with Lourdes.

"I love this house," Willie said, yawning. "But I miss the old neighborhood."

Lourdes kissed her on the forehead. "You'll get used to it."

"Did we move here so we could host bigger parties?"

"We moved here because your father worked hard."

"But why couldn't we stay in our old neighborhood?"

"Because sometimes you have to go where you're not wanted in order to change people's minds."

Willie thought for a moment and stared out the windows. "I'm going to help change people's minds."

"Good girl." Lourdes again kissed Willie on the forehead, leaving behind a faint badge of Vaseline, like the seal on an envelope.

Years ago, in her clients' houses, Lourdes mentally rearranged furniture, swapping out pieces to create a better flow. A chestnut wood worked better than mahogany. A low bench worked better than the Baker card table the woman kept under the TV simply because it came from her mother-in-law. She never made these suggestions to the women, of course, but they picked up on her critical eye. Lourdes always showed up looking immaculate, and they often complimented her on her choice of blush or the scarf tied around her brown bob like a headband. The man who owned the cleaning company, Mr. Wingate, did not require his ladies to wear uniforms, only name tags with his logo, *Wingate Cleaners,* pinned to the front of their shirts. Even so, Lourdes often chose a crisp white button-down tucked into carefully ironed slacks, looking freshly pulled together, varied and bright, despite wearing nearly the same thing every day. One client in particular, Maude, was enamored with Lourdes, following her from room to room while sipping iced tea, asking if she needed anything, inquiring where her scarves were from or how she kept her hair straight despite sweating from the work. Because of Maude's fascination, Lourdes ventured one day to suggest she could help Maude decorate—choose a few pieces to tie the rooms together, add a bit of personality, which is what Lourdes tried to do with her own appearance, see, which Maude seemed so taken with. "Oh, I don't know," Maude said, stiffening. She looked uncomfortable and kept shaking her head. Lourdes refused to feel embarrassed. Maude stopped following her around the house after that.

The joke was on Maude, though, wasn't it? Now Lourdes wore an emerald hummingbird brooch on her blouses instead of a *Wingate Cleaners* name tag, and she has decorated Lewaro Street with a different floral theme in every room and unique antique pieces, which even the white magazines have asked to take pictures of.

"When are you and Nell going to stop serving at those parties?" her brother called out as Willie passed by his open door on the way to her room.

"We like going to the parties," Willie protested, leaning in the doorway.

"It's all a joke."

"No, it's not."

Seb laughed without looking up from the radio he was repairing on the carpet. Willie searched for a comeback. "You don't like the parties but you like the house, don't you?" she said, copying what Max had said to Andrew.

Again, Seb only laughed.

Her brother had not wanted to move and was on a quest to distance himself from the family in an effort not to seem like a sellout to his friends. He tried to bring Willie along with him, regaling her with the unglamorous aspects of Max's business, but she refused to listen. "It's cool Dad runs his own company," she sighed.

While her friends were outside playing double Dutch or tag on the sidewalks in the summer, Willie went to work with Max. She carried a red leather purse she pretended she needed so she could be like her father, who carried an alligator leather briefcase. Really it held only her book, in case she got bored, a few pens, a notepad, and cherry-flavored ChapStick. When they moved houses, Max also moved the company closer to Lewaro Street, into the first floor of a row home that shared space with an insurance agent. It was across the street from a train station, so rent was cheap. In the summer mornings, Willie sat in the bay windows of a spare office and stared at the commuters going into the city for work, making up stories about their jobs and the families left at home. When the phone rang, she sat at a desk and cleared her throat, trying to make her voice deeper, before informing the caller that they had reached the offices of Max Revel Associates. Her father gave her a list of their current projects and people's names. Only if one of those people called was she to transfer them over to his office; otherwise, she took messages on a small notepad that had blank spaces for the caller's name, the time and date, and why they were calling. Every time she had a stack of five messages, she carried them into Max's office and, if he wasn't busy, read them aloud. Or she would leave them on his desk under a small business award that doubled as a paperweight.

When Seb came to MRA's office, Willie noticed how much Max's demeanor changed. He would call his son into his office to show him plans for current projects. Willie had to guess at what needed doing, but Max asked Seb if he wanted to do the payroll or accompany him to a jobsite. The difference, Willie knew, could not simply be attributed to their age difference, which was only three years. Even though Seb was the perfect physical amalgamation of their parents, it was clear he and Lourdes had more in common. They each appreciated the effort it took to make something work, whereas Max and Willie were interested in getting to the outcome as quickly as possible. But because Max focused on Willie's fragility as his only daughter, he ignored or failed to appreciate her love of the business.

Every so often, Willie discovered her father staring angrily at a large and disorderly pile of papers strewn across his desk. What frightened her, on these days, was his stillness. She considered her dad well-rounded (she'd heard a teacher use that phrase once, and she liked the way it sounded). He was stern and tough yet soft and forgiving. He sat at a desk all day but also climbed ladders and played basketball in their driveway. On these days, though, there was no softness. The vacancy of his eyes and his clenched jaw created an uncomfortable contrast, an illumination of something he usually tried to hide.

"Can I help?" she offered.

Max laughed. "There are things about this business you don't need to find out."

Willie did not understand what this meant, and she stood in the doorway pondering it, feeling agitated over her inability to solve the riddle.

"Is it a client?" she pressed. "Are you angry over one of the messages I gave you?"

"Willie. Please. Go on." He flicked his wrist toward the door where Andrew was passing by.

"Why don't you come on with me?" Andrew said, guiding her toward his desk in the main room. "Don't take it personally," he assured her once they were at his desk. "Your dad has a lot on his mind."

She spent the rest of the day trying to guess which of the names on the approved list might disappear the next day.

She began calling these incidents "the Still Moments," and they weren't all bad, because at the end of the day her dad would clap his hands, signaling he was ready to leave, and the two of them walked up to the shops on the main road. These were the days he bought the family nice things. The new neighborhood had not only more stores but an incredible variety. They were all in low-level stone buildings, and the only way to tell them apart was through the color of their shutters. At the top of the hill, Willie and Max passed the furniture store (red shutters) and a store dedicated only to spices (green shutters). There was a store dedicated to olive oil, a florist who let you pick out as many flowers as you wanted for your bouquet, three restaurants, a toy store, and a store for quilts and sheets. Willie's favorite was the florist. It was run by a thin woman named Beatrice, who smelled like the roses she sold. She always placed a stray flower behind Willie's ear. Willie couldn't help but notice how shoppers paid attention to her and Max in these new stores, in a way they didn't in the old neighborhood. They looked by pretending they weren't, glancing sideways, their mouths slightly open, halfway between a smile and a gape. Often, they stared above Willie's eyes, at her hair or an indistinct point behind her.

She and Max stopped in front of the hardware store (yellow shutters). Her father bought Seb a new tool set and her mother a red gardening stool. Max wanted so badly for his family to be happy that he had a hard time noticing what made their happiness distinct from his own. He thought it could be measured by how far he and Lourdes had come, as if the purchases could stop up a hole that might otherwise drag them backward. When they got home, Willie watched as Max presented Lourdes with the stool, and she tried not to notice when her mother's smile didn't reach her eyes. Max carried the stool outside and called for Lourdes, Seb, and Willie to follow him. He began undressing, and Willie was surprised to learn he had swim trunks under his slacks. He bounded toward the pool, his legs moving so fast they looked like the spinning spokes of a Ferris wheel, until he connected with the water, a noise Willie now equated with joy. She ran over in time to see Max emerge from the water with his eyes still closed, his mouth an open circle. When Seb copied Max and dove in, Willie was even more shocked to discover her brother also hid swim trunks underneath his pants.

"Should we join them?" Lourdes asked, tucking Willie into her side.

She and Lourdes changed into their swimming suits and held

hands as they jumped into the deep end of the water. Her mother, wearing a white swim cap, pretended to be angry when Max tossed a palmful of water in her direction.

The next time her dad had a Still Moment, she thought, she would suggest they go home and get in the pool.

The house was big enough that when she wanted to disappear, she could. Her favorite place was a wall in the garden behind where the pumpkins and eggplants grew. Though the leaves were sticky and sharp and sent pricks into her shins, she liked the idea of hiding in an open space. The rest of the garden was sprawling, large enough it could have fit their old house on the lawn next to the pool, with more grass and oak trees to spare. There were other advantages too. At the old house, she had to contend with Seb's discarded projects on the floor, which she tripped over in the night, but here she could decorate her own room. On the flowered wallpaper, Willie hung large sheets of paper on which she wrote her musings about the world. She had a pile of magazines stacked as high as her small blue desk and a dresser littered with notebooks and pens; her own twin bed, covered in a new green-and-blue bedspread, her own desk, her own dresser, even her own globe-shaped rug. For Willie, the house was a dream. The issue was what lay beyond it.

"'I'm Wilhelmina. You can find me by the pool,'" Damien mocked her at lunch.

"She's too uppity to talk to us."

"I'd talk if you said something interesting," Willie retorted, yawning.

"Leave her alone!" Nell yelled. "You're all just jealous you aren't invited to the parties."

"Oh no," another gasped. "Could it be? I think you should go to lost and found and see if they have your Black card."

Willie tried not to care, but she wondered if Damien was right. Were the house and neighborhood changing her? It'd been only a year, but in her room she examined herself in the mirror, turning from side to side, studying her profile. She looked the same, changing out of the cardigans and loafers her mom bought her as soon as she got to school so none of her friends noticed. So if it wasn't looks, what was it? She still joked and laughed and played the same games. But now that she wasn't around on the streets after school, she could count the stories they told about things that happened after she was already back at home. Was she becoming something else without wanting to? On her wall she wrote: *Can you remain the same inside, no matter where you live?*

She figured one way to understand it was to understand more about her family, what made her who she was. On nights when her grandfather Marcus came over for dinner, Willie asked him about his childhood. He told her about Natchez, Mississippi, where he lived on his grandfather's farm. Stories about the river and its vastness, about the bluffs, about the different pace of life above and under the hill. But Willie wanted more than scenery.

"And then you moved here? For work? Did your grandparents come with you?"

Her grandfather's eyes clouded over. "Stop asking all these damn questions," he told her.

—

One summer morning when Willie was approaching eighth grade, Lourdes carried folded laundry into Willie's room and informed her she had an interview at Walton, the private school near their house.

Willie stretched her legs out in front of her and continued reading her book. "I'm not going."

"Excuse me," Lourdes said, handing the laundry to Willie, "don't use that tone in my house. And it wasn't a question, so I don't need a response unless it's to ask for more details about the school."

"Why do I need a new school?" Willie balked. "My grades are fine."

"This isn't about your grades."

"No, it's about you and Dad wanting to fit into this stupid neighborhood." It was out of her mouth before she could stop herself, and it was the obvious cover for why the mothers on the street in the afternoon did not have to welcome Lourdes into their conversations, because their kids did not attend the same school. What was there to talk about if their kids didn't have the same teachers? Play on the same sports teams? Once an idea lodged itself in Willie's mind, it became impossible for her to imagine it any other way. Her mother wanted her to go to this school for selfish reasons, of that she was sure.

"Walton will give you access to worlds your father and I can't. I'm not saying you couldn't go places without it. But if you could take two weeks by train or an hour by plane, wouldn't you choose to fly?"

"Not necessarily."

"Don't backtalk me. It's settled. Don't mess up this interview."

That afternoon, Willie looked to Nell for solidarity. "Can you believe they're making me go to that school? It's all my mom's idea. My dad doesn't care. My dad would have me leave school and work with him if he could. Maybe I should just do that."

Nell was braiding her hair in front of Willie's bedroom mirror. Her eyes remained fixed on her fingers as she sat cross-legged on the carpet. "It might not be that bad," she said, shrugging.

Willie narrowed her eyes. "I thought you would be sad. I thought you'd offer to wheel me away in a suitcase again."

Nell sighed and met Willie's eyes in the mirror. "I am sad," she insisted. "But you might fit in."

"What is that supposed to mean?"

Nell swept her arm around, indicating the room but also the entire house, the neighborhood.

Willie expected nothing much from Walton. Since her old school had been easy for her, she thought Walton wouldn't be much different. But the lessons were convoluted and dragged on. The class size was a third of what she was used to, and when the classroom door clicked shut, the instant hush that overtook the room made her tremble.

She tried, with as much good faith as possible, to approach her new environment with optimism. The classrooms were brighter and cleaner, with plants on the windowsills, growing toward the sun. There were plush leather lounge chairs thoughtfully placed throughout the library, and each classroom had a fresh coat of grayish-beige paint.

For the first couple of weeks, Willie felt like a shop window, one of those opulent displays people stared at during Christmastime. No one was mean to her, but no one was nice either. In the cafeteria she approached a table with the three other Black students in her grade. "Can I sit with you guys?" One girl nodded and pulled out the chair next to her.

"Cool bracelet," she said, gesturing to Willie's wrist.

Willie looked down at the green beads Lourdes had given her and shook her wrist. "Thanks. How do you guys like it here?" Willie asked, pushing the small portions of food around on her plate.

One of the other girls shrugged and told her it was fine, easy but boring. They told her which teachers were insufferable, which ones were not to be trusted. For a few days Willie relaxed, believing she had found her friends, people to make the next few years bearable. But on Friday, Lourdes picked her up in the new Cadillac Max had purchased, and on Monday, when Willie went to sit at her usual table in the cafeteria, the girls laughed and whispered but grew silent when she approached. The group turned mean and dismissive, making fun of the way she pronounced certain words, of the ribbon that she had tied around her relaxed ponytail. Willie folded her hurt into her pride and turned inward. Each morning, she put on the armor of her uniform and a smile that placated both the adults and her classmates and chewed on the plan crystallizing in her mind. She still helped in the MRA office after school and on weekends, and because her dad resisted hiring more people, she knew he needed her—even if he wouldn't admit it. Perhaps she could go to work for Max. She'd be so good, so indispensable to her father, that he might suggest to Lourdes she leave school, maybe be homeschooled. Her mother would agree once she understood how much Max needed her.

In class, Willie smiled to herself, thinking she would one day take over the family business; maybe she could start training after her fifteenth birthday. She would be the first woman to run a construction company and would move the business into a larger building in the city, instead of the small space it was in now. Then, once the business was downtown, she would buy a home in Rittenhouse, close to the restaurants and shops where she would entertain and throw even better parties than her parents had.

For several days, Willie tried to find time alone with her father to update him on her plans, but he was always busy or on his way to an appointment. "When I get home, baby girl," he told her, kissing her on the forehead.

One night at dinner, when she had planned to speak to him, Max was particularly agitated. "They keep pricing me out," he said, referring to suppliers. "I won't break even. They're quoting me three times what they're quoting the other guys."

"I have an idea," Willie said.

Lourdes shook her head. "Not now, baby."

Willie pressed on anyway. "I thought I could leave school and go to work for you, Dad. Just a few days per week at first, and then full-time."

Her parents stopped eating and stared at her. Seb looked on, amused.

"How do you mean?" Max seemed bewildered.

"I help you a lot anyway, so I thought it could make more sense for me to start working full-time. I could be homeschooled."

Lourdes pushed air out between her teeth and stood to take

her plate to the sink. "I see you must be studying comedy at Walton."

"You can't work for me full-time. You're too young. Seb, on the other hand," Max said, turning toward her brother, "we can start considering. I have to go to the job at the hotel tomorrow. Come with me."

Seb feigned remorse. "Sorry. I have a test I need to study for."

"He doesn't want to work for you. I do."

"She's right," Seb added.

"You're not leaving school," Lourdes said. "Have you lost your mind?"

Willie forced herself to remain calm. She only had to explain why it made sense. But when she looked at Max, he was still staring at Seb, hoping Seb would want to work at the company, and it finally dawned on Willie that her father might never see her. Willie realized that being overlooked was beginning to be a theme in her life, and she did not enjoy it. She concluded that she needed a new dream. One in which people took her seriously and respected her opinions.

"Never mind," Willie said, shaking her head. "It was a stupid idea."

Willie searched for new activities to fill her time. She became friends with a girl named Celine, who encouraged Willie to join the school paper.

"We can write about basically anything we want," Celine said, blowing a bubble despite gum being forbidden in school. "I've seen how Mr. Grey reacts to your papers in class. You'd like it."

She thought back to how she interviewed guests at her parents' parties and couldn't believe she hadn't drawn the line. The first time Willie saw her name in print, she understood what she wanted to do with her life. Maybe she had always known but hadn't realized. For the next three years, Willie spent most of her spare time working on stories for the *Walton Gazette*. It led her to think differently, so that in class, at dinner, watching movies with her family, she was both there and not there, always thinking of potential angles. It was how she made sense of and lived in this new world her parents had thrown her into. She clipped out articles she admired, underlining the names of journalists she wanted to emulate, like Alfie Cane. Over time, she convinced Mr. Grey to let them publish stories about what was happening in Philadelphia and the world generally, so long as she interviewed students and teachers about the events, tying it back to how people at Walton might be impacted. She still didn't love the school, but with the paper she was able to look at her environment objectively, like a scientist. The other students might not have liked her, but they grew to respect and even fear her. Nell and her parents complained of her being preoccupied.

"What happened to those ideas you used to have for the business?" Max would ask. "You never talk to me about them anymore. You never stop by."

"I know. I'm sorry. I'll try to come Monday," Willie apologized, but then a story would need editing or she would need to interview one more person before they went to print, and another week passed without her stepping foot in MRA. There were times when she overheard Max and Lourdes talking at night in the sunroom, her father concerned they had overextended themselves financially, and Lourdes comforting him by saying she could still pick up work cleaning houses on the Main Line. Some part of

Willie felt badly about abandoning her father in the office, but then he had made it perfectly clear there was only so much she could do to help.

As they grew older, Seb spent less and less time at home, while Willie stayed home in the library working on her stories or helping Lourdes cook and garden.

"You're going to turn into an old white lady if you don't get out of this neighborhood," Seb said, passing Willie in the library on his way out to meet friends. He leaned against the door frame in wool slacks and a blazer, brushing his edges.

"I'm going to win a Pulitzer and you'll be pruning an old white lady's shrubs," she said, glancing up from her notebook. "But don't worry. I'll lend you money."

Occasionally, with Nell and Celine, Willie continued to help at her parents' parties. Max had gotten a lucky break and won a contract from the city doing plumbing for a municipal building and Willie took note that around that same time she began to recognize fewer and fewer of the guests at her parents' parties. Sonny stopped coming altogether. The conversations she started to overhear no longer inspired her. At best they bored her; at worst they made her question the moral compass in the room.

"I don't know half the people here," Willie commented to Nell one night during a party. "Do you?"

Nell tipped a champagne glass back and swallowed the liquid bobbing at the bottom.

"The beefcake in the vest works for the mayor. I heard him introducing himself."

Willie cracked the door open and peered through. "I don't know what's worse—the fact that a guy who works for our mayor is here or the fact you think he's a beefcake."

"Says the girl who rejects every date offer at Walton," said Celine. The parties had become a testing ground for inappropriate behavior, and Celine stood by the screen door, trying unsuccessfully to light a cigarette.

"That's because those white boys don't want a date, they want an experiment," said Willie, closing the door. "And I'm not a lab."

Willie put on a good show of being self-assured, but she was unsettled, because even though she loved working on the paper and believed her calling was to become a journalist, she felt this didn't define her. This was antithetical to the way the rest of her family approached their lives. Seb was in Temple's engineering program and was glad to be considered an engineer, one who didn't want to work at his dad's construction company. It seemed simple for him: He had his friends, and he had his vision—he knew what he wanted and what he didn't. Lourdes, too, wanted a grand house with a large garden and the status and respect this brought with it. For Willie's father, his business was his identity, which, in his opinion, was as it should be for a man. Perhaps what tugged at her, Willie decided, was loneliness. Nell and Celine were her best friends, but they did little to stem the flow of eyeballs directed at her as she moved around Walton, around the neighborhood. She longed at times for her old friends, her old life, but whenever she went over to Nell's house, she felt she no longer belonged. Her oasis was 512 Lewaro Street, the place where the whole family filled each corner like batter poured into a mold. But what Seb had known and what Willie was coming to realize was that it also created a separation among those in their lives who didn't live that way.

By now she no longer needed to bet Andrew on how many of the neighbors' blinds would be closed for a party. It was no longer fashionable or convenient to be downright rude to the Revels. Instead, the McGuinnesses, Urlachers, and Smiths not only greeted them but occasionally came to a party, although they never invited Max or Lourdes over to their own homes, and it was embarrassing to see her parents' disappointment, subtle yet sharp, like a small shard of broken glass.

Her dad's job required him to put politics aside. Perhaps because of this, Willie refused to. Every now and then, when she interviewed a teacher, they divulged a hint as to their larger value system. Walton was her introduction to the differences between political parties and how these differences showed up in people. Willie found herself both annoyed and fascinated by the duality she saw in others. Her parents, for instance, who cared about civil rights but also cared about preserving their own nice things. Or her teachers, who believed one thing but taught another. She wanted to go deeper, to follow her curiosity. So Willie maintained her tradition of interviewing guests and, as it was no longer the amusing pastime of a child, her father often interjected and relieved her of her duties when the questions became more and more pointed.

Toward the end of the night, before the men retired to the sunroom with Max, Willie approached Nell's beefcake and asked him what he did for the mayor.

As he spoke, an article had taken shape in her mind. She wanted to write something that would make her parents remember who they were. She could see it made her parents uneasy, these new guests; she could see her mother gritting her teeth and smiling at these superficial, boring women. Willie wanted to shake them and ask them if what they were doing was worth it. Sacrificing what they believed in for the sake of success, a house.

"Could I interview you sometime?" Willie asked him, cutting him off mid-sentence.

"Interview me? Why?"

"We're doing a series of articles for the school paper on people working in the administration." As the words escaped her, it didn't sound like a bad idea. She wanted to publish one more important piece before graduating. She knew she could make something out of this profile that was worthwhile. She also knew her father would not want her talking to this man for her school paper, and the thought of agitating Max gave her a small dose of perverse pleasure. "Why don't you come by my office tomorrow morning? I usually go in on Sundays to catch up."

Willie eagerly agreed and, seeing her father headed in their direction, pointed to an empty plate. "I better go replenish these. See you tomorrow."

She told her parents she was going to study at Celine's and instead borrowed their car to drive downtown, parking next to a vacant lot across the street from his office, which was located on the ground floor of the housing-authority building. As she crossed the street, she was startled to realize she was nervous and was scared to admit what she was really after. When they had first moved to Lewaro Street, it had seemed an act of resistance. She wanted, in her own small way, to remind her parents of that. This man shouldn't have been in their home in the first place. So much of who they used to be was focused on helping, on creating opportunity, or at least that's what she thought. Who were they if this was no longer true?

The building was deserted except for a security guard reading a newspaper by the entrance. She nodded and gave an awkward wave to the guard, as sweat gathered like a posse under her headband. She wiped her hand along her hairline before knocking on his door. White blinds pulled halfway down, beige walls with nothing on them except one lonely diploma, a blue carpet, and a blue sofa. She filed these details away until she could write them down. He gestured for her to sit in the chair across from his desk. Willie began recording and she got out her notebook, which she awkwardly balanced on her knee like a small instrument.

She asked him benign questions about how he began working for the housing authority and what he studied in school. He thought she was nothing but a kid, so instead of downplaying her questions, he answered them earnestly. His wrist rattled as he kept hitting his fingernails against the top of his desk, and she wrote this down, how he tried to steady it but then would knock the top of the desk again, almost involuntarily. He talked and talked, and Willie was rewarded for her patience when he began telling her a story about Section 8 vouchers. "Work–life balance," he said. "This is what I do in my personal life because of working

all the time. Section Eight vouchers—you know what those are?"
Willie knew what they were but played dumb. "Can you explain?"
she asked innocently.

"I buy the apartments, then I rent them out for Section Eight
housing. But first I advertise listings to make the surrounding
area look more expensive, so I can get a higher voucher."

"You mean you advertise fake apartments?"

He smiled while nodding.

"Isn't that fraud?"

He glanced at the recorder and Willie relished the look on his
face, the look of someone who considered her to be a real reporter.

"I think that's enough for today. You got what you need?"

She nodded and packed up her things, thanking him once
more as she closed the door behind her. At the end of the hall
next to the stairwell, she stopped in front of a door with a small
glass windowpane along the top. All the other office doors were
solid wood. If she stood on her tiptoes, she could make out folders tossed haphazardly on top of a large rectangular metal table.

Without pausing to think of the consequences, she slid a
bobby pin from the back of her bun and picked the lock like Seb
had shown her. She entered a cold room lined with filing cabinets.
Willie's eyes scanned the folders, hungry for something more to
add to her story. She thumbed through the different labels and
started to tuck a sheet with addresses into her pocket from a
folder with a Section 8 label on it.

"What's going on in here?" The security guard stood, confused, in the doorway.

Willie slowly replaced a document. "I got lost."

The guard's hand moved to a radio clipped to his belt and she hastened to grab her things. "I'm leaving. Sorry. I thought it was the bathroom."

He stepped aside to let her out of the room. "You and I both know this door was locked."

Willie had forgotten that Marcus was spending the day at the house, and her grandfather and her parents sat drinking coffee at the kitchen table when she walked in. Marcus whistled through his teeth and shook his head.

"Where were you?" Lourdes asked, standing.

"What do you mean?"

"Willie, don't be smart with me. I called Celine's house. I know you weren't there."

Max held out his hands for his keys. "Explain."

"I wanted to interview someone from the party to write an article for the paper."

"Then why lie?"

"Because I knew you'd be scared about what I was going to write. Which was also the point," she added under her breath.

Max started to walk out of the room and then turned back, crouching down and putting his face close to Willie's. "I'm doing work for the city. You cannot write little stories about whatever entertains you in the moment."

Willie felt tears forming and bit the inside of her lip to keep them from falling.

"Lo, get me fed, please," Marcus said, trying to change the subject.

"Remember whose house this is," Max said.

"I'll be out of your house soon enough."

"You're right. And maybe we should cancel the graduation party we were planning on throwing you."

Willie stared straight ahead at an indeterminate point, like the people who didn't look at her in the shops. "Go ahead."

Marcus raised his eyebrows at Willie's remark but stayed quiet.

It was her parents, so of course, a few months later, there was a party. Lourdes lined the slate path with tea lights and cooked Willie's favorite foods, chicken and dumplings and apple pie with a vanilla bean custard. In the final days of school, with exams finished and the last issue of the paper having been published, she had plenty of free time in which to reflect. The night before her graduation party, she lay sprawled across her bed, staring up at the magazine articles she'd clipped from her favorite writers, collages of which now replaced the blank paper she had once used to write her naïve notions of the world. She shuffled through old pictures, pausing at one from a family vacation the Revels took shortly after moving into the house. The trip had been her mother's idea. Perhaps a way to ensure their relevance to the movement, Willie now thought. They had aimed straight for the cataclysmic point first: Greenwood, Mississippi, and a town named Money. The Revels met a man named Coov, who took them to Bryant's Grocery. They went to Birmingham and Tuskegee. They drove to Little Rock, Arkansas, and stood on the

steps of Central High School. They drove along U.S. 80, following the Selma to Montgomery National Historic Trail. Lourdes
had wanted them to go to Natchez, but when she tried to press
Marcus for details about where his grandfather's farm was, she
received only vague responses and he claimed he couldn't remember.

Max had preferred to drive, explaining that having their own
car gave them more control. It was the beginning of summer, and
the farther they drove, the more stifling the heat became. Willie
and Seb sat in the back, rubbing ice cubes along their foreheads,
while Lourdes kept changing the radio station and Max smoked a
cigar out the window, his elbow slicing through the air.

The trip might have been Lourdes's idea, but to all of them,
once they were there, it felt less like a vacation and more like a
rite of passage. When they pulled back into 512 Lewaro Street,
Max paused the car at the top of the gravel driveway. The sun
beamed down the allée and hit the yellow stucco and green shutters of the house. Lourdes teasingly asked, "Who lives here?" and
it became an inside joke among them all, to ask that as a way of
never taking their home for granted. Willie understood the meaning: You can't tour a plantation and come home to 512 Lewaro
without understanding its significance. By walking through the
front door of their home, they were rewriting history. The fact
that what they experienced might not have been about their specific people was beside the point. Perhaps this was what her parents were always trying to remind her and Seb—the house itself
would always be an act of resistance, despite whatever moral con-
cessions needed to be made along the way to keep living there.

Throughout the night at her graduation party, people congratulated Willie and told her how proud they were. As she walked around the house, she felt an itching sadness.

"Can I get everyone's attention for a brief moment?" Max asked, standing at the end of the hallway. His voice was deep and loud, and he wore a royal-blue blazer that bulged around his broad shoulders in a purposeful way, accented with a pink-and-white pocket square. He gave the impression of being taller than he really was. Stout and clean-shaven, he didn't have to work hard to capture the room. "Thank you all for coming," he said, nodding. "As most of you know, my brilliant daughter and her best friends, Nell and Celine, graduated from high school this past week. They are off to do incredible things. My daughter, Willie, will be going to Cornell to keep holding powerful people to account and to study journalism. I don't think they're ready for what my little girl will surely uncover." At this, Max paused and found Willie's eyes among the large group of people. He put his arm around Lourdes's waist, and she laced her fingers through his and nodded. "Willie, your mother and I are so proud of you. You are strong-willed. At times, stubborn. You are persistent and brilliant. We can't wait to see what you do next."

Everyone turned to look at Willie, and she knew she was expected to cry or yell out her gratitude. She stood there, one ankle crossed over the other, and yelled instead for everyone to eat up. "My mother spent three days cooking!" she shouted.

She gazed around the room, and her breath came in smaller and smaller doses. Now when she noticed the eyes on her father, she felt something changing, yes, but also something lost.

Chapter 3

Professor Cane stood silently at the front of the classroom to demonstrate a point. Willie absorbed the impatience of her classmates, the left-to-right adjustments of thighs, the bags being opened and closed, the sighing chests, and she sat still, closed her eyes, imagining that the incessant rustling came not from peers but from some unknown wiser being whom she could sense moving closer but couldn't see. Situated in one of the old halls of the media center, the classroom smelled of wet stone and dry-erase markers. She inhaled and let the musk travel through her, coating her with both a sense of discomfort and expectation.

"It doesn't matter how uncomfortable it gets," her professor said. "Your desire to be comfortable has to be less than your need to get the story."

He proffered a nearly imperceptible nod, indicating the end of class. While her classmates quickly gathered their things and filed out of the room, Willie stayed behind to finish writing notes from the class, waving off a friend waiting for her by the door.

In her first year, she was invigorated if not intimidated by the solitude, the anonymity, the promise for reinvention. In Philadelphia, her parents and her parents' friends thought of Willie and Seb as examples of progress. Though she felt alone at Walton, she understood that her presence signaled a change, and therefore the stares, or the different treatment, were all in the name of something good. Without her parents in this strange northern town surrounded by gorges, her loneliness had at first felt purposeless.

But now, in her senior year, she stopped looking like Lourdes's idea of respectability and found her own: simple clothes consisting of loose trousers or jeans, a T-shirt, a large blazer, and the occasional scarf for easy sophistication, dark colors, no more relaxers. Her freshman roommates became her friends. She had dated (sort of). Had her own voice at the paper, a voice her editor described as *unflinchingly pointed*. At night, at parties, her friends knew they had her for only a couple of hours before her mind drifted back to her stories. Constant motion at home might have been a threat—to her friendship with Nell, to her mother's expectations and wishes—but here it was expected and celebrated. What was it that Lukács said of Dostoevsky? *He describes how the soul lives its own life.*

She first met Professor Cane when he ordered from her at the café. It amused her how much one learned from taking a person's coffee order every day for four years. He valued consistency; was embarrassed when he asked Willie to remake his drink with hotter milk. She learned that he missed writing and investigating his own stories, felt teaching was more stable but less fulfilling. When Professor Cane asked her to be his research assistant in senior year, she imagined, self-deprecatingly, that it had as much to do with how well she prepared his cappuccino as it did with how well she performed in his class.

Now Willie took her time putting her notebook and pens into the designated compartments of her bag. She smiled as she approached Professor Cane's desk. "It was a good class," she reassured him.

"It wasn't, but what can you do?" He ran his hands over his hair as though to be sure it was still there. "Are you going anywhere for the holiday?" He bent to put a folder into his leather briefcase. As he did, she noticed that his shirt was untucked, and she shifted positions to keep from reaching out and tucking it back into his jeans. She imagined, for a moment, what would happen if she let her hand linger there.

"No." She shook her head. "I have too much work to catch up on." She said this matter-of-factly, not to feel sorry for herself, but was aware of how it sounded.

"You're going to burn out, and I feel it's partly my fault. Why don't you spend the weekend with us? My son will be visiting too."

Willie shifted her bag to her other shoulder. "I don't want to impose."

"You're not imposing. Come by tomorrow." He stood and smiled as if it was settled.

Afterward, she made her way across campus to the small apartment she shared with friends, knowing if they found out she was going to Professor Cane's house for the holiday, they would tease her relentlessly, aware as they already were of her crush. She looked up at the towering trees, the imposing buildings, the students splayed out in groups or buried in books, indicative of a life built on possibilities, maybe, instead of limitations, and felt content on her walk home.

Professor Cane lived twenty minutes from campus in a large brown-and-white stucco colonial. On Saturday afternoon, carrying a small overnight bag, Willie walked to his house, despite his offer to pick her up. After a while the neighborhood gave way to square houses with stone rabbits and neon plastic eggs decorating the front lawns. She stood in front of the address he had given her and peered up at the large single-pane windows, all of which were sealed shut. She knocked, and Professor Cane's son, David, opened the front door. He was of medium height and stocky build, with hands big enough to be the first thing she noticed. One of them gripped the side of the door as he introduced himself. "You must be my father's favorite student."

He motioned her inside, as though she were an electrician or handyman, and she followed him into the dark hallway, self-consciously looking down at her wide jeans and plain white sneakers. She touched a hand to her hair, which was freshly detangled but pulled back into a small puff, lacking the sheen other women had on campus. Her favorite shirt was several years old and had a small snag in the silk, which she tried her best to hide.

She had never cared much about her appearance, and now she found herself regretting the neglect. Willie took in the framed family photos in the hallway, hanging in a straight line like bread-crumbs leading to the kitchen.

Professor Cane's wife hugged Willie and thanked her for help-ing him keep reasonable hours at work. Willie flushed. She had never considered his wife, beyond being an abstract figure she knew existed. One night Professor Cane and Willie worked late in his office, talking about writing, and Willie found herself pre-tending she and Professor Cane were married, that they would go home, have dinner, and continue the conversation in bed. Lucy, his wife, was beautiful and elegant in a different way from Wil-lie's mother. She had no need for makeup, and her hair formed a gray halo about her face. She showed Willie to her room for the night, a small nook at the end of the hallway that doubled as Lu-cy's library and sewing room. Material was stacked on one side, leaving space on the other for a twin-size bed covered in a floral comforter.

"It's not much. But I hope it's cozier than those dorms they pack you all in. Make yourself at home as much as you can."

Before going downstairs, Willie stared at herself in the small mirror in the room. She had her mother's clear skin, high cheek-bones, and oval face, and she was taller than most. Unlike Lourdes, though, Willie's beauty was understated—but only because she never tried. She rubbed Vaseline onto the wrinkly crease between her thumb and forefinger and on her lips. "There is no need to be nervous," she told herself out loud.

Dinner at 512 Lewaro Street was a predictable affair. Her mother cooked, her dad sermonized, Seb ignored everyone. But in her professor's house, loud music played as Professor Cane and David set the table for dinner. Whereas Lourdes moved slowly and calmly, Lucy bounced around the kitchen, from one corner to the next. Artwork with splashes of orange and green and black covered the walls, and the ceiling was crisscrossed with wooden beams. Professor Cane patted Willie on the back when she entered.

"We're glad you're here. I told Lucy I'm mentoring the next Gwen Ifill."

Willie offered to help, but Lucy walked toward the table carrying a large serving platter and David carried out the remaining dishes behind her. "Sit, sit."

Dinner went by easily, with Lucy and Professor Cane asking her polite questions about Lourdes, Max, and Seb. Much of it Professor Cane already knew, but he laughed and commented as if learning about her life in Philadelphia for the first time. She charmed Professor Cane and Lucy, joking about her last name being an antonym to describe her personality.

"Although it could be used to describe my parents' salons, I suppose. The parties are partly what made me want to become a journalist. I used to save Professor Cane's articles in high school as inspiration." She had never told him this, and she looked over for his reaction.

Professor Cane smiled sheepishly, and Willie watched his hands as he speared fish. They were smaller than David's, though they appeared stronger, more capable.

"How did the parties make you want to become a journalist?" David asked. When he spoke to her with intention, Willie saw how much he resembled his father, and it made a whirlpool churn in her stomach. His teeth were a brilliant white and his voice was deep, giving Willie the impression he was self-assured.

"Well." She considered his question. "I was always interested in learning from the guests about why they were there and what they cared about. The parties made me realize I liked questioning people. Getting to the truth beyond what was apparent."

After dinner, David borrowed his parents' car and Lucy took leftovers to their recently widowed neighbor. Professor Cane invited Willie into his study and closed the door. The wood-paneled room was brightly lit with two metal floor lamps, and an armchair sat in a corner by the window next to a small brown sofa. Books reached to the ceiling, and newspapers were in lopsided piles on the floor. He gestured to a chair in front of his desk for her to sit on. Her professor riffled through a laminated stack of articles on a shelf behind his desk before pulling out one long page and tapping the front of it.

"This was the piece that put me on the map," he said.

Willie knew what it was without having to look. *"Jet,"* she said, taking the paper from her professor. She read his byline and looked back up.

Professor Cane sighed and leaned forward in his chair.

"Your writing is impeccable. You have the right instincts. But you write as though you have something to prove other than the argument you're making. If you're going to be successful at this, you need to stop caring what other people think of you. White people, Black people. None of it matters. Write the truth."

"I'm scared people will wonder what right I have given how I grew up."

"You're not writing personal essays."

Willie nodded and looked down at her lap. His words, she understood, were her professor's way of telling her he supported her. She imagined herself in five or ten years, accepting an award from the National Association of Black Journalists and thinking of this night, evidence she should keep pursuing this path.

Professor Cane stood and picked the article from between her fingers. He leaned against the desk, and she felt compelled to stand so she was facing him instead of looking up. Still, he was taller than she was. She wondered what it would feel like to be the type of person who acted in this moment without thinking of the consequences. Celine, for example, would act. Celine would reach up and kiss him, blaming it on their mutual attraction. Willie could do it. She could be the type of person who went for everything she wanted, including people. Reckless ambition could become reckless abandon. She had the overwhelming urge to kiss him; his lips, parted by a few degrees, looked soft yet firm. His hand held steady on the desk like a conductor pausing mid-symphony, as though he was vividly aware of every part of her body and what he had the power to make her do. For the first time, Cane seemed younger, timid, and so Willie moved closer. Cane placed his arm on her bare shoulder and rubbed his thumb in small circles on her skin, like he was trying to start a fire. When he bent down, his lips landed on her forehead, though, instead of on her own. Disappointed, she looked up.

"I should . . . I'll go start on the kitchen."

"Willie, wait. Sorry, I—"

"No. I'm sorry." She left quickly without closing the door behind her.

When Willie went upstairs for the night, she allowed her hand to travel between her legs until she cupped herself. She pictured Professor Cane downstairs, lifting her up onto his desk. He peeled off her jeans as she arched her back, and he told her they needed to be silent for as long as it took while he slipped into her and moved back and forth urgently, his eyes closed. Willie flipped over onto her stomach, so her hand was trapped underneath and her face was buried in the pillows. She moved forward and backward, picturing him unable to remain silent, as her body spasmed.

Downstairs, she heard the front door open and listened as David opened the refrigerator. She pulled on pants and a shawl and padded down the steps. David sat in the living room, drinking a glass of water. The shine of his eyes and the way his feet were propped on the coffee table told her he had been drinking. She sat down on the sofa next to him, and he offered her a sip of his water like they were siblings. Folding her legs underneath her, she turned so her back was against the arm of the sofa. She reached out and touched his forearms, which were exposed in a white polo shirt. She grazed his arm where it met his sleeve and he continued staring ahead, his jaw pulsing. She took off her shawl and folded it neatly into her lap. He set down his water glass and then leaned over, placing his lips on hers, his hands traveling to her pants. There was no feeling in the kiss. She tried to imagine his father and opened wider, finding his tongue, massaging it with her own.

She leaned back and watched his chest heave up and down. When he tried to kiss her again she held up her hand, blocking him.

"You fucking tease," he whispered. "I didn't even want you."

Willie pulled on her shawl and stood. "I know."

"Don't tell anyone about this," David told her, fastening his belt.

"I was going to say the same to you."

Early the next morning, she left a note on the kitchen counter explaining that she didn't feel well and thanking them for their hospitality. She ran all the way back to campus, her overnight bag slapping against her like a form of punishment.

Everyone else in her apartment was away for the weekend. She let herself in and collapsed on the couch. What had she done? Had she ruined her only chance at success by putting a journalist she respected in a position where sex felt attainable? She was not experienced, but she had been through enough brief relationships to know when a person wanted more than polite conversation. Though perhaps she had misread the situation. He was, after all, in his own house. His wife had just made them dinner. What could Cane possibly have seen in her except a student enamored? She brought her legs underneath her and pulled the throw hanging from the back of the couch around her shoulders. It was nearly three in the afternoon and raining outside so she convinced herself it would be dark soon and laid her head on the arm of the sofa, falling asleep. She skipped dinner and awoke at nearly nine in the evening at the sound of one of her roommates.

"Willie?" Eddie came and sat next to her, placing a bag of takeout down on the table.

She looked around her.

"Are you okay?" he asked.

She shook her head. "I'm fine."

"How was your weekend? Didn't you stay here?"

"My weekend?"

"Yes. What the hell is going on?" Eddie asked, confused.

"Nothing. Maybe I am a little sick. I'm going to go lie down."

Eddie stared at her, unbelieving, and began taking out several small containers of food. She was suddenly so hungry she wanted to take the soup from him and drink directly from the cardboard bowl. Then the image came back to her: Professor Cane touching her shoulder. She picked up her overnight bag, which was still leaning against the sofa, and went into her room. The next day she skipped class. The day after that she skipped class and called in sick to the café. "Can I bring you anything?" Eddie called. She told him no, to leave her alone. When he knocked the next day, she opened her door to find Eddie and Nell holding a plastic take-out bag and a liter of soda.

"Yell at me later for calling her. You need to eat."

"You smell like Mr. Graves," Nell said, tossing her jacket onto the floor and spreading out a blanket on top of Willie's bed. They crawled on top and ate spring rolls.

"I messed up," Willie said, sharing with Nell everything that happened in Cane's study. "He invited me over to his house and I tried to kiss him. He's never going to trust me enough to make recommendations so I can get a job after graduation."

"First of all, you didn't do anything. Why did he lean against the desk right in front of you and touch your arm? He probably didn't know what he wanted. And you were smart enough to leave before it went further. It's not your fault. You didn't do anything."

She didn't tell Nell what she had done with his son. Sometimes she thought something was askew inside her. Sex was a means to exploring an otherwise unexplored depth, yet she could never lose herself completely enough to enjoy it, and this constant awareness made her feel dangerous and untrustworthy. Men, it seemed, could have both—the control and the unexplored depths. She, on the other hand, didn't want to know what would happen if she lost herself.

After Nell left, the only way she could stop replaying the scenes from Cane's house was to work harder. She focused on her other classes and took on more articles at the paper. She kept her interactions with Cane to a minimum, nothing beyond what was required, leaving his office or classroom as soon as she could. Their communications became stilted, neither of them mentioning what happened. Once, she thought he was going to apologize, but instead he cleared his throat and thanked her.

One class Willie began focusing on was taught by a woman named Elizabeth Johnson. Professor Johnson often discussed her distant relation to President Andrew Johnson and how her lineage informed her thinking. She conducted fieldwork on economic theory and pushed students to examine their personal views about the law and society through their own experiences and upbringings. She internalized the reversal of Sherman's order and viewed civil rights as a direct outgrowth of her family's actions. A true and yet narcissistic notion, Willie thought, but she was fascinated by how much it colored the way Johnson viewed herself. The Revels weren't the type of family who sat around saying *We come from a long line of . . .* well, anything. Their conversations focused on how much Max's business would set them up for the future. Her grandfather didn't like talking about the past, and her mother didn't know her past before the Solomons, so it was hard for Willie to imagine feeling so completely compelled by the actions of your blood, generations earlier. The Revels had direction, but it was like standing on a ledge and looking upward— there was a perpetual feeling of the bottom falling out from underneath them.

One afternoon, Professor Johnson walked back and forth across the front of the classroom and asked the class whether forgiveness could be political and, if so, could it last. There were only fifteen students in the room, and she looked each one in the eye, waiting for an answer. Finally, Willie raised her hand. "No. It can't."

"Why?"

"Because forgiveness is personal. And the government can't facilitate mass forgiveness among a large group of people."

"But what if the government becomes personal? What if it's one face, connected to the original act, asking for forgiveness?"

After a few moments, Professor Johnson resumed her pacing, no longer expecting Willie alone to answer the question. Class ended before anyone else attempted to respond.

Afterward, Willie stayed behind. "I think it's more complicated than what I said," she told Johnson, approaching her desk. "I think forgiveness can be political, but for forgiveness to work, the government has to ask citizens how it can make amends. And not only ask but listen."

"Do you think forgiveness is quantifiable?"

After what happened with Professor Cane, Willie needed to

find another mentor. She knew Professor Johnson favored candor, so she pressed on. "To be clear," Willie ventured, "we're talking about whether it's possible to make amends for slavery, right? Whether you could be the face of the government and make some sort of gesture?"

Professor Johnson shifted in her chair. "Sure. That could be one aspect of political forgiveness. Yes."

"In that case, forgiveness isn't the point. But it's a nice way to convey it's not only about money."

"Forgiveness might not be possible, but we will be a weak country until we can acknowledge and apologize for our history."

"Apologies can come without the expectation of forgiveness, though, right? People have tried for reparations before, and it's never gone anywhere."

Professor Johnson nodded. "You're doing good work in this class. What are your plans after graduation?"

Willie tilted her head back uncomfortably. "I'd like to work for a magazine or paper. I'm meeting with Professor Cane next week to discuss recommendations."

Professor Johnson nodded, and Willie detected an air of annoyance. "I can also put you in touch with former students who are working in journalism if you like. Depending on how your meeting goes. Let me know."

Every year the university hosted a party for students of various majors and the donors whose money had gotten them there. As an editor at the paper, Willie was expected to attend. The room was sweltering, and all she could think about was the perpetual itch of the nylon against her warming legs. As older men asked her what she was doing there, Willie scratched her calf with her high heel.

"I'm so sorry," she said, excusing herself from a conversation. "I'm going to see if I can snatch one of those tarts I saw being passed around."

Willie stood at the pastry table and let the cascading crumbs from the tart fall into a balled-up napkin in her hand.

"Dull, isn't it?" Professor Johnson said, appearing next to Willie.

"But the tarts are good," Willie said, smiling briefly with her mouth full.

Professor Johnson laughed. "I feel like we're all playing dress-up and dancing for the devil."

"I'm not sure you can say that."

"What are they going to do? Fire me?"

Professor Cane approached and stood next to Willie at the table.

"I didn't mean to interrupt." He tapped his tumbler with his thumb and looked between the two women.

"You're not," Willie said, transferring her napkin to her other hand. "We were just talking about—"

She looked to Professor Johnson for help finishing the sentence, but her professor sipped her wine and stared at him blankly.

"Our meeting tomorrow," Professor Cane said, addressing Willie. "Could we move it to four o'clock?"

"Sure. Of course."

"Willie, there's someone I want to introduce you to." Professor Johnson set her wineglass down and walked toward the center of the room. Grateful, Willie followed. She wiped the sweat from her hands before tossing the napkin into the trash.

Maybe it was because Willie was the most outspoken in her class or because Professor Johnson was a chronic do-gooder cloaked in white guilt. Or maybe she simply disliked Professor Cane. Whatever the reason, Professor Johnson made several introductions over the course of the next few weeks. One, a former student, an editor at *The Village Voice*, offered Willie her first job.

Chapter 4

As Willie hurtled underground, the blank faces of the other passengers stared back at her in silent contemplation, and the thought of what her brother had said disturbed her. *You're living a dreamer's life.* It was said with admiration, and the hint of an accusation. Not *you're living* the *dream. A dreamer's life.* Like it didn't belong to her. Like someone else deserved it. She slid over for a woman with two large shopping bags and tried to focus on the interview. Focus instead on what her editor had said, which was, *You have potential.*

Magda Lerner, her boss, was a severe woman with a slicing laugh who initially hadn't liked Willie. "You're overeager and don't know your station," she told her during the first week. "Can't you go faster?" Willie carried a tray of coffees in one hand and a stack of interview transcripts in the other. If Magda hadn't changed her order three times and had given her exact change, yes, she could go faster. Willie balanced the tray on her knee and set the stack of papers carefully down on Magda's desk in front of her computer.

When senior staffers went out for drinks, Magda stayed behind, and Willie began doing the same, telling the other entry-level assistants she would meet them later. But often Magda didn't leave the office until after eleven P.M., and Willie ended up eating instant noodles from a bowl of hot water in her studio above a slice shop in Washington Heights. Magda didn't like to be interrupted when she worked, so Willie began leaving treats outside her door, like she was a dog being lured out of a cage. Sometimes it was food, sometimes a photo or a paragraph clipped out from another newspaper relating to a story Magda was working on.

One evening, when they were the only two left in the office, Magda approached her desk, holding out the baklava between her thumb and index finger.

"Did you bring this?"

Willie looked up from the pages she was highlighting and glanced around. Of course she had brought it.

"It's delicious." Magda jerked her head toward her office and began walking away.

An uncomfortable silence ensued once they were in the small windowless room. There was only one picture on Magda's desk, of her arms wrapped around a woman's neck, both smiling. As far as Willie could tell, Magda wasn't in a relationship and didn't have children. She never discussed family or friends. *My future,*

Willie feared yet hoped. Magda sat down at her desk and took out the deck of cards she kept in her desk drawer.

"What is it you want?"

It was an easy question to answer. "I want to be on staff as a reporter."

Magda nodded, shuffling the cards. "They will try to pigeon-hole you, you know. Give you the Black stories. The stories no one else wants."

Willie said what she believed, which was, "I want those stories."

After a silence, she asked Magda, "Well, what do you want?"

Magda sat back, surprised. They both laughed because they didn't know what else to do and because the moment seemed to call for it. "I want to be executive editor," Magda said. "I want to run my own newsroom. I want it to win Pulitzers. But you know"—Magda sat back and blew out air as though she had smelled something unpleasant—"no one understands women who want to work more than they want a family. We get punished for it."

"So, what do we do?"

"Be the best. Choose ourselves."

Selfishness, as a concept, Willie thought about often. Here she was now, thinking about it on the train. On nights when she arrived home and couldn't sleep—which was most nights—she tugged at the nagging feeling, hoping to unravel it. Her parents had sent her to Walton, sent her off to school, but now her freedom carried the expectation of a thank-you note. Nell had said much the same thing, in different words. What should they be doing for their parents? It wasn't about money—she had none of that, and neither did Nell—so much as it was about their time, their physical presence. Of course, Celine didn't understand this. There were families who believed that older generations propped the newer generations up, and then there were those who believed the opposite.

Willie had become Magda's favorite, and although Magda would never think in those terms, Willie was now the one on the subway, assigned to cover the severe beating of a Black sculptor by a white cop in Harlem.

On the train Willie kept touching the edge of her notebook, touching her pens, switching her bag from one shoulder to the other, kept smoothing her hand down the back of her head, where she used to have a pillow of curls but in a moment of brashness had cut it off before her first day at the paper.

Officer Halborne was in plainclothes at the back of the diner wearing an expression of misplaced importance when she arrived. She knew it was him—or, similarly, he knew it was her—by their mutual hesitation. She looked around, and he gave a wave that looked as if he was telling her to stop. Two discarded sugar packets, soggy from spilled coffee, clung to the saucer in front of him.

"Can I get you a coffee?" he asked her.

"No. I'm alright." She placed the recorder in the middle of the table. "Thank you for agreeing to meet with me."

He shrugged and tilted his head. When the waitress came, he ordered two coffees anyway.

He told her how he had been standing several feet away when he saw two of his colleagues confront the man. He could have stepped in when he heard raised voices, but his innate reaction was to defend, not defuse. Then everything happened quickly, though in his mind the moments slowed to an almost painful pace. He should have stepped in then, when the moments were collapsing into themselves. While he talked, she listened, and she noticed how she could hear the change in his pocket as his knee moved like a metronome, how his lips and eyes grew smaller like he wanted to keep what he was saying inside but his body was expelling it involuntarily like a bad meal. She recorded these details, all of the coffees and the hand movements and the loose change, and Magda said later those details had made the difference between her article resonating or being forgotten.

A week after the article was published, her phone rang while she was on her way out of the apartment. She assumed it was her mom, whom she had accidentally hung up on in a rush to make it to work on time.

"I'm sorry," she answered without waiting to see who it was. "I didn't mean to hang up. I'll call you back tonight, okay? I'm late."

"Hello?"

"Who is this?"

"My name is Lou. I work for Elizabeth Johnson. She was wondering if you have time on Wednesday to meet with her? She'll be in New York."

She hadn't spoken to her professor in a year, and the thought crossed Willie's mind that perhaps her professor expected more from her than she had thought. *Freedom with the expectation of a thank-you note.* "Okay," Willie said. "Sure. Where should I meet her?"

Willie, dreading the reunion with her professor, thought it could only mean admonishments for a lack of gratitude. Why else would she be summoned? A burgeoning young Black female journalist was an attractive candidate for a mentee, and the price for admission was not freedom to do as you please. She should have written her professor to share her success and sent her the article with a personal note. She was only twenty-three, but it was possible to believe she knew everything while also constantly discovering she knew nothing at all.

Professor Johnson welcomed her into a spare carpeted office with a water dispenser in the corner. "Don't worry, it's temporary," she said, gesturing to the room. They hugged, Willie relaxing against the firmness of her former professor's arms. "How have you been? I saw your article. Congratulations."

"I'm sorry," Willie blurted, immediately losing all conviction that her success was her own. "I should have sent you a copy when it came out and thanked you again. It's only because of you—"

Professor Johnson laughed, holding up her hands. "It's definitely not because of me."

"Well. You helped me get the job."

"You got the job because you're qualified."

Willie sat down, relieved. "So, what do you mean the office is temporary? You're still at the school, right?"

"I'm going to run for Senate, Willie. I have a full-time job I think you would be perfect for."

"A full-time job?"

"I'd like you to join the campaign. If you're interested."

She knew the appropriate answer, and the appropriate re-action, the one her former professor expected, was one of ela-tion. "Wow. I don't know what to say," she said, pausing. "Can I think about it?"

Professor Johnson tapped her index finger twice on top of her closed fist. "This is a good opportunity, Willie. I know you're doing what you set out to do, but you've got to keep your eyes open. There's more than one way to do what you love."

How to stay respectful?

"Of course. It's just . . . My boss and I are finally getting along, I'm finally getting assigned stories. I think I could be really good at this."

"I'm hosting an event tonight for prospective staff. Will you come?"

The event was in a restaurant off the East River. Professor Johnson, talking easily with different clusters of people scattered throughout the room, wasn't a tall woman, and preferred to stand and project her voice rather than hold a microphone. Her assistant, Lou, introduced her and she stood still, her face serious, her spine erect, and the room grew quiet. It was strange, seeing her, to think how intimately Willie once interacted with Profes-sor Johnson in the small classroom. Because of political figures wandering around Lewaro Street throughout her childhood, watching her former professor speak felt like an odd form of des-tiny she was supposed to latch on to.

Her professor spoke about her plans for governing, her plans for the campaign, and Willie glanced around at the faces conveying the same awe that used to inhabit the faces of Professor Johnson's students. Her professor had a way of taking what had been said before and recasting it as both new and inevitable.

The next evening, Willie sat in the middle of her floor and tried to reason things out. She believed Professor Johnson when she said it was a good opportunity; Willie just wasn't sure if it was the *right* opportunity for her. She couldn't help recalling *Don't fix what ain't broken* and other clichés as she made out her list of pros and cons. If she read the signs—the conversation they had when Willie was in school, the book Johnson had written, the television appearances—she guessed the Senate was only the beginning of what her former professor, a woman guided by her legacy, had planned. Willie would be stupid to miss it.

The phone rang. "Willie," her mother said when she answered. "Willie." Her mother repeated her name two more times.

"What is it?" Willie asked, frightened. "What happened?"

"You need to come home."

When she arrived at the hospital, Lourdes and Seb were sitting side by side on small white plastic chairs. She hadn't seen her mother in several months and was struck by her beauty. Her hair was straightened into a bob, and she wore a blouse unbuttoned beneath her collarbone. Seb rubbed their mother's shoulders, and Lourdes explained that Max had been up on a short ladder inspecting the HVAC at a site downtown when he suddenly fell backward, unconscious. His head had hit the ground but, luckily, he had missed the concrete by a few inches. "They think he had a heart attack." Willie took a seat next to her brother and tried to think of what to say. She had never seen her mother cry before, and she found this preoccupying her as much as the uncertainty around her father. An hour or so later her grandfather arrived, and they all sat in silence on the white chairs until the doctor came and gave them an update.

When they went in to see Max, Marcus's skinny fingers gripped his son's protruding shoulder. "You always were clumsy on a ladder, goddammit." Lourdes smoothed the sheets over Max's legs. Willie kissed her father on the cheek and stepped back, glancing out the window. She hated hospitals.

She and Seb walked in search of food, feeling uncomfortable at the sight of their father confined to the narrow bed. Seb stood back, appraising his options at the vending machine. "I have to head out soon," he said. "Can you hold down the fort for a while?"

Her brother was oblivious to the differences in how their parents treated them. He was encouraged to experiment, get his PhD, stay single for as long as he wanted. But her choices, from her parents' perspective, held the slightest undertone of selfishness. Why had she moved to New York? Why didn't she come home more? Why was she off living a dreamer's life?

When they got back to the hospital room, Max was yelling at the doctor, a forty-something athletic redhead who looked like he'd rather be anywhere than telling Max Revel he'd have to take it easy from now on. The doctor turned to face Lourdes, preferring her calm nodding to Max's insults.

"These are permanent changes, then?" Lourdes asked. "And if he makes them, you expect he'll make a full recovery?"

"These aren't suggestions. We discovered his kidneys are releasing too much renin, which is causing his blood pressure to skyrocket." The doctor turned to Max. "This is rare for someone your age. We need to take precautions. I'll give you something for the swelling in your legs, but you're not going to be able to walk more than a handful of steps at a time for the next couple of weeks. No stairs. We're going to see how the medication works for a month. Then, depending on how that goes, we'll adjust as needed. But either way there will have to be permanent lifestyle changes, or you will end up back here and next time you won't be lucky enough to have this conversation."

Max leaned back and stared at the ceiling. "You call this lucky."

The truth was, none of them had a plan for if Max couldn't work or if the business failed.

Back at home after the hospital, Lourdes heated up leftover soup for herself and Willie and sat down at the kitchen table. Instead of picking up her spoon, she stared at her daughter like she was an insurance salesman. "The recovery is going to take months, you know. He can't just rush back to work. He's going to need help running the business."

"Good thing he has employees who can help," Willie responded, pushing the limits of an acceptable tone under her mother's roof.

Lourdes shook her head. "They're journeymen," Lourdes said. "They don't know how to manage the payroll and accounting."

"Why can't Seb help?"

"He's in the thick of his program. Plus, he'd be bored. And bored people make mistakes."

"Why can't you do it? You're smarter than Dad anyway."

"I'll do some of the administrative duties. But your father thinks I wouldn't know the first thing about running that company. It would cause more stress than it's worth. He trusts you because you used to help him."

"Mom, what are you asking?" Willie began eating to quell her nerves.

Lourdes was unreachable. "You need to come home and help. At least for a while. You're hardly making any money in New York. And we can't send you any—it's too tight."

"I don't need any money from you, I told you that."

"Your dad needs you, baby."

A few days later, the doctor discharged Max with a strict regimen, and Willie stayed the night to cook dinner while Lourdes set up a cot in the sunroom so Max wouldn't have to climb the stairs.

"Sit down a minute," Max told her after they ate, as Lourdes lowered the volume on the television.

Willie scratched at a spot on her wrist while her father began a more direct version of her mother's speech from a few days prior.

"I want you to work in the business," Max said. "I want you to start now so you can learn closely how the business works."

"But I'm a journalist. I'm going to be promoted soon. And my professor, Elizabeth Johnson—do you remember I told you about her? She's going to run for senator. She wants me to work on her campaign."

They looked at her sympathetically, as if what she was saying was the furthest thing from a reality they cared anything about.

"The idea will be for you to take over MRA," Max said. "I thought you'd be excited about that. It's what you wanted."

"When I was fifteen."

"All I built will go away unless you step in. This is your legacy."

Willie searched her parents' faces for some sign of understanding. They must see how much she had made of herself in New York and how much would be lost by giving it all up.

"But I really think I could be good at this if I keep working."

"Why don't you come home for a year or two as your father gets back on his feet?" Lourdes suggested.

Her mother continued to look at her as Max nodded. He told the story he had told her so many times before, about how he had started MRA from nothing, how he had fought to be accepted into the union, how he had succeeded on his own despite his mother leaving and Marcus's drinking. The tired old tune: how they were a family trying to define a more perfect future.

"And if I refuse?" she asked.

"Disappointment carries the same weight as guilt," Lourdes said. "Remember that."

She could see now that if Max was unable to work, it was cause for panic. In her room, she called Seb and asked him if he would consider working in the business.

"No way," he said. "I can't."

"Neither can I."

"Tell them no. Dad is still young. They're worried because of the accident, but he'll be fine."

When Willie heard her mother come up the steps, she went into the bedroom and pleaded. "I can't do this," she said. "Please."

Lourdes sat down on the edge of the bed, appraising Willie. "I remember one of the first weeks at home after the Solomons adopted me. They were rushing about, trying to pull my room together, make me feel at home. And at night I would hear them whispering about how to make the numbers work. What could they give up in order to get that shirt or that piece of meat. It all seemed so hard for them. Not like they didn't enjoy having me, but the work of having me didn't seem worth it. So I asked Ida one day what made them adopt me if they couldn't afford it. She said they couldn't afford *not* to have me. Their faith told them they should have a child. They wanted one so badly that the money or lack of money didn't matter. Ida said to me, 'Money shouldn't determine whether your soul gets fulfilled.' And then this girl I was friends with growing up—beautiful, shy Italian girl—her family had no money either. She used to tell me how embarrassed she felt about her clothes, her house, her lunches. But people spoke to her in stores in a way they never spoke to me. They looked her in the eye. I never wanted you or Seb to feel shame because of a lack of money. And I wanted you to go to a nice school so even if you didn't have money, you'd have a dignity that forced people to see you. I just want to make sure we'll be okay. And I don't know how to do that without securing what your father has built. And you are the best chance at securing it."

—

Back in New York, her apartment was just as she had left it, and yet all the pieces looked more brilliant. The green vase caught and distorted the sunlight onto the thrift-store coffee table, making a comforting puddle. Her refrigerator hummed and the spatulas, laid out to dry, were in a neat row next to the sink. On the train, she had played out different scenarios. Not returning at all; waiting a few months before calling home again. But when she walked back into her apartment, she slid to the floor and cried. She knew she would not disappoint her parents, and she knew that everything in that room—in that city—was now worthless. Her answering machine blinked with several messages. She deleted the messages and showered. She put on lipstick and went to work.

Eleven Years Later

As Willie made her way to Fern Jacobs's office, walking through the muted halls of Walton—most students were gone, leaving behind only the most and least ambitious—she felt like an Episcopalian in a Catholic church.

The innards of Walton's hallways were the same, though dressed more modestly. The furniture less opulent. The carpet understated. Willie had not expected to send her child here. Then again, she hadn't expected to have a child. The road to understanding had grown shorter and more frequently traveled since her daughter, Paloma, was born, and she could see now why Lourdes had insisted Willie go to school here. She was willing to make trade-offs for Paloma's future success, even as she still dealt with the repercussions of those trade-offs herself.

Inside her office, Paloma's history teacher gestured to a low leather couch with a black-and-gold crochet pillow in the middle.

Willie sat on the edge while Fern lowered herself into a chair and smiled.

"Thank you for coming in," she said, although she didn't sound grateful. "As I mentioned on the phone, there was a little incident in class this morning." She raised her thumb and pointer finger and slowly brought them to touch to demonstrate the minuscule size of the issue, which of course Willie knew meant it was the opposite. "I asked the class to complete an assignment, and Paloma refused to complete it," Fern continued.

Willie scooted backward on the couch, tucking her purse behind her for support, both feet on the ground.

"Can you back up and explain exactly what happened?"

"I asked the students to create presentations explaining their family's history and to draw flags of the countries represented in their family tree. The children had questions about everything they've been hearing about the Forgiveness Act, and I thought it would also be a good icebreaker to have each of them discuss their lineage."

Fern leaned forward, and Willie noticed she had accidentally colored outside her top lip line. Willie looked at Fern's lipstick and drew a thin red line to her grandfather sitting in the VA office in a low chair, being told by a man in a cheap suit he didn't qualify for benefits. *There is hypocrisy in all authority,* Willie thought.

Fern lowered her voice. "I'm concerned Paloma is looking for special treatment. I don't want to start the school year by giving her a pass any more than I would give another student."

Someone closed a door down the hall, and it felt like the jamb had clicked into place at the base of Willie's spine.

Fern parted her lips, pushing her tongue through the gap between her two front teeth. Willie felt, when looking at Fern, as if all the eyes she had encountered in the stores when they first moved to Lewaro Street, in the halls at Walton when she first enrolled, in the classrooms at college, were staring back at her, still asking why she had the audacity to think she and her family belonged there.

She looked at Fern's smudged lipstick and fought the urge to hand her a napkin.

"Paloma is the only Black girl in her class. Can you not see how this might be uncomfortable for her?"

Fern inhaled and shifted in her chair, placing one hand on top of the other. "Well, I . . . no, but I mean, I wasn't asking about race. There's a difference between race and ethnicity. It was supposed to be a fun exercise."

Willie was struck multiple times a day by how many worlds can coexist. The world where the Revels existed as a middle-class Black family. The world of Waltons and Ferns, where they pretended to be liberal and color-blind but were just blind to reality, until it inconvenienced them enough to pay attention. The world of herself, where she wanted to be a certain type of person, living a certain kind of life. Paloma was on scholarship at Walton, just like Willie had been. And while this was its own type of legacy, Willie knew Fern was taking the conversation less seriously than she would have if the Revels were paying customers.

"I don't need to be told that there's a difference between race and ethnicity," Willie responded. "Can you get Steve in here, please?"

"I don't think we need to involve Mr. Wallace. I'm sorry if you think this assignment was inappropriate. I can see now how it might have been misconstrued."

"I think we should all have a conversation about it," Willie said, starting to walk toward the door, her purse still on the couch.

Fern stood and opened the door before Willie could reach it. "Let me see if he's available."

Willie took a deep breath, reflecting on how, once you make certain decisions, people expect you to live with the consequences: Because she chose to send Paloma to Walton, she had no right to argue when indignities such as this one happened. When she first envisioned the Forgiveness Act passing, it had not occurred to her the small ways a person's world would change. How she would need to explain to her daughter that the Revels didn't know their ancestors, that she didn't know Paloma's dad's last name. That a national policy acknowledging that slavery was wrong would change the way non-Black people thought of their own relevance.

The principal entered, his face red, as if he had been dangling upside down and was about to burst like a balloon. He apologized to Willie immediately and silenced Fern when she tried to interrupt. "We want to make sure the students understand how important the Forgiveness Act is," he explained. "That's all this is. But we would love to work with you to make sure you feel comfortable about what's being taught." He asked if Willie had any interest in presiding over a standards board.

"It's not my job to create your curriculum."

Steve backtracked, and Fern tried again to speak.

"Forget that it singled out Paloma for multiple reasons," Willie continued. "Did you think about what it would feel like for a child who perhaps doesn't know who one of their parents is? For someone who is adopted? Of course not, because it's not *your* reality."

"*My* reality," Fern said, growing defensive, "is that I'm a first-generation American. I would never intentionally make someone feel like they didn't fit in."

Willie yanked the chain of her purse from where it had slithered down between the cushions and brushed past them. "At least you know which generation American you are," Willie said under her breath, reverting back to childish ways.

In the car, Paloma sulked in the seat next to her, fumbling with a small drama-mask key chain attached to her backpack. Willie fought the urge to say, *Turn that frown upside down.*

"Are you mad?" Paloma asked.

"Not at you."

"Ms. Jacobs sucks."

"Language," Willie said, laughing. "You never should have been put in the position of having to do that assignment."

She flicked on her turn signal, and Paloma looked out the window.

Willie braked behind a black SUV letting out a carload of boys with football helmets tucked under their arms. She wished, fleetingly, for a partner to share the weight. But she hadn't been in contact with Paloma's father since she was pregnant and was not going to call him now for help giving a history lesson to their daughter.

"You understand what the Forgiveness Act is, right?" Willie asked.

"Yes. I'm a kid, I'm not deaf."

"Watch your tone. And there are children who are deaf, so your point doesn't hold."

Paloma looked at her. "I understand what it is," she said.

"Okay, well. Do you understand what it means if it passes?"

"It means the government is finally going to admit they screwed over Black people." Paloma turned back to the window. "But there's no way it's actually going to pass."

"Where did you hear that?" Willie asked, startled.

"Olivia told me. It's the truth, isn't it?"

"It is going to pass. And your teacher should have been more thoughtful in how she approached the assignment."

"Where is my dad from?" Paloma asked the window.

Willie sighed. "I told you, baby. You were my out-of-the blue present. He wasn't ready for such a big gift."

Paloma leaned her forehead against the window, unsatisfied.

When they got home, Willie paused the car at the top of the driveway of 512 Lewaro, as Max had done when they returned home from the road trip when she was a child. "Who lives here?" she asked.

Paloma smiled despite herself. "I do."

Chapter 6

A large taxidermy deer head poking out of the library greeted Willie and Paloma when they walked into the house.

"Come grab one of his antlers," Max yelled at them.

He grunted, trying to maneuver the deer so its nose wouldn't hit the rubber padding lining the doorframe. He now looked like a gently aged, tall cherub. His stomach, which had grown rounder and softer since his accident, made the job of getting the taxidermy through the door more difficult than it would have been, say, a dozen years ago, when he had scurried up ladders to inspect faulty insulation or storm drains. Despite the limitations of his body, if you squinted your eyes and ignored his rapidly increasing bald spot, you might mistake him for a founder to envy—or, at least, so he hoped. His job had become an exercise in proving both his physicality and his competence.

When you live with your parents as an adult, it's easier to see the hidden corners behind which they pretend to have control. Willie used to see Max's Still Moments and think he bought the family things out of anger. But now she stood behind her father, knowing he was hiding something by the way he heaved and grunted; the more useless things he brought into the house, the more she knew he was simply afraid. Afraid of falling, afraid of being pulled backward. Max wanted so much for his family that his actions obstructed his intentions. He wanted her to be happy at work—so he hid problems from her "for her own good." He wanted his family to be wealthy and to have nice things—so he compounded junk instead of interest. He assumed his family would forgive him his trespasses so long as he provided.

Max finally got the deer head through the door and propped it against a wall in the library.

"Come grab one of his antlers," he repeated, panting and wiping sweat from his forehead.

Paloma backed up with her hands in front of her like stop signs, a lollipop from school conveniently jammed into her mouth. "Uh-uh, no way."

"Where did you even get this thing?" Willie asked, dropping her bag on a chair.

"McGuinness gave it to me." Max grunted again, trying to lift it on top of the desk, sweat now dotting his shirt like grease spots on a paper towel.

Willie pictured old-man Calvin waving to Max from his driveway, eager to give him a taxidermy deer like he was doing Max a favor, although she had a hard time seeing him offering it to anyone else and an even harder time picturing anyone else on the street taking it.

She took off her shoes and climbed atop the desk. Max stood on a stool, and together they hoisted the deer up like they were trying to fly a heavy kite. Max hammered in a nail as Willie balanced the head against her thigh, feeling the cold of the antler dig into her skin like a finger in her ribs.

"I want to ask what you think about the Soteria job," Max said, raising his voice over the hammering. "You read the note he sent us?"

Willie kept staring at the deer, imagining other lives lived, to withstand her current moment. Max gestured for her to hoist the deer so he could hang it, and then they climbed down and looked up at the new creature in their home.

"I read it."

"We need the work."

"I know we need the work. But not with him."

"Your morality won't pay the bills, you know."

Max had watched the local news as protesters threw paper bags filled with brown putty at Soteria's Philadelphia office to protest the company winning the city's recycling contract, holding picket signs with cheeky slogans like, WE NEED LESS SHIT, NOT BULLSHIT! Hank Lasure's politics would be comical if not for the fact that they shaped their city. Hank was not the only businessman in the area opposed to the Forgiveness Act. A few times in the last month, Max and Willie went to meetings for potential jobs, and the meetings progressed normally, with the client outlining the specifics, Max explaining MRA's process and rates.

Then Willie would see the white client glance at Max's watch, a silver Rolex that Lourdes gave him for Christmas one year. Or they would study the cut of his suit, their eyes moving downward. Or they would look at her small diamond earrings for a second too long. If you weren't watching you might miss it, but Willie was watching, and she made note of how those same people phoned MRA a week later to tell them they did not get the job. The disdain because of the Forgiveness Act suddenly palpable.

After two years as senator, Elizabeth Johnson had run for president and won, with the Forgiveness Act as her major pillar. It took almost her entire presidency, but now that it had the contours of a real policy, sprouts had grown on people's hatred. For people who opposed the money, withholding more became a source of power. What they were saying on television and in the newspaper was that it would have to get worse before it got better. President Johnson warned that Black businesses might see a periodic decline in revenue. There was also a growing group of Black business owners who opposed the Forgiveness Act on moral grounds, either because they claimed they didn't need it, or they didn't want a handout, or they thought the money was part of a wider conspiracy to track their movements. There was a certain pressure, led by men like Hank Lasure, on Black families in the Revels' position to walk away from the money if the bill did pass. Max was so fatigued that morals were beside the point. He supported the Forgiveness Act, of course he supported the Forgiveness Act, but he also supported free healthcare and less war—it just wasn't up to him.

"You don't want to work with him either."

Max sighed, setting the hammer down on the ottoman with an understated finality. "I don't want this to turn into the Inquisition. If I only worked with people I agreed with, we wouldn't be standing here."

"This time is different. This time it matters what he believes."

"Why? Why does it matter? We have no control over the Forgiveness Act. Tell me, has your life been so terrible," Max continued, "that you're willing to risk it all for reparations? We have to dig ourselves out of this hole."

"You mean the $150,000?"

"I mean the rent, the payroll, the lease payments for the equipment. All of it." Max laughed without kindness. "It's not my business what he believes about the Forgiveness Act."

"Give us time is all I'm saying."

"We don't have time." Max shook his head. "I'm worried we raised you too right."

Willie watched him walk off into the kitchen and she looked back up at the deer, which was frozen in a perpetual state of fear and longing. "Welcome home, Bambi."

In times of uncertainty, in times of celebration, they ate, and on Friday afternoons, whether they were uncertain or celebrating or both, the Revels gathered in the kitchen at 512 Lewaro.

Seb walked in the door carrying a six-pack of Heineken in one hand and a small brown paper–wrapped book in the other.

She considered how much to fill her brother in, feeling too tired to parse through her own frustrations or his feelings. He never wanted to know specifics because he felt guilty that she was the one stuck working with Max. He liked the broad strokes: Any exciting contracts? Ridiculous "Max as a boss" stories? Willie built a life on doing what was expected and it had led to feeling like she had no life at all. But look at Seb. So unencumbered. He lived in an apartment downtown and taught at Temple. "What's that?" Willie asked, pointing to the parcel and stepping back to let him into the hallway.

"For Paloma. And what the hell is that?" Seb asked, pointing at the deer mounted on the wall.

"From McGuinness."

Seb emptied his arms on the hallway chairs and untied his black sneakers while Willie told him about what had happened with Paloma at school. Lourdes stepped out of the kitchen holding a spatula.

"What are you two whispering about out here?"

"Nothing, Mom."

"Well, come on then. Paloma's helping me slice potatoes."

Seb entered the kitchen, roughing up Paloma's blossoming afro to which she, wide-eyed, patted it back down before elbowing her uncle good-naturedly in the stomach.

"Paloma, what's this I hear about trouble at school?" Seb said, picking up and biting into a string bean from a colander.

"Mom! You told him?"

Willie put her hands up in defense. "I didn't say there was trouble." Paloma placed the knife back on the wood cutting board and calmly walked out of the kitchen.

Willie set the table while Seb sat on a barstool at the kitchen island. "How was your date last night?" she asked.

"Potential. There's potential there," Seb replied, opening a beer.

"Speaking of potential," Lourdes interjected, pointing the

knife at him. "Your job has potential, Seb. Don't lose focus over a girl, please." There were no "girls" in his life. Only women looking to settle down with a man holding a respectable job and capable of stimulating conversations enough to stimulate other parts of themselves. But Lourdes still saw Seb as a "promising young man." And when Willie tried to remind her that her son was no longer young, Lourdes flapped her hand and sucked her teeth and told Willie bitterness wasn't becoming.

"Yes, I know, Mom," he responded.

Willie rolled her eyes. Discussions about Seb's love life centered around his choices. He could choose to have a woman or his job or both. But Willie's love life was seen as an inconvenient disappointment. A man hadn't chosen her; she failed to land a man like she was a fisherman hunting for food, dependent on the ensnarement of her net for survival. Her romantic failing was the pregnant pause in the room. But nobody asked whether she wanted for romance. They all just assumed it hadn't chosen her and therefore was better left unsaid.

After years of convincing herself Paloma was proof enough her body was capable of lust and longing, she became frustrated when the occasional stirring happened between her legs, reminding her she was missing something. As Willie folded napkins and tucked them underneath the silverware, she thought about Paloma's curiosity about her own dad.

When she had moved home all those years ago, Max tried to help her forget her old life. He flooded her desk with papers needing to be filed and taught her how to run the payroll every week. Max tried to get her excited about work again, like she used to be as a child when he told her *HVAC* stood for *Heaven's Vaults and Closets,* but all she could see in the papers and projects was the mundane, like the results of God's blueprints turned out to be a hall of fun-house mirrors. When Willie offered her resignation, Magda had been, if not sympathetic, at least mildly understanding. She told Willie to continue pitching ideas and to keep in touch in case she ever decided to move back. But once Willie had left, she ceased to matter, as though now that she lived in Philadelphia her ideas were less interesting. First Magda sent her polite rejections, then she sent her nothing at all. There was no creativity involved in Willie's new job, and with every rejection she got from her editor, she worried her talent was slipping through her.

A few months after Willie moved home, Max came back part-time. She tried applying to other jobs, until the silent replies whittled down her confidence to an unrecognizable thing. Max made Willie accompany him on business pitches, but in the meetings, oblivious, he introduced her proudly as his daughter, not as a director in the company, and the men turned their attention to Max as she sat silently by his side, doodling fake headlines. WOMAN DIES IN CONSTRUCTION ZONE—CRUSHED BY SILENCE.

She was bored, so she drank. Nell and Celine saw her return as their blessing.

"Quit acting like someone has a gun to your head," Celine told her, passing her another drink.

Celine's apartment in the city was where the three of them extended the optimism of their youth. Philly, she liked to think during those moments, was for loyalists and masochists. People who knew their worth and people who didn't know how or didn't want to free themselves from the past.

One Friday night while out dancing, Willie noticed three men leaning against the bar watching her and her friends as they circled their hips to the reggae playing over the speakers. She had been home four months and it had been a particularly soul-crushing week at MRA. The men were handsome. Willie waved them over. The tallest one peered down at her and smiled, shy and tentative but with a palatable danger. She took his hand and wrapped it around her waist, pulling herself in close enough to smell his aftershave. Willie closed her eyes and pretended she was in a nightclub in Harlem. Standing on her toes, reaching up for his shoulders, hanging from them like they were a coat rack, she asked, "Do you live nearby?"

In the bathroom, Nell furrowed her brows and asked her, "How will you get home?"

"A bus," Willie said, reapplying lipstick in the mirror.

His name was Arman. At the front door of his apartment, Willie took off her shoes. A faint smell of leftover Chinese food wafted from the trash next to the refrigerator, and he had left the ceiling fan on, causing his black curtains to blow up at the corners in a serene way. A mug on the island was empty and rimmed with something brown. She went to the bathroom and stared at herself in the mirror with the water running.

Arman waited on the sofa with a bottle of liquor and two mugs. When she walked out, he sloshed liquid into her cup and held it out to her. She sat down next to him and connected her glass to his. They sat, talking about their childhoods in Philadelphia. He ran his hand up and down her thigh and they drank, until she could no longer tell what time it was on the clock opposite them, her vision blurring the clock hands into one. She remembers stumbling to her feet and pointing toward the bedroom, the feel of his chest weighing heavily against her breasts, and the taste of the liquor on his breath.

In the office the next day, Willie stared blankly at the numbers on her desk. Every time she tried to complete a form, she had to pause and go stand at the open window and hang her head outside in the fresh air like a dog. She wanted to arrive at work early so her parents could not comment on how late she had stayed out, but once there, she longed for bed. She didn't know Arman's phone number, nor his last name. She realized that being with him only made her miss her freedom more, that the heightened awareness she had of what her parents might think of her was suffocating, and now it took too much effort to separate the longing from her hangover, so it all morphed together into one large, uncomfortable mass in her stomach.

Normally she cross-referenced the names and hours before sending over the completed payroll document, but because it had taken her so long, she submitted the report without looking it over. She told herself that the extra due diligence was no longer necessary.

The next day Max knocked on her door. "Can I see you in my office, please?"

He sat behind his desk and held up a sheet from the payroll.

"I have just gotten off the phone with the foreman, who tells me we paid one of his guys ten hours of overtime." He cleared his throat. "Can you explain to me why that is?"

She ran through the names and numbers. Ten hours of over-time she would remember.

"Dad," she said, realizing her mistake too late. "I'm so sorry."

The paper drifted back down to his desk, slow as a snowflake.

"This business helped you discover what you love—you ever think about that?"

She had thought about it, but not in the way he intended. Max hadn't seen her as capable, which is why she went looking for other passions to begin with. *Women can't work in construction* used to be his unspoken but strongly held belief, and now that he had changed his mind, she was supposed to forget he had ever made her feel that way. He waved his hand and watched her leave. She waited for the indifference to come, to stop her from feeling guilty about messing up, to make her focus only on herself and what was being done to *her*. Instead, her hands shuffled papers, and she resisted reflection. She cared what he thought of her. She cared about being good at her job, whatever that job may be.

Off and on, a month later, the nausea was incessant, but she refused to ask for time off. One night at Celine's apartment, she ran from the living room to the bathroom, hinging at her waist over the toilet bowl like her insides were a bucket of dirty water being tossed onto the sidewalk. Nell silently gestured to her stomach.

"You're late, right?" Nell reluctantly asked when Willie returned.

Willie ran a dish towel under water and wiped her lips. "Late for what?"

"She's trying to ask if you're pregnant," Celine said.

Willie looked at them, slowly replacing the dish towel.

"Is it the guy from the bar?" Celine asked.

"Who else would it be?" Nell snapped at her. "It's okay. We'll figure it out."

On the couch, Willie pulled her legs underneath her and sat back. "What if I am? Maybe it could be a good thing. I need purpose."

"You don't even know the guy!" Celine exclaimed. "What if he has some chronic disease that can be passed down?"

"Your life's not over just because you live here and work with your dad, you know. You can still make choices."

"I know," Willie said. "I know. You're right."

Lourdes guessed before Willie could tell her.

"What do you want to do?"

"I don't know."

"Do you know who the father is?"

"Yes" was all Willie replied.

Lourdes nodded. "We'll help you." Then she went out to the garden as if the matter was settled.

Her father had pressed his lips together and nodded. He started to slam his fist on the table but stopped and left the room.

"Do I need to beat someone up?" Seb asked, baffled.

It had been a difficult pregnancy, and there were many times when Willie felt grateful for working at MRA. She was nauseous, her feet swollen. At her desk, she unclasped the buckles from her shoes and leaned back in her chair like she was an editor yelling at an inept reporter. Because she was still embarrassed by her payroll mistake and Max yelling at her, and because she didn't want any of the employees to think she was receiving special treatment from being both pregnant and the boss's daughter, she tried especially hard to engage in work, more so than before she was pregnant. She realized the job had plenty of creativity if she allowed herself to find it, and there were even elements of what she loved about journalism: It was fast-paced when she set herself deadlines and goals; it required concentration and attention to detail; she could devise unique solutions to problems and new ways of finding clients.

Once Willie could no longer ignore the changing shape of her body and the new fit of her clothes, she drove to Arman's apartment and parked across the street, working up the nerve to buzz. For several minutes she sat in the car, watching the building. It was so overcast that fog obscured the windows on the top floor. Few people had entered or left the building. The street, too, was sparsely populated.

In front of the door, she zipped her coat and pulled her fingers through her curls a final time. She buzzed his door and waited. After several minutes she tried again, holding the button down for longer. As she was turning to leave, Arman rounded the corner, carrying a coffee from a store down the street. When he saw Willie, he paused, as if contemplating whether he could slip past and ignore her.

"Hi," he mumbled. "What are you doing here?"

With her coat on, it wasn't obvious that she was pregnant. She stuffed her hands into her pockets.

"Can we go upstairs and talk for a minute?" she suggested, pointing to his door.

Upstairs, she remained standing. In the light of day the black curtains no longer looked serene but depressing. The apartment was filthy.

"You want water?" He walked around quickly, putting dishes in the sink.

He continued moving about the apartment, until she realized he wasn't going to invite her to sit down.

"I'm pregnant."

He kept cleaning the kitchen, as though he hadn't heard her.

"I'm pregnant," she repeated. "It's yours."

She felt exposed, standing there against the door, and as she looked around at the disarray of the room, she wondered why she had come. She wanted nothing from him, and she didn't ever want to return to this room again.

"I can't manage that right now." He kept rubbing his hand back and forth over his head like Max did when he was frustrated.

"I don't need anything from you. I just thought you should know."

"Okay," he said, finally looking up at her. "Thanks."

She turned and left, and she started her car still without knowing his last name.

While driving downtown away from Arman's apartment, she felt a release of her former self. She would have a daughter, and she would create a world where her daughter could create any life at all that she wanted.

Then, when Johnson became president, Willie hoped the relationship could be a tether back to her old life, and she followed President Johnson to a near-obsessive degree. In her bedroom on Lewaro Street, she pored over the newspapers and tried getting in touch with Johnson's administration to share her ideas for how Johnson could improve her messaging. A staff member finally had to tell her to get a life. During dinner, Willie preached to her family about all she could be doing instead. When President Johnson launched her commission to study the impact of slavery, promising to pass the Forgiveness Act, the Revels dismissed it all as the theater of a guilty white woman. Willie told them to wait. "You'll see. And I could have been a part of it."

Willie heard the garage door open and placed the last floral napkin underneath a knife and fork. She walked to the door to help her grandfather Marcus up the garage steps.

"Y'all add another goddamn step to these every time I come here. I know it. I know you do. Just to see if I notice."

"You know we have to keep you on your toes. Here, hand me your walker. Dad's got you from behind."

Marcus lived in Wissahickon Senior Living, half an hour away. Most people, when they get older, wanted to stay at home as long as possible or else go live with family. Her parents had offered for Marcus to come and live with them—Lourdes prepared a basket of his favorite fruits and brought photos of a room she planned to redecorate for him—but he refused. The next day he told them he inquired about a room at Wissahickon. "If you want to help, pay for the bill," he'd said.

Marcus gingerly lifted one leg at a time like he was Neil Armstrong until he made it into the back hall of the kitchen. Willie opened beers for her father and grandfather. Paloma walked back in with a book open in front of her face, stopping to kiss Marcus on the cheek.

"What are you up to, Grandpop?" Paloma asked.

"Five-foot-nine these days. When I can stand up straight."

Willie and Lourdes carried out the roast beef, potatoes, and salad.

"Seb, tell us about the classes you're teaching this semester." Lourdes poured a slow drizzle of gravy over the potatoes.

Seb, ever eager to talk about his work, could barely swallow before answering. He told them he was teaching three undergraduate engineering courses. "There's also a new one my friend is teaching that I'm excited about. It's Human Rights versus Animal Rights. They're going to dissect different theories about fundamental rights." He stopped to shovel food into his mouth. "Fascinating, really. Especially with the Forgiveness Act approaching the House and Senate."

"Why would they group the Forgiveness Act with animal rights? I don't like that," Willie said.

"We're not talking about politics during this meal," Max cut in.

"It's a good point, Wil," Seb said, ignoring Max. "But the discussion she wants the class to have is whether, under the UN Declaration of Human Rights, slavery meant a violation of human rights. Obviously, the answer is yes, right? But legally it's more complicated than that. Because Black people weren't even considered human. So, you have people who were in favor of slavery arguing that legally no rights were being violated. For the Japanese American Evacuation Claims Act, for instance, the whole reason Japanese Americans were ever able to claim redress payments was that they claimed their rights as citizens—as humans—were violated. But how do you claim rights were violated if Black people weren't even considered human in the Constitution?"

"Fine," Willie said, cutting into her meat and looking at the inside to check its doneness. "But don't group it with animal rights. How many of their students will even be Black? They won't get it."

"You have to take your emotion out of everything. It's just a class."

"Well, it's about time there's some emotion in politics again," Lourdes said.

Paloma looked up from the book she was trying to hide on her lap under the table. "People at school say the Forgiveness Act's not going to pass."

"What did I say about this conversation?" Max interrupted. "The Forgiveness Act is not going to mean shit for us. As a family, as a race, as a country. Nothing. It's all optics. It's all hidden meanings and optics."

Lourdes narrowed her eyes and looked down at her plate. Seb, oblivious, needled Max to the point of explosion. "I think you're wrong, Dad," he said. "It would be huge if this passed. And the intention is there. You have the right people pushing for it. The entire way slavery is taught in schools would change."

Marcus watched his family go back and forth like ping-pong balls. "It's all theoretical to you little shits," he finally said, his voice deep, yet wobbly with age. Paloma's eyes widened but she remained quiet, writing on a piece of paper balanced on top of the book on her lap. "This isn't abstract. This is real," Marcus continued. "That money is real and it's not nearly enough for what I've been through. What my parents have been through. What my grandparents have been through. What's funny is that it's even a question." Marcus laughed heartily to himself, as though he forgot the rest of the Revels were even at the table, his dentures rattling like loose coins in a jar. "A Black man robs a convenience store to feed his family, they put him in jail for life. A white man steals a Black man's wages, children, labor, and fingers, they get rich, their kids get rich, their grandkids run for office."

Yells from kids across the street drifted in through the open screen door. Willie thought about how to make the conversation as pleasant as the day passing them by outside. "We'll just have to see once it passes," she said. She disagreed with Max—and she saw through his fear. Because fear was all it came down to. Fear the bill's passing would backfire or disappoint. And when her father was overwhelmed with the potential enormity of something, he put his head in the sand and refused to change course.

"Grandpop," Seb said, "$175,000, help with buying a home, and free college tuition. You don't think it's good enough?"

"What's enough?" Marcus said. "You'll be a porko pigo if you think the score is even."

"Anyway," Lourdes said. "Enough politics, Max is right. There's dessert in the oven. Apple pie."

Other families feasted on oral tradition and stories from their elders. The Revels skirted around the issues. They were loud and they laughed and they got angry but they rarely got into it. Just as the risk of deep water emerged, someone always backed away, paddling to safety.

Seb turned to Paloma. "Hey, I do want to talk to you about that assignment, though. Hey, hey, don't roll your eyes. Ever. But especially not at family. There's nothing wrong with us knowing what's happening at your school."

"Sorry," Paloma said.

"Next time someone asks you to draw the flag of your ancestral homeland, you draw the American flag and you feel proud doing it. And you remember that this country would literally not exist without the work of your ancestors." Seb pointed at Paloma's chest and repeated, "They're yours. The White House, the Capitol in Washington, D.C. We built them. We worked in the fields to make America rich. Before I forget, I brought you a book."

Seb went into the hallway and came back with the wrapped parcel. Paloma tore into the paper bag, pulling out a book on how to write screenplays. There was a drawing of a Black girl with a small afro wearing a pink ribbon as a headband on the cover, writing in a notebook. Willie silently mouthed "thank you" to Seb across the table.

After dinner they went into the sunroom and watched various anchors debating the Forgiveness Act ahead of the House vote. Willie was still smarting from Max's earlier comment. *Raised you too right.* She knew what he meant, that they had raised her *too white,* that she hadn't suffered the indignities he had suffered and therefore didn't have a right to lecture him on sacrifices. But whose fault was that?

The television was loud, and everyone was talking at the TV like they were watching a sports team they were suddenly indebted to, pausing only to watch a highlight of President Johnson.

"Are you frustrated that Republicans in the Senate have discussed a filibuster?" a reporter asked the president.

"I care that it passes," Johnson replied. "A few misguided Republicans will not stop us. We have enough votes to make sure it passes."

Max changed the station, looking for a reprieve from the coverage, but every station he turned to was discussing the Forgiveness Act.

"Would you stop?" Lourdes protested, taking the remote.

"You're right. I don't know what I'm expecting. All of this is pointless, though. It's never going to be as simple as each of us getting a check for $175,000."

"It's going to pass," Willie said patiently. "Johnson knows what she's doing."

"When has the government ever done anything for us you can trust? You think you know her, but people change once they have power. You don't know her."

"I don't know what you're mad about," Marcus said. "All the government ever did for you was give you work."

"Everyone be quiet," Lourdes demanded as the news panned to the House floor.

A final vote count from the House appeared along the bottom of the screen: 220–211. The Forgiveness Act had officially passed the House of Representatives.

"This is a historic moment," the Speaker of the House said. "And now we look to our colleagues in the Senate to keep the momentum going."

To cheer would have been too crass. The Forgiveness Act still needed to pass the Senate. So the Revels all made small gestures of hope without sacrificing their dignity. Lourdes's shoulders went down while Max's went up. Seb's lips pointed outward in a gesture that communicated his skepticism. Willie sighed heavily and noticed all of this while also noticing the white orchid in the window, which in her mind had looked the same—curved spine, pink nucleus—for the past ten or twelve years, and now it seemed to glow in its solitude like a beacon. "We'll see," Seb said, voicing his thoughts. He paraphrased the lyrics of a Police song. "The doctor tells me it's delusions. I tell him, 'No, it's just optical illusions.'"

Willie opened the door to the back porch, where music from the neighbor's house drifted in as Mrs. Robinson clinked champagne flutes with her husband. Lewaro Street had changed since she was a child, with more families who looked like the Revels, and Willie appreciated that now at least two of their neighbors were the sort of people who celebrated this type of news.

"Many governors have already begun taking precautions and initiated an increased police presence in major cities across the nation," an anchor explained. "We're following the killing of an unarmed twenty-five-year-old Black man who was shot and killed while jogging in the subdivision of Satilla Shores in Brunswick, Georgia. Rashad Jones was out for a jog when two white men, a father and a son, took a .357 revolver and a shotgun and pursued Jones, shooting him in broad daylight. When authorities arrived on the scene, the father claimed they were, quote, 'getting their own reparations.'"

"This is the shit," Max said, "I'm talking about." Lourdes switched off the television. They gathered their plates. The orchid continued glowing in the window like some sort of omen.

Chapter 7

Paloma bit down hard on a lollipop, shattering the sweet mold into a million sharp blood-red pieces, and trudged upstairs, leaving her family behind in the sunroom. She chucked her backpack against the floral armchair in the corner and watched as it bounced pitifully onto the carpet, also covered in wide-mouthed florals. Her grandmother loved flowers—decorated every room with them—and they implored her to cheer up, that things weren't so bad.

But today had been about as bad as it gets in the fifth grade—and she had only been a fifth grader for two weeks! "We'll all get to know one another a bit better!" Ms. Jacobs chirped halfway through class, standing in front of the whiteboard. Paloma didn't know her family's history, not the way Ms. Jacobs meant. The other kids pranced across the checkered linoleum floor to pick out markers. Back at her desk, she looked down at the white paper. She could faintly smell herself—never a good sign. She glanced to her left and saw Anthony drawing the Italian flag, his tongue poking out from the side of his mouth. He was using a ruler to get the lines achingly straight. She only knew it was the Italian flag because he always bragged about visiting Italy in the summer like he was some kind of diplomat. He glanced up, asking Paloma if he could borrow the red marker on her desk, his black hair flopping over and into his eyes. She handed it to him and surreptitiously looked to her right, where Billy drew the American flag. The sweat began to form a shallow pool in her hands' hollows.

She could feel Anthony staring at her. "Why aren't you drawing?"

"Leave me alone, Anthony, I'm thinking."

"No talking, please." Ms. Jacobs pivoted in their direction, pressing her index finger to her lips. "Paloma, here," she said, handing Paloma a sheet with a list of five countries. "You can choose from one of these."

Paloma focused on the paper and refused to look back up except at the clock, which proclaimed a tortuous twelve minutes left to go. *God, I hate this, get me out of here.* She started to close her eyes and point her index finger at a country at random and then stopped, listening to her classmates confidently polishing off their emblems. Instead, she raised her hand to go to the bathroom, where she planned to stay long enough to miss the rest of the excruciating introduction to the fifth grade. And this would have worked; her bathroom plan would have worked fabulously if not for the fact that today (of all days) she'd forgotten that history on Fridays meant a double period.

When she strolled back into the classroom, she realized her spectacular misjudgment of time. Sixteen pairs of eyes turned to stare at her as she walked to her seat.

"Great, Paloma," Ms. Jacobs said, smiling her devilish smile. "You're next."

She peered around the room. "I didn't draw anything. I'm not presenting."

Ms. Jacobs shook her head back and forth, as if she didn't hear correctly or had water stuck in her abnormally small ears. "What do you mean? Didn't you choose a country from the list I gave you?" Ms. Jacobs said, pointing at Paloma's desk from the front of the room.

"Can I skip this assignment, please?"

"Why would you want to skip the assignment? Please, Paloma, we're just practicing public-speaking skills and learning about our family trees before we learn about the Forgiveness Act. There aren't any wrong answers."

"You live with, like, five generations—how do you not know where you're from?" Nick yelled from the front row.

Her classmates burst out laughing. Paloma's face grew hot. She touched one of the plastic tortoiseshell barrettes clasped to the end of her braids.

Ms. Jacobs clapped her hands twice, sharply. "Enough, Nick. That's enough. Quiet down." Turning to Paloma, she said, "Just tell us about your family's traditions, then. No need to draw."

Paloma had been the only Black girl in her grade at Walton

since she started in kindergarten. Then in her third year a girl named Flora joined, and Paloma breathed a sigh of relief, realizing for the first time why she was always defensive, building a wall around herself to keep out the eyes of her classmates. Why she felt self-conscious and on display and anxious, like a walking target. Her reprieve was short-lived—before they could even get to middle school, Flora transferred, and here she was, back to being the lone wolf except for her friend Olivia, which made it slightly more bearable. Paloma had gotten adept at convincing herself that the anxiety and angst she felt were simply a part of her internal fabric, ingrained in her personality, like her mom's bitterness and ambition or her grandmother's grace.

Paloma narrowed her eyes to keep from rolling them. *Why can't Ms. Jacobs just let this go?* She glanced at the clock. Thirty minutes left. Her other classmates talked about traveling abroad or family reunions. The Revels had a family reunion once, a barbecue in the Wissahickon with her great-grandfather Marcus's brother and his family. But once didn't count as a tradition. And her grandfather had all but thrown her grandmother's potato salad out the window and kept driving. Max might feel like a father to her, but Max couldn't fill the missing half of her history. Years later, she would think about how Ms. Jacobs's assignment opened something inside her, like a rusty spigot turned on, causing little trickles of questions about what her father looked like, what he smelled like, the foods he preferred.

Then it was suddenly as if someone put words into a soup and force-fed her that soup to see what would come out. "Nick, I do not live with five generations. But thank you for that comment. Very insightful." She put on her best I-think-you're-an-idiot smile.

"My grandparents live with my mom and me because of the family business. So, in terms of family traditions," she said, turning to face her teacher, "that's probably the biggest one. My grandfather started the company, and now my mom works there. That's all I have to say." What a stupid, humiliating experience. Why had she lied about Max and Lourdes living with her and Willie, instead of being honest that it was the other way around?

Paloma sat back down at her desk and stared straight ahead for the remainder of class. She moved only to give a sympathetic smile to Reese, who apparently also didn't have many family traditions and who had reluctantly drawn the American flag despite clearly being more than American. More chuckling in the back of the room. Backpacks being zipped and gathered. Ms. Jacobs looking angry as she released her little prisoners to their next period.

The Forgiveness Act seemed to be responsible for the nerves and anxiety emanating from the adults around her. No one knew how to talk to one another. Everyone acted as if they might turn a corner and be spooked by what was on the other side.

Now she glanced around her room—so large she often spent entire weekend afternoons in it, leaving only to eat or go to the bathroom. Paloma set up different zones in her room for different times of day. In the morning she sat in the chair and read, swiveling it around to face the window, giving her a view of the pine trees set farther back from the driveway, where sometimes she climbed to the top with her book or pen and paper. In the afternoon she sat at her white wooden desk painted with pink flowers along the edges, writing and revising her stories and plays. In the evening she climbed on top of her bed and sang—belting out melodies she made up in her head. Paloma imagined herself stood too. "I know what it feels like to wish you knew the people who made you. To wish for some answers about yourself. Believe me, I know. But what you must remember is that you are not lacking in love. Under this roof, which is your home and your history, we all love you very much. Nothing else matters." Her grandmother unclasped the small gold quill brooch she was wearing and handed it to Paloma. "Whenever you need a little strength," she said, "you picture holding on to this quill and letting its strength fly into you. Put your energy into those amazing stories you write. You can write your own definition of yourself. You don't need an invisible father to do that."

Paloma turned the quill over in her palm, brought it to her chest, and held it there.

"I have to go back downstairs. You hold on to that for now."

Paloma gritted her teeth and looked out the window. It wasn't even that she hated Walton, or her teachers, or her classmates. She was indifferent to it all, aside from Mr. Jeremy's class, where she got to write plays, the thing she loved to do the most. When she wrote stories about girls exploring strange lands, it didn't matter that no one else had her hair; the only thing that mattered was her characters and whether their questions got answered. Otherwise, her philosophy about school was a simple one: Get it over with.

At school on Monday, Paloma found Mr. Jeremy arranging chairs in his classroom, the radio playing a talk show in the background. The monotony of the voices compared to the eccentricity of her drama teacher felt mismatched, like a wrong pair of socks. She

a contestant on a show, judging the quality of her sin
by how long Willie kept the door to her own room op
long it took for Lourdes to appear in the doorway and s
ing with her. Paloma sat with her back against the armc
arm draped over her backpack, waiting for her mother t
up the stairs. It was clear her mother didn't know wha
with her.

"Can I come in?" Lourdes asked, knocking on the door.

Sometimes it seemed like her grandmother was the only
who understood. For Lourdes, Paloma was purpose. Lou
took care of Paloma when Willie went out, and it seemed
liked to have children to raise up and make in her mold. Palo
was eager to hear her grandmother's stories, to try on her jewel
and listen to her thoughts about the world, her stories about th
salons. Motherhood for Willie seemed like a role she played, hop
ing no one would notice it was a poor casting decision.

"Of course," Paloma said, standing as her grandmother entered the room.

The two of them sat on Paloma's bed, and she held her breath
for a moment before asking, "Am I weird?"

Lourdes chuckled. She shook her head and cupped Paloma's
cheek. "You are a gift."

"I lied at school and said you lived with Mom and me instead
of the other way around."

"Are you embarrassed you live with us?"

"Do you know anything about my dad?" Paloma asked instead of answering.

Lourdes brushed both hands down her slacks and stood in
front of Paloma. They were almost the same height if Paloma

entered without knocking, testing his ability to always "know the space." He professed to noticing even the slightest change in a room. "Know the space and you will know yourself." It became a running joke that on the first day of class students secretly adjusted objects before class to see if he could guess what changed. He turned the moment Paloma's left foot crossed the threshold, and she shook her head in amazement. "How? How?" she asked.

"Out of necessity, my dear. Out of necessity."

Mr. Jeremy was one of the few Black teachers at Walton, and Paloma gravitated toward him not only because she loved his classes but because he trusted the students to know their space. He treated each student like an adult with fully formed opinions and legitimate reasons for liking the things they liked and disliking the things they didn't. He taught them from a place of trust instead of a place of condescension. The kids created all sorts of rumors about how someone as interesting as Mr. Jeremy ended up at Walton: He was in the witness-protection program. He had been banned from Broadway. His teaching there was all an experiment, some sort of elaborate living-art installation.

The first week of school, Mr. Jeremy had asked the class to choose an iconic figure to write a play about. The best play, he said, would be produced for Walton's annual Flash Festival, the arts festival the school put on every year featuring short productions by students. Paloma had been looking forward to sweet revenge ever since last year, when her spoken-word poem wasn't selected. This was the reason for Paloma's visit to his class so early in the day.

"I picked the person I want to write a play about," she announced to her teacher.

As he bent to move another chair, Mr. Jeremy's fedora slid downward, and he tipped his head back to replace it. "And you couldn't wait until Friday to tell me this?"

"Well, I wanted to get your opinion. Before I say it in front of the whole class. It's a weird choice."

"Go ahead."

"Phillis Wheatley," she told him.

"What goes on in that mind of yours?"

Paloma shrugged.

"I knew I needed to keep an eye on you. I love it. A bit conflicted about her work, but I think it's just what this school needs. How did you learn of her?"

"My mom has a book of her poetry."

Mr. Jeremy nodded vigorously. "I doubt anyone else in your class will know who she is. Are you prepared to educate?"

"Educate?" Paloma asked, squinting with confusion. "As in, give a presentation?"

"Speak to who she was and why she is significant. Here, practice. Go. Tell me who she is."

Paloma arranged her feet hip-distance apart like Mr. Jeremy's and cleared her throat. "Phillis Wheatley was, um, the first Black woman to write a book of poetry," Paloma said.

"Lose the 'um' and try again. Say it confidently. Like you're proud to be connected to her."

Paloma dropped her backpack on the floor and broadened her shoulders. "Phillis Wheatley was the first Black woman to write a book of poetry in the United States," she tried again.

"Yes. Better. Yes." Mr. Jeremy checked his watch. "I'll see you Friday for class. In the meantime: Start outlining. We're going to make this the best damn play Walton has ever seen." Mr. Jeremy winked at her and waved her dismissal like he was fanning a royal.

Paloma moved through homeroom, moved through the rest of her day, buoyed by a new creative energy. Her thoughts about the play overpowered any lingering anxiety about what had happened in Ms. Jacobs's class last Friday. Had it not been for Sia, a girl two grades older than Paloma, she might have succeeded in forgetting about it completely. But during recess, Sia ran to catch up with Paloma, who was heading for a tree in the far corner of the field. "Hey, wait up!" she yelled.

Sia had never spoken to Paloma before—at least not directly. Paloma looked around her. "Me?"

"Do you see anyone else all the way out here?"

Paloma stopped and waited. Sia wore a denim jacket with her name written in rhinestones on the collar, over the requisite yellow polo shirt tucked into Walton's plaid uniform skirt. "I heard about what happened in Ms. Jacobs's class," Sia said. "Good for you."

"Why? What are people saying?" The air smelled like fall even though both girls were nearly sweating. Sia pushed up the sleeves of her jacket, rolling the cuffs in perfect half circles.

"That you schooled Ms. Jacobs."

Sia straightened her hair, and it hung below her shoulders like black fringe. Her skin looked like the slabs of caramel Paloma asked for on the boardwalk when the Revels went to Cape May in the summer.

"I honestly didn't know what to draw, you know? I mean, what would you draw?"

"Me? Oh, well, I'm Haitian. I drew the Haitian flag when she asked our class. But that's not really the point. The point is, you stood your ground. And I just wanted to say I respect that." Sia shrugged her shoulders like it was no big deal, despite Paloma feeling mortified that her speech had made the rounds. "See you around." Sia turned and sprinted back toward the basketball courts.

Paloma continued to her original destination under the oak tree at the far edge of the field, feeling significantly less buoyant than before. Some days this school just . . . How to make sense of Walton? The only school she'd ever attended still felt like a foreign country for which she might never have a passport. How to feel normal in a school where the average wealth of her classmates' families exceeded the GDP of a small nation? Paloma was fine, though, she really was. She knew her mom worried, but she didn't have to. Paloma was a survivor, and she had friends and she would be okay, really. Because here was the thing: Paloma knew how to be a chameleon. She could change colors with the best of them. Around the popular kids she was deferential. Around the bookworms she was herself. Around the drama kids she played down her abilities. Around the older kids she laughed at all the right times. Paloma knew what she was doing. She did what she had to. Paloma could become whoever she wanted to become; she just needed to be who they wanted her to be first.

The changing of colors was as routine as the changing of the guard. This she could control. What Paloma couldn't control was her family. Three generations living as two, operating as one unit. Tracy, Olivia, Summer—her closest friends at Walton—all had a set of parents, and those parents made those families do normal family things. Tracy's mom and dad enrolled her in overnight camp during the summer. Olivia's moms played card games at night after dinner with their kids. Summer's mom and dad took her and her siblings to stay at her grandparents' farm three times a year. Paloma loved each member of her family individually. But did they all have to be together all the time? Couldn't she and Willie have some traditions that were theirs alone?

"Your dad's old," Olivia once said to her, referring to Max.

"Oh, he's not my dad, he's my grandfather," Paloma replied. And then she went on to clarify how Max helped raise her and she thought of him as her own father. And it occurred to Paloma, as she was explaining Max to her friend, that maybe the Revels weren't normal. Maybe it wasn't normal to live with your grandparents and to think of your grandfather as your father and to not have any inkling whatsoever as to who your real father was. But Paloma couldn't square this, because it never felt odd to her. The only thing that felt odd was a need to justify it.

Paloma peeled herself from the grass like the slow removal of a Band-Aid. She ran back to the main building, where the rest of the day was spent in avoidance as she tried to make herself as small and as unlike a person who stood their ground as possible, until Lourdes picked her up to take her home, reminding her there was no changing of the guard required.

Chapter 8

Willie learned Jamaican proverbs once, either researching for a story or for a class, she can't remember, and they began coming back to her in flashes, like prophecy. Here was one now: *Seven years no 'nough to wash speckle off guinea hen back—human nature never changes.* Another: *Sharp spur mek maugre horse cut caper—the pinch of human circumstances forces people to do what they thought impossible.* Willie's thoughts were like a movie played in reverse. Out of sequence, jumbled, racing to a point that by the time she got there had already passed. Compromise was, at this point, of no consequence, but morality bugged her like a hangnail. Her dad wanted to talk about morals? She had already compromised to work with Max, but it had been a compromise of ego, not ethics. Working with Hank Lasure stretched the limits of her imagination, not because she couldn't, but because if she did, what would it mean? The Sunday after Forgiveness passed the House, Willie and Paloma sat in their respective rooms while Max and Lourdes were at church. She suspected Max had already signed with Hank, she suspected there were things he wasn't telling her, and so, ignoring the voice in her head saying she was trying to imitate a woman searching for a story, she yelled for Paloma to pack her things and they drove to the office. It smelled closed-up and deserted, and Willie opened a window. Paloma spread her things over the table in Willie's office and Willie went into Max's.

The company was stuck in a paper slog. Despite Willie's efforts to get Max to digitize, he insisted on keeping paper records of everything. He still used a typewriter, placed in the middle of a small mahogany table in the corner facing the window. There was enough paper in his office and across tables in the main room to start a fire that would last for days. She stared at his desk and perched on the edge of his wingback chair swiveling left and right like a child twirling a tutu. From this vantage point, with the door open, her father could look out into the office and at all times see two or three employees typing or filing or taking calls, employed because of him, creating a euphoria of power and purpose he tried to emulate at home. The misfortune was that she was proud of her father. Without the pride she could have probably left, but the pride showed her something of herself she couldn't lose. Her mother knew this, Seb knew it, though for him the pride produced shame. The pride was the problem. The pride in what her father had built, the pride in what it afforded the family, the pride in 512 Lewaro Street, the pride of running it, now, even if with a small bitterness.

Willie took a sip of coffee and lifted one page at a time, careful to replace each one where she had found it, not out of meticulousness but from the insistence of her conscience. She told herself it would be like she hadn't even been there. There was correspondence between her father and suppliers, men whom she would need to call later in the week to discuss the terms of unrealistic deals he might have agreed to. There were receipts. Faxes from two months ago. There were bank statements.

She picked one up and examined it more closely. Almost all of her parents' 401(k), it seemed, had been transferred into the business account. "Shit," she whispered aloud. The journey from dependability to accountability is incredibly short in a family business. She was looking at the distance in numbers.

For as close as they all were, in both physical and emotional proximity, Lourdes, Max, and Willie rarely talked about money. They didn't share insights or ideas about how to invest or whether it was better to open a savings account or spend the money on stocks and bonds. It was the blind leading the blind when it came to smart financial sense, so no one led anyone. Lourdes and Max never asked Willie if she was being smart with her money. And Willie never asked her parents, because it wasn't her place. The Revels were one-generation deep into a world that required financial literacy to continue as residents—and they still didn't have the right dictionary in their library to talk about it. What kind of child can watch their parents walk to the edge of a cliff without extending an arm to stop them from falling? Their choices pained her, stirred some anchor that dragged across the ocean floor of her stomach, drudging up responsibility and emotion she'd rather keep buried.

"Mom," Paloma said, walking into the office. "How much longer are we going to be here?"

Willie stared at her daughter for a moment, trying to make sense of why she was there. "Let's go." She replaced the paper where she had found it.

Downtown on Monday evening, groups of police officers and boarded-up windows, spray-painted with looping spirals of graffiti, were signs of an impending carnage that never arrived.

In the car Willie lowered her window, inhaling fall, enjoying the scent of foliage and humidity, glad for a few moments of solitude. She turned up the volume of the president's voice on NPR: "I want to correct my familial legacy of wrongs, and we need to correct the nation's legacy of wrongs. I am urging the Senate to approve the Forgiveness Act as quickly as possible. Our nation is hurting. We need to officially ask for forgiveness from the Black community and begin our nation's long-overdue healing process." How often had she listened to Elizabeth Johnson's voice over the years? Her former professor had ended up being one of the great constants of her life.

President Johnson's speech ended, and the NPR host spoke next with a senator from New York.

Host: *You have been an outspoken advocate of the Forgiveness Act. Can you give us an update on where things stand and how you're feeling about the chances of it passing the Senate?*

Senator Walker: *As you know, Rachel, this bill would be monumental if it passes. We have never issued any sort of reparations payment to African Americans in the United States. Think about that for a moment. After the murder of Rashad Jones and countless other* *innocent, unarmed men and women, the nation desperately needs a catalyst for healing. People are tired. And two men being sent to jail will not solve the problem. The Forgiveness Act would start to put a dent in the racial wealth gap in America. But—and this is why I have been such an outspoken advocate of this—it's not just about what it means for African Americans. It is about what it means for every American citizen to finally reckon with their country's past so we can live up to our true potential. And in terms of whether I'm optimistic about it passing, I would say I'm extremely optimistic. I mean, look. We have a record number of African Americans in Congress—the most since the founding of this country. Now, clearly, there are members who oppose the Forgiveness Act. Who think they should not be responsible for the sins of previous genera-tions. But what I ask them is whether they drive on roads that were built before their generation. Do they pay taxes for public services that will benefit other people? Do they want to save the planet for future generations? I'm excited for the benefits our society will reap when a country is spiritually and financially liberated.*

Host: *There have been comparisons between the Forgiveness Act and the Civil Liberties Act. Are those accurate?*

Senator Walker: *The Civil Liberties Act was necessary because Japa-nese Americans who were subjected to the racism and brutality of internment camps deserved recourse. The CLA proves that repara-tions can work in this country. I want to be clear that one of the differences with the Forgiveness Act is that it's not only an acknowl-edgment of wrongdoing. With Forgiveness we are looking to create systemic change.*

Host: *We've been hearing that there are proof requirements to qualify for the funds and there is some concern about what will be required.*

What's your opinion of that criticism and do you think it's a valid concern?

Senator Walker: *Anytime you're implementing something of this magnitude, there will be growing pains. We saw that with the multiple iterations of the Civil Liberties Act. The final iteration of that bill took forty years, partially because of the failed proof requirements the first time around. We hopefully learned from those lessons and will course correct as quickly as we can if there are problems.*

There was so much change in the country and in the business, Willie felt physical sensations—the smell of the air, the texture of the soil in the garden—were all she could trust. Every day there was a new headline, another event, which made her regret taking the stability of previous years for granted. Yes, she had always wanted the Forgiveness Act, but in a consistent and vague way, the way one might want their favorite television show to end. When she found herself feeling excited over the possibility of the Forgiveness Act, she questioned whether it was foolish to feel optimism. There was no policy in America that had ever done entirely right by her people. It was a country built on hypocrisy; she had been taught to hold this skepticism in her heart since she was a child.

Willie found a parking spot near Celine's apartment in front of the Mother Bethel AME Church, its stained-glass windows refracting rainbows onto the sidewalk as the bell continued its steadfast stride to six chimes. The statue of Richard Allen, the church's founder, raised a hand in blessing while his other hand rested on top of a Bible. It was the oldest African Methodist Episcopal congregation in the country, in the oldest church property continuously owned by Black people. Philadelphia was the only true home she'd ever known, and the city, while at times stifling and too small, defined her as much as anything else. You could walk almost anywhere and feel like you were part of a larger piece of the story, a cornerstone for the entire country. Willie looked once more at the church, feeling briefly the connection among all things. The Forgiveness Act and the creation of this church, the history of this parish. She noticed how two different colors of brick made up the exterior and how the copper of the bell had faded into an off-kilter green. The multistoried homes near the church, with their small balconies and brass door knockers glinting in the sun, somehow carried a similar stately aura. Philadelphia was filled with these beautiful reminders of the past, but they asked something of her, a respect to be repaid, which most times she felt unable to give. New York, on the other hand, had asked nothing, needed nothing. Here what she did mattered, and if it didn't, she felt it had the potential to.

In front of Celine's apartment was a welcome mat that said *Bienvenu*, a pair of tall black boots, and a grungy set of sneakers. Willie slid out of her leather loafers and pushed open the door, which was propped against the deadbolt, then let it close softly behind her. As an adult, Celine wanted to be a bohemian who survived on her grit and charm with little comfort, but signs of her wealth were apparent in subtle ways, like the artwork gracing the walls of her new apartment, gifted after her grandmother died, or the location of the apartment itself, two rooms above a bakery in Old City, modest but filled with her parents' furniture.

"Hello!" Willie called, and made her way down the narrow hallway.

Nell and Celine answered in unison. Celine grabbed the wine out of Willie's hand, hugging her with one arm. The kitchen smelled of onions and garlic, and Annie Lennox played loudly from a room away, the thick walls muting the singer's impact. Willie poured herself a glass of wine and walked over to the window, taking in the skyline. Celine had recently accepted a full-time position as an editor with Penn's alumni magazine, and what Willie felt wasn't jealousy exactly—she had harbored greater ambitions than a university magazine—but it was close enough to the type of life Willie once imagined for herself that she had to work to conceal flashes of coldness. She imagined herself in Celine's position. Living downtown with her daughter, not feeling like every decision made factored in whether Max and Lourdes were okay. What would it have been like to live and breathe your work because it consumed you? Working at MRA was fulfilling on a basic, superficial level. She was organized and efficient, and she knew the company had survived for as long as it had only because of her. And yet she fueled it, not the other way around. Nell and Celine used to tell her how impressive it was, a woman running a construction company, at which point Willie explained well, no, she wasn't running it. Max was.

They wanted her to want more from life within the confines of what she had. They used to prod her to move out of Lewaro Street, until one day she finally told them to stop. Lewaro Street was comfortable; Lourdes helped take care of Paloma; it didn't make sense to spend money on rent. They both knew her the best and yet sometimes not at all. Wanting more from life wasn't the problem. The problem might have been that she wanted too much, spent her formative years around people who expected to get what they wanted. At a certain point she had stayed so long at MRA because she was scared to leave. What if she couldn't get another job in journalism? What if editors laughed at her for trying? What if the only job she could get wouldn't be enough to take care of Paloma? Familiarity—a powerful enough drug to dull the senses, chain you to a place, making you insecure.

Willie helped Nell arrange taco materials on the table as Celine carried over the salad and wine. "My dad's retirement party is next week," Celine announced, biting into a taco, not noticing that half of the insides had fallen back onto her plate, "and my parents begged me to bring a date. Apparently I'm only as important as the person I'm with."

"I thought you were still seeing what's-his-name."

Celine laughed, coughing on her food. "He complained I wasn't available enough. And that when I was available, I wasn't present." Celine held up her hands in air quotes around the word *present*.

"That's why I asked you both here tonight," she said, cupping her hands together and resting them behind her plate.

Nell rolled her eyes. "We have dinner here every Monday."

"Yes, but I have a special request. There is an editor in my office who could be a contender for a date, and I want to throw a party as an excuse to get to know him. Will you two come?"

"You think dating someone you work with is the best idea?" Nell asked. "You just started this job."

Celine nodded and continued eating. "It will be fine."

"When's the party?" Willie asked.

"This Friday."

Nell shook her head. "That's the day the Senate is voting on the Forgiveness Act."

"Oh, I didn't realize it was this week," Celine said, embarrassed.

There was an awkward silence, each clasping on to their own resentments.

"How are you two feeling about it?"

Willie and Nell glanced at each other. It was hard to hear Celine's question without feeling its deficiencies, the meat of which was that the Forgiveness Act had no bearing on her.

"What's to feel?" Nell said, carrying her plate into the kitchen, returning with another bottle of wine. "I feel great about it if it passes. But I really don't want to be around a bunch of white people the day we find out."

"It will pass," Willie said, raising up one knee and resting it against the edge of the table. When it came to politics, they let her speak with an authority she didn't possess because of her former relationship with President Johnson. She looked at Celine, who sat nodding with an unspecific smile, and wondered if anything was real to her friend. After a moment she said the thing that had been on her mind since morning. "I think my dad has wiped out their retirement to keep the business going. The only prospective job Max and I have coming in is with Hank Lasure's company."

"You can't work with him," Celine said, shaking her head.

"Easy for you to say. I don't want to work with Hank either, but what choice do I have?"

"You act like you're chained to your desk. Get another job."

"What other job? The only experience I have is working for a newspaper for less than a year."

"Remember Aunt Terry?" Nell said. "She runs that recruiting firm. I'm sure she'd help you."

"I can't just leave."

Her friends sighed, both visibly and audibly annoyed.

"You have a right to be happy. You can't always do what you think is the right thing if it makes you so miserable."

She looked at her friends, feeling so utterly not of their world that it made her shiver. There was always a fourth presence among the three of them that no one wanted to acknowledge. All the hurt parts and embarrassments they thought no one could see. They thought not speaking about them made them invisible, but all it did was make each person seem less real, slightly more condescending. Could she be the first to acknowledge it? Could she tell them how sometimes at night she wrote fake book reviews and articles? How one time she pitched ten publications and didn't hear a single thing back. How she'd hate herself too much, feel like too much of a failure, if she left MRA now. She knew it made no sense. She cleared her throat as if to say it. She wanted to say it. But if Nell and Celine responded with anything other than, *We love you and we're here for you, we understand,* she wouldn't be able to bear it. "I don't want to talk about it," she said instead.

She felt lonely walking back to her car and paused to look at the church and houses around her. Two men shook hands on the brick steps of a home across the street, and when one of them laughed, she looked closer, realizing it was Max. The other man stood in the doorway, leaning casually against the frame as though seeing a friend off. Willie had never seen Hank Lasure in person, though his face—his mannerisms—were recognizable. His brown hair parted to the side, a few tendrils gracing his forehead. Bright-blue eyes, almost physically piercing in their clarity. In all the pictures she had seen of Hank, he was always dressed impeccably, as though it were by accident, an expensive-looking navy-blue suit with a starched white shirt and no tie.

She crossed the street and approached them, smiling manically at her father. Max opened his mouth to speak and then closed it. "Hank," he said finally. "This is my daughter."

Hank gave her a confused look and made a half-hearted gesture, as if unsure whether to descend the stairs to shake her hand on the sidewalk.

"What are you doing here?" Max asked, his eyes pleading with her not to make a scene.

"I was having dinner at Celine's. Nice to meet you, Hank."

"Likewise. Your dad is a great guy. Hopefully we'll be able to work together," he said, nodding.

Willie cleared her throat and turned to look at Max.

"Well," Hank said, banging the door twice with a flat palm, "I better get back inside. If the kitchen is already clean, I'll be in trouble." He pointed an index finger at both of them. "We'll talk soon."

She turned on Max once the door was closed. "Meeting? At his house?"

"Don't," Max said. "Not here. Please. I'll meet you at home."

—

Back home, the house was quiet. Part of what Willie hadn't been able to explain to Nell and Celine was that she felt incapable of continuing to take the moral high ground, because she wasn't good. She *wanted* to be good, and her desire meant she held positions that she thought were the right ones, but they were aspirational, and that was all. She felt physically uncomfortable about Hank's position about the Forgiveness Act because people like that—of which there were so many—didn't understand the reverberating costs of slavery. It wasn't a real word to them, only a word they were tired of hearing, so they heard nothing. He was against reparations? Plenty of people had been against reparations. But how could she go to Max and tell him it was wrong to work with Hank when they had no viable alternatives except getting the Forgiveness money itself, which had no timeline attached to it?

Willie boiled water and stared at family photos on the credenza while she waited for Max to get home. Her favorite photo was from a road trip the family had taken several years ago. Willie and Lourdes are posing in large straw hats, each with one hand resting on the brim. Paloma is balanced on Willie's slim hip, and Max is standing behind Lourdes, gripping her shoulders like he's guiding a boat to shore. She remembers Seb yelling "Smile!" and for the first time in months, she smiled without thinking about it, without forcing herself to. The trip had come at the right time, when the fog from Paloma's birth finally cleared and she was able to feel good again, whole and like herself.

The kettle whistled and Willie turned off the heat. Lourdes walked in carrying her own mug and the two of them sat at the kitchen table, each lost in her own thoughts. "Where's Paloma?" Willie asked.

Her mother chuckled and turned a small spoon in tiny circles in her cup, despite not taking sugar or milk, fearing anything settling at the bottom. "She told me not to disturb her artistic process. I haven't seen her since dinner."

Willie sat thinking. "How much do you all have in savings?" she asked carefully.

Lourdes sipped, staring at the pattern of dark lines making waves in the wood table and pretending not to be startled by the question. "We have enough."

Willie pictured her mother cleaning houses again in her sixties, her wrinkles becoming more pronounced, her back stooped, living in an apartment or a smaller house without any of the antiques and furniture she had acquired over the years for 512 Lewaro. For the first time, a seed of worry planted itself firmly in Willie's stomach. She had been naïve when she first wanted the Forgiveness Act to pass. She had partially viewed it as symbolic, a way for the country to move forward, even as she also believed in its urgency. If you understood where wealth came from in this country, how could you dispute the necessity of the Forgiveness Act to close the gap? She found it unfathomable. Still, she had understood the act in an academic sense, but her understanding lacked experience and, to a certain extent, empathy. She understood now. How it could be both not about money and how money was necessary. The truth was that no matter how secure you thought you were, how far removed you thought you were from the inevitable fight and strength that made it possible for you, Willie, to be sitting at this kitchen table with your mother in a beautiful house, you were never that far at all. Today, tomorrow, twenty years from now—the worry was going to come eventually. The fight was going to resume, because that was the country they lived in.

"Willie, come in here a minute," Max called to her from the sunroom, where he had gone straight to after arriving home.

"It's fine," she said, preempting him, as she walked into the room. "I know you're doing what you think is best. I just don't know if I can do it with you."

"It's worse than you think, okay? I've already transferred the money from our retirement account into the business."

"I know."

"What do you mean you know? How do you know that?"

"It doesn't matter."

Max sighed. "Just because we work with him doesn't mean we believe what he believes. Someone will take his money. Might as well be us."

"But that isn't who we are."

"What's the alternative? I don't have a degree from a fancy college. I don't have any degree."

"I do."

"Then use it."

"I planned to."

Max looked up at the ceiling. "We're meeting at their offices tomorrow. Come with me. Please."

She left the sunroom and walked into the library, where she swallowed a sip of tea and scooted closer to the computer. Like anyone scared of the inevitable, she had avoided looking too closely at the details. Now she clicked and read about the man whose company could supposedly save them.

Hank Lasure grew up in Louisville, Kentucky, the son of an insurance salesman and a fifth-grade teacher. When he was two, a polio attack paralyzed his right leg, leaving him with a slight limp. His classmates used to call him Hoppity Hank. To avoid the taunts, he spent most of his childhood inside, creating imaginary worlds where he was the leader.

At the age of twenty-three, with a chemical-engineering degree from Harvard and a five-thousand-dollar loan from his uncle, Hank started a chemical-manufacturing company. His first customers were also his uncle's customers—farms east to west along I-64 and I-80. By the time Hank turned forty-three, Soteria Industries was one of the most profitable manufacturing companies in the country.

There was an article about a recent fundraiser for Senator Mark Lee where Hank was quoted as calling the Forgiveness Act "an embarrassment for the country and a moral stain on the Constitution." Willie clicked on the link but couldn't stomach more than the first two paragraphs. He had penned a letter to Congress with several other CEOs, proclaiming, *Hard work and personal re-*

sponsibility are core American values. These values lead me to oppose the Forgiveness Act, which will not only increase the United States deficit but will send a message to African Americans that their own hard work is not adequately valued, and time and energy taken away from building the U.S. economy will instead be spent reviewing the mistakes of the past. She knew Hank Lasure wasn't influenced by the video of a man being murdered or a mother's relentless anguish. He said it was terrible and a tragedy, but you could see in his eyes that, really, he believed these men and women and children were at fault, somehow putting themselves in that situation, that it wasn't his problem. In addition to owning the manufacturing company, he now also had significant real estate holdings throughout the city. He relied heavily on contractors, whom he paid very little compared to his own profits. Willie tried to ignore the pressure in her chest, the swirl in her stomach like a tossed coin before a game.

She scanned the headlines, searching for some sort of unequivocal sign, but of course nobody had written a piece saying *Hank Lasure is evil, Willie. Don't work with him.* But if she was going to tell Max to walk away from the deal, she had to have more than a vague idea of who Hank was and what he stood for.

Her mind worked in the wrong direction. Her instinct was to further expose Hank for who he was, not work with him despite it. She thought back to the night in Alfie Cane's study. *Write the truth,* he had said. She clicked away from the article about Hank and looked up Alfie Cane's biography on the university website. He was still teaching the same classes and had barely published anything new since she graduated. Neither of them had spoken about what happened, and she had tried to spend as little time alone with him as possible after that. What would he think about her life now? He would tell her to write anyway. She thought about emailing him and asking for advice, but what would she say? The distance from that night had given her perspective, and she was able to see it for what it was. *He* had stood close to her in his study. He had stared at her, he had wanted her and he hadn't done a good job of hiding it. They were both to blame. But just looking at his picture made her throat close and her face turn into a grimace because she still hated herself when she looked at him.

Willie jumped when Paloma came into the library with a stack of papers tucked under her arm. Ann Peebles sang about tearing down a playhouse and Willie turned down the volume, nodding at the papers in her daughter's arm. "I'm guessing you're still awake because that's the play you're working on?"

"Mr. Jeremy had us pick someone famous to write a play about. I chose Phillis Wheatley."

"How do you know who Phillis Wheatley is?"

"I found a book of her poetry in here."

"You're amazing, you know that?"

Willie wanted to reach into a bag of their history and encourage her daughter with a story about a relative or an ancestor who had been an author or an artist. *We come from a long line of being the few Black girls in school,* Willie thought.

"I decided I want to be a playwright," Paloma told her, settling down in the armchair and spreading her papers out before her.

Chapter 9

Paloma came to slowly from the dreams, as though someone softly touched her shoulder to wake her. This time she dreamed she was standing alone in a circle, and people kept wanting her to speak, to justify something, but each time she tried to use her voice, nothing happened. She was trying to find her father in the faces, she wanted her father's help, but in the dream she knew he had been taken the night before; she knew she would never see him again.

Paloma lay in her bed, staring at the ceiling, a corner of which was covered with several glow-in-the-dark star stickers. She felt queasy and sad, her comforter pressing her to the bed the same way Max had once pressed the stars to the wall.

The dreams had begun when she started researching Phillis, and she wasn't sure what to make of them. Now she tried to swallow and felt jagged glass carving a path down her esophagus. She looked at the clock on her bedside table and realized it was twenty minutes later than she typically got out of bed. Willie came in and asked if she was feeling all right, while walking to the curtains and pulling the drawstring, sending them cascading in opposite directions.

Paloma shook her head. "My throat hurts."

"You've been staying up too late working on that play." Willie laid the back of her hand against Paloma's forehead. "You're staying home." When Paloma tried to argue, Willie held up her hands. "Your grandmother will be here. Try to go down and at least have some breakfast." She kissed Paloma on the forehead and was gone.

By the time Paloma had brushed her teeth and pulled on a sweatshirt to go downstairs, her mother had left for work.

Lourdes stood at the sink, holding a cup of coffee and looking out at the pool and garden. Paloma didn't like missing school, but she and Lourdes relished being in the house by themselves. When Paloma was home sick with her grandmother, she would read in an armchair in the kitchen while Lourdes cooked or, if she felt well enough, would help with ironing or delivering fresh laundry throughout the rooms. During lunch they would take a break from chores and share a meal of chicken soup and saltines while watching soap operas. She appreciated the quiet elegance with which her grandmother moved about 512 Lewaro Street, dusting the antique surfaces, making beds, ironing clothes. They didn't feel like chores—at least not to Paloma—only the honorable acts necessary to inhabit a home so majestic. When Lourdes was alone, though, she spent the mornings leafing through Willie's old college brochures and mapping out imaginary course loads for herself. At the library she took out books on each subject and spent the mornings talking to the librarian or with Doris at the diner, where she would go sometimes to read.

It had become a ritual for sick days to double as wash days, and now Paloma positioned herself in front of Lourdes, next to the pomade and brushes and flat iron, while her grandmother turned on the news.

Paloma's favorite anchor appeared, a serious woman with braided hair and pink lipstick. "The Senate majority leader has been vocal about pushing the Forgiveness Act through," she told viewers. "Here he is discussing the act with reporters earlier today."

Nathan Townsend stood in a marble hallway, two thick columns on either side of his small frame. He spoke slowly and carefully, like one of Paloma's old windup dolls:

Eight years ago, we passed the Commission to Study and Develop Reparations Proposals for African Americans, to address the fundamental injustice, cruelty, brutality, and inhumanity of slavery in the United States. The results from this study were undeniable. For hundreds of years, the United States government has successfully evaded responsibility for constitutionally and statutorily sanctioning the unspeakable exploitation of African Americans.

The deprivation of freedom; the exploitation of labor; the destruction of culture, religion, language, and families; and the denial of humanity. The United States government willingly engaged in these acts. Today, the African American community continues to suffer

the consequences of deliberate prejudiced choices made by the gov-
ernment of the United States of America—the consequences of
redlining, of exclusion from the G.I. Bill, of police brutality, of
mass incarceration, of unequal education in Black communities.

To heal a wound, you must first acknowledge its existence. While
no amount of money can ever make up for the wrongs committed by
the United States government against its own citizens—citizens
who made this country possible—America now takes the first im-
portant step. A country that does not acknowledge its moral wrongs
cannot move forward. With the Forgiveness Act, America accepts
both moral and financial responsibility for the wrongs committed
against African Americans and starts its long process of healing in
order to deserve the words written in one of its founding docu-
ments: All men are created equal.

We are recommending that families begin considering how they
will qualify for the Forgiveness funds. We will release a genealogy
guide, but families are strongly encouraged to think about which
ancestral line they will use to prove qualification and who will be in
charge of documentation.

The flat iron singed Paloma's ear as her grandmother inhaled
sharply and stared at the screen. Paloma knew to keep her pain to
herself, so she sat there, her left ear burning until Lourdes set the
iron down on the glass coffee table, while the screen panned to
senators shaking hands. Her grandmother grabbed her shoulders
and swiveled Paloma around to face her. Paloma saw she was
smiling, and Lourdes's expression turned Paloma's face into a re-

flection of her grandmother's. The two of them sat like that for a few moments, beaming at each other, as the news continued playing in the background. Paloma saw in her grandmother's face an accessibility and openness that she wished she saw in Willie's.

"You look happy," Paloma told Lourdes.

"I just can't believe it's actually happening."

Chapter 10

Willie drove them downtown to the meeting with Hank, while Max, sitting quietly in the passenger seat, pretended to be engrossed in something on his phone. Hank's office had laid out pastries and cardboard boxes of coffee on a skinny frosted table along one side of the room.

This time she did shake his hand and sat next to the head of the table, taking out a notebook and her laptop.

Three of Hank's colleagues joined, and Willie stared at each one, trying to deduce their motives, making excuses for why they were there. One man covered half of his mouth as he spoke and she pictured his lips morphing into a zipper and him stepping out of his skin.

She walked through their standard timeline for jobs. What

she felt when speaking was not what she expected, or what Max likely thought, watching her as he was from the other end of the table. Despite her tense muscles, hatred, agitation, she still wanted to come across as competent, and she was disgusted with herself that, after everything, this was what she focused on. Max, who hadn't spoken much, drummed his fingers on the table. "Where's your bathroom?" he asked suddenly, looking around the room. One of Hank's colleagues stood and pointed down the hall to the right.

"Is that your daughter?" Hank asked Willie after Max had left.

Willie followed the line of Hank's finger and saw that Paloma's newest school headshot, a photo she had tucked into a page of her notebook, had fallen onto the table. She reached out and slid it back between the pages. "It is."

"Looks to be about the same age as my daughter," Hank continued.

Willie smiled politely. "Why don't we take a quick break while we wait for my father?" she suggested. People nodded and stood.

Moments later, a man who hadn't been in the meeting pushed open the door. "Are you all missing anyone? Someone collapsed in the bathroom." He looked at Willie, given that there were no other Black people in the office.

Willie stood, panicked. "What happened? Where is he?"

"I had the secretary call an ambulance."

Her heartbeat drummed in her ears as she moved quickly to where Max was lying on the floor outside the bathroom, a few people kneeling in front of him. "Dad. What happened? Are you okay?"

Sweat dotted his upper lip and hairline. He opened his eyes

briefly but didn't respond. "Who called the ambulance? Where is it?" Willie screamed, and the faces around her looked distorted, like cartoons. She tried to help Max sit up.

"I don't think we should move him," a man on her left said. "Let's wait until they get here."

She was staring down at Max, who was breathing heavily, when three EMTs arrived, pushing a stretcher down the hallway, disconcertingly calm.

"Make room, please," one commanded.

Most people moved away and went back to their desks or conference rooms. One person from her meeting stayed, pulling her out of the way so that she could no longer see Max. The calm voices became rushed. Max was hoisted onto the stretcher, and one of the EMTs got on the radio to say they were coming down with a male patient, "nonresponsive." She hesitated, frozen, and didn't know whether to run after them when they left with the stretcher. By the time she realized she should have followed, they were already in the elevator with Max.

Hank stood next to her. "I can drive you to the hospital."

She looked up and met his gaze. She felt like an imitation of a woman, a daughter, an employee. *How terrible,* she thought. *How terrible.* The two words kept repeating themselves in her mind, and she wasn't even sure why or what they meant. But what if it didn't matter at all what they did? So what if they worked with him? "I have a car," she managed. "It's okay."

He had already gone back to the conference room and gotten her bag. "It will take too long to get it out of the garage. I have a parking spot."

She sat in the passenger seat of Hank's Range Rover and kept swallowing like there was something stuck in her throat. He didn't try to make small talk or make her feel better, which she appreciated. They drove in silence. The car smelled like expensively pungent perfume and he had a picture of his daughter stuck to the dashboard with a pink bunny magnet.

He pulled up to the emergency entrance and she jumped out of the car. "Thank you," she said. "I appreciate the ride."

"Let me know if there's anything I can do."

She gave a brief nod and closed the door.

A nurse told her where to wait. For one reason or another she couldn't bring herself to call Lourdes. If she called, it would mean acknowledging that something terrible was happening (or perhaps had already happened). She needed to delay the knowing, so she sat hugging herself.

"Ms. Revel?" A man with a clipboard stood in front of her and told her Max was stable.

"Can I see him?"

Max was in the bed, alert and embarrassed. The heart monitor was background noise. "I'm okay," he said when he saw her. "I'm okay."

The nurse had told Willie that Max had passed out from low blood sugar and a complication because of a new medication.

Max and Willie looked at each other and then looked away. "You scared the shit out of me."

"You know," he said, "I've been thinking a lot about what I will leave behind. I don't want it to disappear. I didn't even think I'd make it one year. Thirty years and what? I'm supposed to let it vanish? I want to leave you and Paloma with something. Can you understand that? Real inheritance. Our people don't get that kind of thing every day. I know this isn't what you wanted to do with your life," he continued. "I know that. But you've done good. You're doing good."

She reached out and placed her hand over his.

Chapter 11

Years ago, Seb interrogated Willie about President Johnson's plan to pass the Forgiveness Act, how she planned to do it and why she planned to do it, as though Willie had great insight into her former professor's character. What Willie knew was that Professor Johnson was the most skilled communicator she'd ever witnessed. While the male students in her class challenged her often, Professor Johnson listened respectfully and then presented counterarguments as if she were entering a house through the side door, so that by the end of the discussion the students barely realized they'd changed their own positions. The press frequently covered her tactics, how expertly she sweet-talked the moderate Republicans and conservative Democrats, moving them to her side like pieces on a chessboard. Her strength in office was the same as in the classroom: a lack of ego and a willingness to play dumb and pretend to have the weaknesses that were assumed inherent to her gender.

The night after Max's incident, while the family consumed unceasing coverage about the Forgiveness Act and the upcoming Senate vote and the apparent risk of a filibuster, Willie announced that she would be in charge of getting their records together.

"What records?" Marcus asked.

"The records we need to qualify."

"We don't have records," Marcus said. "And even if we do, sounds like it might not matter anyway."

"It's going to pass. And every family has records; we just haven't traced anything yet."

Willie looked at her mother to agree, but Lourdes ignored her gaze and heaped more roast chicken onto Max's plate, still angry that neither of them had told her about Max's trip to the hospital until she discovered the forgotten white bracelet limply clasped around his wrist.

As a family they had made no real plans for once the Forgiveness Act passed, as though planning were a form of superstitious sabotage. Willie wanted to shake each of them and ask if they understood what it meant? The lack of planning was the same way they approached the business. She knew it was self-preservation, not ignorance. While planning and preparation might mean accepting disappointment, stasis was a more comfortable perpetual extension of the present.

At seven-thirty on Friday night, Willie pushed open Celine's apartment door to the sound of loud voices and the smell of hot, expensively catered food. Celine, wearing a black skirt and a white silk top, gripped her arm in the foyer. "I'm so glad you're here," she whispered. Most of Celine's friends, Willie assumed, were supportive of Forgiveness yet indifferent to its implications, so she was wary of the false smiles she might end up wearing, but she needed to get out of the house, even if for an hour.

Small groups of people were dotted throughout the kitchen and living room, sipping wine and choking down scotch and vodka on the rocks. Willie selected a beer from the bucket on the kitchen counter and stood next to Nell. The two of them surveyed the room, trying to figure out how everyone knew one another.

"I'm staying for twenty more minutes," Nell said sullenly, "and then she can't say we didn't try." They connected glasses and returned to their observation. Five other Black people stood around the room, looking distracted. A few men sat on the couch, watching sports.

Celine appeared next to Nell and Willie, gesturing toward a man in the middle of the sofa. "That's him," she said, pointing out her reason for the party. She twisted her skirt so it rested lower on her hip.

"Go tell him you want to show him something in your bedroom," Willie teased.

Celine grunted and wandered off, continuing to adjust her skirt. Because of the music, or because Willie felt she shouldn't be there, the cacophony of voices sounded to her like tin.

"Well, anyway, the statues are beside the point," a man behind the couch was saying. "The novelist Émile Zola believed if you were born poor, you lived with the soil inside you. Meaning you can't escape your fate."

Nell and Willie approached the group, and one of the men, who had introduced himself as Jared, looked confused and irritated. "What the hell does that have to do with anything? People don't want racists immortalized in stone throughout the country. That has nothing to do with your fate." As he talked, Willie couldn't help glancing at a vein bulging in his neck.

"People who want to rebel will always find something to rebel about."

Nell rolled her eyes, twirling her keys around a finger on her left hand. "On second thought, I'm leaving. Want to come with me?"

Willie glanced around and shook her head. "I'll leave soon."

She wandered over to a hallway lined with artwork, and gazed at a painting—the back of a man staring into a dark cave, holding a lantern under a sky of stars—and thought how maybe Celine's whole persona, her parties, her friends, even her art, were just attempts at believing in things she felt she should believe in but didn't, really.

She moved to the next painting and wished for more light in the hallway, squinting. At first glance it was a sketch of a house, but now Willie noticed there were lots of other tiny details. A birdbath and a canvas set up in the outline of a garden, a painter working en plein air.

Celine's brother, Daniel, appeared next to her, nodding at the sketch. "This is my favorite."

Though she hadn't seen him for several years, Celine, Nell,

and Willie once visited Daniel in New York when he was in college. The two of them hugged and Willie asked what brought him to town.

"Talking to my dad about investing in my company."

"Since when do you own a company?"

"Since I realized people in New York want to get out of the city but don't own any of the right equipment to go camping or hiking or skiing. I'm starting an outdoor sporting company that covers the full gamut. Rentals, advice on where to go. I want to make it an entire experience." He paused, narrowing his eyes. "Doesn't your family own a business?" he asked.

"We do. But hardly comparable to what you're trying to do."

"Still, you must have some advice."

Willie took a long drink from her second beer. "Just don't work with family."

He laughed. She excused herself and went to the bathroom.

When she came out, Jared from the other group was there, admiring the cave painting. Willie pointed at the artwork and continued standing behind him, leaning on the doorframe. "Haunting, isn't it?"

The voices from the other rooms pushed them deeper into the apartment and closer together to hear each other. He told her he worked for *The Inquirer*.

"Sometimes I feel I'm not a very good journalist," he said, laughing. "I care too much about the people I interview. You have to be more ruthless in this job."

She nodded. "I used to want to be a journalist. But"—she shrugged—"I couldn't figure out a way to make it work."

Jared nodded like he understood. "My dad found my journal

once where I wrote down stories. He walked into my room one night, holding it, and said, 'I will finance you for two years if you can figure out how to turn this into something.' It was all the encouragement I needed."

Willie contemplated how different her life might look had her parents done the same.

The apartment grew quiet, and Willie realized quite a few people had already left.

She glanced up at the television to check the time, and someone had changed the channel to the news. On the screen was a view of the Senate floor. Lots of dark suits standing around and a countdown clock in the corner slowly ticking upward. Two hours fourteen minutes thirty seconds, thirty-one seconds, thirty-two seconds. Willie silently read the words on the screen: *Senator Mark Lee (R-PA) Filibusters Forgiveness Act Vote.* She glanced at Jared, who had moved to lean against the edge of the sofa. Despite everything she knew, the filibuster had seemed symbolic and theoretical and now that it was happening, her chest tightened at the cruel inevitability of resistance.

"I didn't think they were really going to let him go through with this," he said.

"He can't actually stall the vote," Willie said, sounding more confident than she felt.

Jared walked closer to the television, angling himself to the side of it, cradling his drink in one hand like a grenade. "He's banking on trying to delay it enough to make Townsend nervous. There's a bill he knows Townsend wants to push through, and the longer he delays Forgiveness, the harder it is."

A woman in a long floral dress and high boots approached

and sat on the arm of the couch. She pointed at the television. "What's going on?"

"Filibuster," Willie said, without turning to look at her. "Against the Forgiveness Act."

Jared looked back at Willie. "I have to go," he said. "My friend is doing a story on this now. I'm going to go watch at his apartment." He walked over and held out his hand. "It was really nice to meet you." They shook hands and he was gone. She realized it was time for her to go too, but she couldn't pull her eyes away from the screen. She worried if she left, she would miss a crucial element of the vote—as if by watching she could control the outcome.

"He has a point," the woman was saying, grabbing the remote. "If it passes, the deficit will be too high. There's no way the United States can afford this."

Willie set her glass carefully on the table.

"There are ways to solve inequality other than spending money the country doesn't have on things no one alive today is responsible for." The woman pointed up at Willie. "I mean, didn't you go to a private school with Celine? Why should you get the same amount as another family?" It wasn't the question itself that made Willie want to shove the woman off the couch; rather, it was the tone and intention, a question that couldn't be answered without Willie digging into her bag of good manners for a calm she couldn't procure.

The woman stood and held her palm out, continuing, "I get issuing a formal apology. I do. I think the country needs to acknowledge that the way we have treated African Americans is wrong. But I don't think this is the right way to go about it."

Celine, who had been standing in the kitchen and overheard, came to stand between Willie and the woman, putting her hands on the small of their backs.

Willie held up her palm and pivoted, removing Celine's hand and distancing herself from both of them.

Because there it was. The pitiful justification she had heard so many times before as someone tried to convince themselves they were still a good person, both patriotic and liberal.

"It's not about the money," Willie said. It was and it wasn't. Either way, she felt she wasn't required to explain. "And how could you possibly know what the right way to go about it is?" She didn't wait for the woman to stammer out an answer. Willie grabbed her jacket from the coat rack and brushed past Daniel in the hallway without saying goodbye.

On the drive home, she listened to NPR's coverage of the filibuster. The Democrats had pre-filed a cloture motion, a procedure that limits debate on a bill, but they hadn't yet voted. Other Republican senators kept asking long-winded questions to give Mark a break from speaking and to drag out his time on the floor. The streets were mostly empty, so Willie pushed the speed limit. A PennDOT vehicle with blinking yellow lights moved along slowly down Lincoln Drive.

Willie threw her bag on an armchair behind the kitchen table and walked to the sunroom, where Lourdes, Paloma, Max, and Marcus all stared at the television.

CNN kept breaking away from the filibuster to replay clips from earlier in the night. Willie was struck by the general disarray and lack of professionalism on the Senate floor—men with cuffs rolled up like Jared's had been; people looking tired and whispering in the background. It looked similar to MRA's office. The government seems like a formal notion until you see its innards, Willie thought. And then you realize it's just made up of people. Sloppy, messy, imperfect people, with the same small wants and fears as the rest of us. Mark Lee was saying, *This is not about partisanship. I have allowed the president to indulge whimsical notions of righting the wrongs committed by her ancestor. But it is not the nation's responsibility to atone for her family's perceived moral wrongs. It is not the nation's responsibility to assuage her guilt. I will not sit by quietly while she makes a mockery of the United States government by raising our deficit and opening the door to future redress payments for unworthy groups. The fact is, no one alive today is responsible for slavery. No one alive today was a slave. Therefore, no one alive today should be taking money from the United States government on behalf of slavery. At this moment in time, we have nothing to ask forgiveness for. I urge every member of this body to consider this bill most carefully. I hope the Senate will see fit to kill it.*

Max suddenly picked up a pillow and punched it, and Willie felt justified at the outburst from a man who supposedly didn't care about the Forgiveness Act.

Lourdes told him to be quiet and removed the pillow from his grasp.

Paloma turned to Willie. "Does this mean it won't pass?"

Willie placed a hand on Paloma's knee. "It is only to prove a point."

Rationally, Willie knew this was true. But it was the making of a comedic skit, the way it felt like every second counted, their eyes glued to the countdown clock. It wasn't so much the filibuster itself (the group of Republican senators who opposed Forgiveness had been vocal about it all along) as it was the listening in real time to those who didn't think people like the Revels had the same rights they did, that they didn't have any lingering pain that deserved to be accounted for. To them, slavery wasn't bad. It was the natural order of things. And how do you correct something that to certain people was never wrong to begin with?

The rest of the house was dark. The television illuminated the Revels like little specks in a model home. For some reason Willie thought of a time when she was younger and had overheard people at one of her parents' parties recalling the murder of Fred Hampton. "They didn't charge not one of those bastards," she remembered Max saying and then finishing his drink. Afterward, she had looked up who Fred Hampton was in the library, confused at the differences between the headlines and what the people she knew were saying. The first time it occurred to her the news didn't always tell the truth.

The mood shifted on the Senate floor. The news anchors, who had been trying to fill the airtime like they were performing their own filibuster, stopped talking. As Mark Lee spoke, a Democratic senator started whispering to a colleague and then stood, gripping a microphone in her hand. Mark Lee was saying, "Blacks commit, as a percentage of their race, more violent crimes than white Americans."

A point of order from the Democratic senator: "The crime rate among Black Americans is not germane to the Forgiveness Act."

Then the gavel: Point of order sustained. It was slightly after eleven o'clock at night, and Willie couldn't hear what else was being said, because she heard a guttural scream and realized it was coming from her.

"It passed?" Paloma asked, jumping up.

Willie pulled Paloma to her chest. "Not yet. But they will vote on it and then, yes, it will pass."

The phone rang. "You were right," Seb conceded, laughing.

Marcus sat in an armchair and in a raspy voice kept repeating, "I never thought in my lifetime, son. Not in my lifetime." She heard cheers from the Robinsons' house next door and could see, through the windows, the family hugging. The local news stations had reporters sprinkled across the city to catch what was to come. A Channel 10 news camera, stationed near her old neighborhood, panned to people embracing where, not unlike the Revels, people laughed at the unbidden sincerity of their own gestures.

Chapter 12

Police officers dragged three Black Panthers from their beds in the middle of the night, stripped them down to their underwear, and lined them up in front of the district center for Panther literature, not far from where Max and Lourdes were living at the time. If Willie's parents had wanted to, they could have walked there and watched as the men were shoved like crates of canned goods into the back of a police truck. When Willie later looked at pictures from that night, she looked at them transfixed as if wishing to make the images something foreign instead of the drama of America playing out down her parents' street. When Max and Lourdes invited a former Panther to their salon, Willie understood this history was all of theirs, regardless of whether you were alive when it happened or reading about it afterward.

On Friday, November 2, President Johnson prepared to sign the Forgiveness Act into law. Marcus sat in the sunroom, reclining in one of Max's large overstuffed chairs. Roy, Max and Lourdes's friend from the old neighborhood, sat next to Marcus, cradling a cold beer against his stomach while his wife, Eva, helped Lourdes make black-eyed peas in the kitchen. Willie picked Paloma up early from school so she could watch the signing with the rest of the family. Max paced around the house with one hand stuck stubbornly in his pocket; the other kept a cognac glued to his side, to hide it from Lourdes, who had tried banning alcohol since the hospital. Seb brought a date and potato salad. Downtown there were several haphazard parades taking place, streets blocked off to accommodate the celebrations. On television, the national news programs showed clips of parties across the country, kids stepping, adults laughing. The collective aura of hope and optimism with a continued dose of disbelief was hard to contain.

Willie watched as President Johnson made her slow walk to the podium. The camera panned out, showing the perimeter of the room, men and women dressed in elegant suits and beautiful dresses of scorched orange, their cameras held high. Democrats lined up along the wall, trying unsuccessfully to look humble.

Thank you all very much. Members of Congress and distinguished guests. My fellow Americans. We gather here today to right a grave wrong. More than four hundred years ago, the first ship carrying twenty enslaved souls from Africa arrived on the shores of America. For two hundred fifty years, America engaged in the most brutal capitalist system of modern civilization. Millions of human beings were forcibly removed from their homes and brought to the United

States to work this land so that America might prosper and become the great nation that it is today. The enslaved were denied their rights as human beings so that their owners might reap the rewards of their labor. They were separated from those whom they loved. Denied the right to learn. Denied the right to life, liberty, and the pursuit of happiness. The Declaration of Independence states that all men are created equal. But the human beings who helped power the American economy were denied humanity. I stand here today to sign the Forgiveness Act into law not only to right the wrongs committed by slavery but to help right the wrongs that persist to this day.

The American government sanctioned racist policies against African Americans who fought for us in our wars. The American government sanctioned racist policies against African Americans who sought to purchase homes. The American government sanctioned racist policies against African Americans who sought to learn. No amount of money can ever compensate for the loss of life, the loss of family, the loss of heritage, the loss of property, and the loss of wealth that African Americans have suffered. But on behalf of my nation, I look every African American in the eye and I say, "We apologize. We ask for your forgiveness." Mr. William Draper, to my left, is the great-grandson of a man whose business was destroyed in the 1921 Tulsa Race Massacre. His great-grandfather's insurance company was prosperous and successful until men burned it to the ground. No suspects were ever charged in this event.

Today I sign the Forgiveness Act into law to give compensation to citizens of our country who have been denied what they deserve for *far too long. I sign the Forgiveness Act into law to let every African American know that America accepts responsibility for failing to live up to the ideals we claim to profess. We ask for your forgiveness.*

The legislation I am about to sign provides for a restitution payment to every African American over the age of eighteen in the United States who proves they are a descendant of an enslaved person. This bill has less to do with money than with honor. For here we finally admit a wrong. Here we reaffirm our commitment as a nation to equal justice under the law. Here we unite as a country and finally move toward the realization of America. Thank you and God bless you. And now let me sign H.R. 619.

During moments of national importance, time melts and slips. Strangers huddle shoulder to shoulder to hear the news together. Invisible barriers crumble. A primal sense of community pulses once again through the streets. The Revels watched as Willie's former professor walked over to a table on the edge of the stage. They watched as she took out a ballpoint pen and turned the Forgiveness Act into law.

Willie glanced at Marcus. A cautious smile played along the corners of his lips, and his hands were folded in his lap as if finishing a prayer. Lourdes stood with her hands on her hips, one knee angled forward, her body a defiant statue, her face a mask of joy. Max's mood lifted, and he hugged his wife, then pressed PLAY on the nearby stereo, filling the sunroom with Stevie Wonder. Everyone paused, looking at one another and laughing, yielding to the moment. Roy and Eva embraced. Seb grabbed Willie by the shoulders and slapped her on the back. Willie hugged Paloma and whispered into her ear, "See, I told you it would pass." This time it was hope unbridled, joy uncensored. As though preparing for battle, a tribe fighting a common enemy, Max and Willie looked at each other for a long time as everyone continued moving around them.

During moments of national importance, it feels as though bills will be paid and mortgages covered, dreams no longer deferred. It feels as though, maybe, it can be less about money than about honor.

Chapter 13

By Sunday, the National Guard had to be called into Ladera Heights and Baldwin Hills in California. Police in DeSoto, Texas, arrested twenty people on charges of hate crimes. Two Baptist churches in South Carolina burned to the ground as parishioners arrived for Sunday services. Several armed protesters were arrested in Washington, D.C. Willie picked up her keys and looked out the window at Calvin McGuinness raking orphaned leaves into orderly piles—one world carrying on while another smoldered. When she drove downtown to run errands, it was a city divided. Signs in the libraries advertised genealogy workshops and sidewalk tables sold Forgiveness T-shirts, but many large businesses remained closed. She stopped at a red light and a man motioned at her to lower her window, like she had a missing taillight or a flat tire.

"Disgusting," he yelled, pointing at her and Paloma. "You're disgusting."

"Mom, what is he talking about?" Paloma asked, turning to her.

It took several moments for Willie to realize what, in fact, he *was* talking about. She rolled up the window and double-checked the locks. "Don't look at him." She gestured at the dashboard. "Look straight ahead." Willie glanced at the man sideways. He was crouched low in his seat staring at them.

A city divided: On Monday there was music playing when she got in to work. Andrew waved a gold party hat in a semicircle like he was directing traffic. "I'm partying like I just got my reparations check, baby! Smile!" He pushed his phone into her face.

She took the hat and looked at it like it was a key to a room she'd forgotten she wanted to enter.

"It's a joke, Wil. Lighten up."

She put on the hat and adjusted the strap under her chin while Andrew grabbed her by the shoulders, steering her into the kitchen. "I knew you were broke, but not that broke," she teased him.

Carol, a project coordinator who had been with MRA for longer than Willie could remember, stirred half-and-half into her coffee and waved to Willie. "Get one of these," she said, pointing at the sticky buns. "They're amazing." MRA was full of journeymen—guys who typically went straight to jobsites but were instead drinking coffee and chatting in the warm office.

Willie followed Andrew back to his desk and sat on the edge. She fingered a raisin out of a sticky bun and popped it into her mouth. "You mean the boss is okay with everyone being here instead of onsite?"

"Who do you think bought the sticky buns?" Andrew winked and bit into one, dropping crumbs on top of his keyboard.

She looked at the crumbs on Andrew's desk, scattered like he was at home. She had been taught to look at her environment with detachment, but she was able to stay because she *was* attached. When Andrew needed help paying for his mom's breast cancer surgery, she advanced him two weeks' pay. Sometimes she came in on Saturdays to fix faulty time sheets so no one would miss a paycheck. She gave Carol spa gift certificates for Christmases and birthdays because Willie knew she raised three teenage boys and took care of her father. Max had built this and it was authentic and his and, yes, to some extent, hers. So why couldn't she detach herself from ethics and do what needed to be done to preserve it? Since she was a girl, she had seen work not as pay but as purpose. And what did that say about who she was if she could work with someone like Hank, who so adamantly opposed Forgiveness? Her parents had been through more difficult situations than she ever would, so the hard choices defined them. They never had to define her, because she'd never had to make them.

She found Max in his office standing at the window, his back to the door.

"I'm going to make sure we qualify for the money," Willie told him.

"I'm sure you'll try," he said, turning slowly. "You should try. But I won't depend on that. We can't right now."

—

Where was she going to start to get the records they needed? Would they even be able to qualify? The man who'd pulled up next to her car had left her twitchy, and in bed that night she couldn't sleep. Overnight, the momentum had changed. She got out of bed and paced her room, pressing her fingertips into the dark circles she knew were underneath her eyes. She peered between her curtains, looking out at the empty and dimly lit lawn where she saw a pickup idling at the top of their driveway. Telling herself to stop being paranoid, Willie moved away from the window, when suddenly the truck pulled into the Revels' driveway and an outstretched arm hurled two objects in quick succession at the downstairs windows. A moment later, glass exploded. Willie was brought back to the day she came home from school to the burning emblem on their lawn. What had saved her then was the house. She scrambled to write down the license-plate number, but the car was too far away for her to make it out.

"What was that?" Paloma ran yelling into her room.

They went into the hallway, and she called out to ask if Max and Lourdes were okay. "We're okay. Are you okay?"

Downstairs, Max and Lourdes stood in their pajamas by the shattered dining room windows. Two bricks were in the middle of the carpet, red dust flaked around them in a faint halo. Max bent down and examined them.

"Go get two sheets and tape," Lourdes told Willie. Her voice was hard, but her hand encircled her neck like a collar.

On her way to get the sheets, Willie phoned Seb and asked him to come over. They sat in the kitchen, Max trying to hide his gratitude at there being another man in the house, all of them pretending to ignore the gusts of bitter air coming from the dining room windows and rattling the sliding door in the kitchen. Lourdes got up and fastened twine around the handles to stop them from banging in the wind. The doorbell rang. "It's just us," they heard Mr. Robinson yell. "Let us in."

Mrs. Robinson was a good foot taller than her husband, and the robe that Mr. Robinson wore, which was too big for him and possibly belonged to his wife, dragged on the floor like a ragged ballgown.

"I just replaced that goddamn window, would you believe it?" Mr. Robinson groaned. "A brick. Landed on the dining room table. Thank God Rhonda had gone upstairs. Usually she sits up late reading."

"I'm just glad everyone's okay."

There was talk of calling the cops. Willie dialed and was told the precinct was dealing with a string of attacks. She was instructed to leave her information and an officer would be in touch.

"Who do you think it was?"

"I hate to say it, but I swear it was the truck that Peterson guy on the corner owns."

"How did you see the truck?"

"I saw it pulling away."

"The cops won't do anything. They pass a law like this, and no one is prepared for the consequences. They sit around and pat themselves on the back, but no one is prepared for the consequences."

"Why can't they just let us be?"

"Is it worth it?" Max asked. "Is all of this worth it?"

Everyone looked down, embarrassed by his question.

—

Several groups offered to help families with their genealogy research, and Nell and Willie signed up for a workshop off the park-
way, figuring they had nothing to lose and otherwise no idea
where to start. The room was crowded and they found two chairs
near the projector in back, where they could still see the screen.
They looked around the room to get a sense of who was there—it
had the feeling of a community center, convivial, with people of
all ages. The woman leading the workshop, who looked to be in
her forties, stood smiling eagerly at the front of the room.

"Genealogy," she began, "is the key to the past and the future.
My name is Rebecca. Thank you all for being here. I look forward
to guiding you on one of the most important journeys you will
undertake. It took the government passing the Forgiveness Act
for people to realize the importance of this beautiful art and sci-
ence. But better late than never." People weren't sure if they
should clap. A few half-hearted hands were put together in the
front of the room.

The House Appropriations Committee had mailed a packet
of information to families who requested the materials. In the
packet was guidance on how to begin a genealogy search to prove
eligibility for the funds. Rebecca projected slides and began walking the room through the information.

Assign one person in your family to be the family historian. This will
make your application easier to manage and will ultimately make the
approval process faster. She shared a list of recommended questions
to ask older relatives to start narrowing down the search for documents:

1. Where and when were you born?
2. Who were the most important relatives to you when you were growing up, and where are they now?
3. Did you know your grandparents? (Ask for information about their lives that will aid your search, including all the places they might have lived and when and where they died.)
4. Did anyone in the family ever talk about slavery and sharecropping?
5. What church did your family go to when you were growing up?
6. When relatives started moving to the North, what cities did they go to?
7. Did anyone keep family Bibles? Do you know where the Bible is now?
8. Can you tell me about your own life, starting from when you were young through today? Cover childhood, teenage years, marriages, and aging.

At the end of the workshop, Rebecca switched off the projector. "The last and most important piece of advice I can give you is to listen to your elders." This prompted both laughter and applause from a group of old folks in the front. "'Bout damn time!" someone yelled.

Willie and Nell lined up to get copies of Rebecca's printouts. "Hey," Nell said, nudging Willie. "Isn't that the guy from Celine's party?"

Willie looked over to where Nell was gesturing and saw Jared bending down to tie his shoe. Her breath caught as seeing him, wanting him, felt familiar, like smelling a pleasant but long-faded scent. He looked up and Willie waved.

"Nice to see you here," he said, approaching. He shuffled like he was about to kiss Willie on the cheek and then changed his mind, instead smiling politely at Nell.

"Yeah, well, I need all the help I can get," Willie joked.

Nell looked between the two of them. "I'm going to run to the bathroom before we head out. Nice to see you again."

Willie and Jared made small talk, and when there was nothing else to say he cleared his throat. "When we're not both playing Henry Louis Gates, would you like to get a drink with me?"

A woman in line behind them cleared her throat and told them to keep moving.

Willie kept her eyes on him. "I'd love to."

Chapter 14

Saturday morning, Willie sat on the back patio with a cup of coffee and again considered Professor Johnson's question from all those years ago: *Can forgiveness be political, and can it be lasting?* Willie imagined that if she were still working as a journalist, she would be trying to answer this question. Professor Cane had wanted her to be clear about the distinction between her stories and personal essays, but Willie thought the best journalists could do both. She had been too insecure to tell him that then. Right now all the Black journalists covering the Forgiveness Act were being asked to do both. They were being asked to flaunt their excitement for the cameras and for the pages, to spread their lineages out for the masses. Should all Black families get the same amount? Should families like the Revels get less because their house was an asset? Forgiveness was neither the point nor a possibility, but did people see a better future for themselves in America after the Forgiveness Act? Could they call themselves patriots and believe it? Willie thought those were questions worth trying to answer.

The government requiring them to unearth their past to prove they qualified was personal. Politicians wanted the concept of Forgiveness to be the focus because it shifted the lens, but the work of forgiving is never on the person—or the country—asking for it. A country is a concept, and maybe the country could be forgiven but the government couldn't. Her thoughts and feelings were jumbled, like puzzle pieces tossed on the floor. She leaned back in the chair and zipped up her sweatshirt, closing her eyes and inhaling the crisp, fire-laced air.

Seb had agreed that it made the most sense for Willie to be in charge of the process for their family. She'd presented a plan to make him feel included and explained how first she would go talk to Marcus, to extract more-specific names and dates from their grandfather. Willie imagined Marcus's reaction when she showed up at his senior-living community. Neither she nor Seb ever went to visit him, instead relying on Lourdes or Max to bring him to Lewaro Street every week.

Lourdes walked out onto the porch, sat down, and nodded in the direction of Willie's notebook. Willie handed over the list of genealogy questions, and Lourdes read them silently, handing back the book without comment. Then Paloma appeared and took the list of questions out of Willie's hand. "Are you going to let Grandma and me help?"

Lourdes pulled on Paloma's braid until she fell into her lap. "I don't know if we can," Lourdes whispered to Paloma.

—

Wissahickon Senior Living was a large white building with orange statues on the front lawn, evoking an aesthetic more similar to California than Philadelphia. Willie entered, signed in at the front desk, and asked the attendant to remind her of her grandfather's room number. The woman lowered her glasses and smiled at Willie. "You his grandbaby? Look just like him."

The hallways were long and bright but not cold. On either end were plush seating areas against floor-to-ceiling windows. Deep couches, books, and puzzles. Groups of people laughing and eating like they were playing bridge on vacation. No wonder Marcus looked disgruntled when he came to 512 Lewaro. He had a nice setup, which slightly assuaged Willie's guilt over not having come sooner.

Marcus's door was open. Willie knocked softly as she entered the room and her heart dropped when a genuine smile replaced the look of permanent boredom that had been painted on his face.

"Who died?" he asked, muting the television.

"No one died." Willie walked over and gave Marcus a kiss on the cheek.

He sucked his teeth. "Thought someone had to die to see your face here."

She tried to laugh, but it came out sounding like a choked cough, and he looked at her sideways, chuckling. She did a quick scan of the room: one Styrofoam cup, a Bible, half-eaten saltines piled onto a tray next to an unopened Coca-Cola. Willie's eyes landed on a small Old Spice deodorant with the top jammed back on so that some of the deodorant oozed out of the side. She cast her eyes around for somewhere to sit, but none of the places felt right.

"I thought we could go for a walk in the garden." She cleared her throat and zipped her jacket. "There's something I want to talk to you about."

Marcus laughed. "You know, we're all in here making bets on when everyone's grandkids are going to show up. Forgiveness makes you all finally want to listen to us. Bobbie's kids won the cake. Ink wasn't even dry." He slapped his knee like Bobbie's kids were the punch line to the funniest joke he'd ever heard. "You're respectful at least, I'll give you that. You always were the curious one, weren't you?"

Marcus pulled himself off the couch and she hurried over, cupping one of his elbows. He flapped his hand toward his walker, and she reached behind her, pulling it over with her right hand. Marcus slipped one arm in a parka, letting the other dangle, limp, until she guided it through the hole. Once in the hallway, Marcus moved gingerly, smiling at the attendant who came out and clasped his shoulders from behind.

Willie and Marcus emerged from the elevators into a rooftop garden, with glass guardrails that were so high it felt like a greenhouse. Willie had expected the weightlessness of open air to hit them, alleviating, she hoped, some of her anxiety. She pictured herself and her grandfather winding down a path, Marcus carefully unpacking generations of familial history for his granddaughter. But the path was not winding, and it proved difficult to maneuver his walker on top of, so they chose a bench on the east side of the building, overlooking the Wissahickon.

"Your father know you here?" Marcus asked, staring up at the clouds.

Willie nodded. "He's busy," she said.

Marcus snorted, unconvinced. "I'm surprised he even wants to apply for the money. He hates the government even more than I do. Although I don't know why. He never fought in no war. He never had anything to be angry about, but he always was. Always was."

There were so many misunderstandings in her family; Willie wished she could spend the morning just talking with Marcus and setting the record straight, like righting a picture frame turned crooked. If somehow she could explain to her grandfather how desperate Max was about the business, how scared he was of failing, maybe the wounds could be healed and they could all begin operating together, flowing as one current instead of fighting the forces of one another.

"What happened between you and Dad when he was a kid?"

"Pssht. I wasn't the best, I'll admit that."

"But have you ever admitted it to him?"

"After his mother left, I couldn't keep my kettle full. I did the best I could. I had no money. The VA promised me benefits and I never saw a thing. I had friends who made something of themselves after the war because of what the government did for them. I got nothing. I lost my dignity, my vision, and my wife."

"I know you were hurting. But he also lost his mom."

"Listen, did you come here to figure out how we're going to get this money or did you come here to be my therapist?"

Willie gazed out at the tops of the trees swaying against the sky. She had never seen Marcus at his worst, but she believed Max when he told her and Seb stories about his childhood, about Marcus's drinking and how Max had to take care of him after his mother left. She knew Marcus had the capacity for cruelty, but as he'd gotten older, his hard edges had blunted so that she'd never seen them. In the same way that she held on to resentments, though, her father had held on to his.

"But this is about more than money, you know that," Willie said.

Marcus studied his granddaughter. "Look. Should I apologize to your dad for some of the things I said and did after his mom left? For what? It would be too little, too late. Just like what they're trying to do with this act. What am I going to do with this money at my age? I'm happy about this passing. Never thought I would see it in my day. But what I want is earnest remorse from those currently in power. Not some Monopoly money that doesn't come close to what is owed. They can't afford what is owed to me. They want proof? Should I show them the stamp of that bullshit temporary construction gig and compare it to the checks my friends got for their degrees and mortgages? Should I get in a goddamn time machine and take them back to my grandfather's house before it was destroyed? They don't want that kind of proof. Knowing something and proving it are two different things."

Marcus had raised his voice, and a frail lady nearby made frantic gestures to her nurse to go back inside.

Marcus's hand rested on his lap and Willie reached out to hold it. "None of it's right. Let's just talk and then I'll see what records I can get together."

Marcus scoffed but relented. "I'll tell you what I remember."

She pressed a button and began to record, making the moment seem far more ominous and heavier than it really was—or maybe this was all that mattered, Willie considered, learning the little truths of yourself from your grandfather.

Willie scanned the list of questions. "Can you tell me more about your grandparents?"

Marcus laughed softly with a pinch of melancholy. "My dad's parents, yes. I never met my mother's parents." He again watched the clouds crown the tops of the trees. "Hemp and Minnie—we lived with them in Natchez before my parents moved us to Philadelphia. Hemp owned a couple of acres of land."

"He was a farmer?"

"That's right." Marcus nodded. "He sold okra and worked odd repair jobs under the hill. He was a good carpenter but loved his land. Used to say, 'You can grow anything you put your mind to.' He was real short, but I thought he was the biggest man I'd ever seen. Not rough, just confident. He used to predict the weather. Folks would come by and stand in the yard and he'd yell out his prediction at four, five in the morning. Sometimes he'd lift me up on his shoulders as he said it."

"Do you remember when he was born?"

"Probably 1865 or '66. I'm not sure."

"His parents were slaves, then?" There was a disassociation when she said it, like the word itself replaced the beating hearts behind it.

Marcus raised his shoulders. "He never talked about them."

"Did Hemp and Minnie come to Philadelphia with you?"

"No. Hemp owned land near the school where Minnie taught. That's how they met. He was always out working, and she would walk by, until one day he persuaded her to have some sweet tea with him. It was good land—a good location with it being right near the school. When my parents got married, they moved in with them, slept in the room at the back of the house where Minnie laid her peppers out to dry. That's where we all slept once I came. It was simple and quiet, that life was. Then one night we heard horses. It sounded like there were hundreds of them, but it couldn't have been more than five or six. Next thing I knew was the heat. They burned it all down—they didn't like a Black man owning so much, you see. Living so comfortable. And we left. We ran is more like it."

Willie tried to steady her breathing. "Who burned it down?" she asked, picturing the arm hurling bricks from the pickup truck through the Revels' and Robinsons' windows.

Marcus sighed and leaned his head back as if a chair supported it, but nothing did, and it tilted at an unnatural angle. "I don't want to remember all this," he said. "Leave it where it belongs. In the past."

She asked again, raising her voice, even though the voice in her head screamed at her to stop. "Who burned it down?"

"Who do you think?" he yelled. "Some white folks in from Louisiana. I don't know their goddamn names." Marcus continued, "My parents and I left that night, after we realized there was nothing to save. We tried to get Hemp and Minnie to come with us, but they wouldn't leave Natchez. It was home to them. They weren't going to start over at their age. So they stayed. And they became our relatives in the South who I never saw again. I heard later they found Hemp and finished the job."

So her great-great-grandfather was murdered. Is this what she wanted to find out? She hadn't known what she expected. She wanted to "know" her history in a blurred sense, but the specifics had always eluded her. And not only the specifics, but what she would do with them. "What happened to Minnie?"

Marcus shrugged. "I don't know. We couldn't find her."

"And they never talked about their own parents? Their parents would be whose records we need. Do you know their names?"

"I was just a boy," Marcus replied. "I never asked them about their own family, their own troubles. And I guess I didn't listen if they ever talked about it neither. You're a grown woman—a curious one at that—and you're just now making me tell you about my grandparents. Think about that."

Willie pressed STOP on the recording. She wanted to ask more about Minnie, if Marcus knew when she was born. But she couldn't bring herself to ask the practical questions. "I'm sorry, Pop." They sat in silence, looking at the sky through the glass with a vacancy between them. A shared, unspoken heaviness over their inability to allow the past to connect them. Names and facts bouncing between the two of them and lost to the clouds.

"Help me back to my room. It's time for my nap." Marcus fumbled but failed to pull himself up from the bench.

Willie grabbed his walker and steadied it. Back in his room, she helped him into bed, where he stared at the muted television. She asked if he wanted her to turn the sound on, but he flapped his hand, closing his eyes.

Willie closed the door to Marcus's room and leaned her back against it in the hallway. A nurse walking by asked if she was okay and Willie held up her hand—a gesture, depending on the interpretation, that could have meant either yes or no. She stood up straight and made her way out of the building.

Last year, the product of Willie's salivary glands had traveled to a lab in Marlborough, Massachusetts. She'd expected to feel a seismic shift when she read *23 percent Nigerian; 20 percent Benin & Togo; 16 percent Cameroon.* And so on. Along with her results, an explanation: *Most African Americans in the Carolinas, Maryland, and Virginia can trace their ancestry back to West Africa.* She was supposed to be comforted and satisfied with this? All she felt was a brief spark and then an absence, a lack of anything real to hold on to.

But now there were names and stories: Just hearing the details made them, if not knowable to her, at least anchors to grasp for.

She navigated to one of the websites the government suggested people use to find their official submission documents. A table of contents explained what to do to begin your search.

START WITH YOURSELF *There's no better time to preserve your genealogy. Start by opening a free account. GrowYourTree gives you access to your genealogy and allows other family members to access your information. Preserve data, stories, photographs, and memories. Keep your history alive.*

FIND AND IDENTIFY LOOSE RECORDS *Search for birth certificates, death certificates, property titles, photos—anything that will help you fill in the blanks.*

When they helped Marcus pack up his house, her grandfather had called Willie over and showed her his uniform from the war, folded carefully in a cardboard box, his heavy green helmet on top. "We used to eat lunch from our helmets," he told her, flipping it over and pretending to spoon out stew. He showed her his shoulder bag, empty shells still in the pockets. The gators to protect his shins from shrapnel were brown from dust and dirt. But aside from his uniform, there had been almost nothing else. No mountains of papers or photographs. When she asked him where everything was, he told her he didn't want to get too comfortable.

Willie scanned the rest of the page. Advice on creating a genealogy *To Do* list, recording sources, how to question family members. A sidebar linked to public census records. She acknowledged how much space the Forgiveness Act occupied in the back of her mind. *We'll be okay once the Forgiveness Act passes. We'll be fine once we get money from Forgiveness. I'll worry about that after the Forgiveness Act.* It colored her excuses, allowed her a shudder of hope every time she imagined the Revels getting their check. In truth, it wasn't just about helping her family but about helping herself. It was a second chance, an opportunity to be both a better person and a better mother, and, whether or not she needed Forgiveness money to become those things, the prospect of it made the concept easier to imagine.

She clicked on the 1920 census, guessing at a year that seemed realistic enough to learn some basic information.

First name: She typed *Hemp.*

Last name: *Revel.*

Birth year? She tried 1865.

Location: *Natchez, Mississippi.*

County? She did a quick search and then typed in *Adams*.

Keywords: There were a few grayed-out examples, like *Air Force* or *secretary*. What keywords described Hemp? She typed *farmer*.

She hit SEARCH and readjusted herself, cracking a bone in the middle of her back.

There were 9,896 results.

Almost ten thousand people named H. C. Revel or H. V. Revel, Henry H. Revel or W. H. Revel.

She stared at *Henry H. Revel* (born 1862) and *H. C. Revel* (born 1865) and *W. H. Revel* (born 1875). Willie leaned back in her chair, teetering on its two back legs, unsure whether she would be able to make all the missing pieces fit together.

She scratched her scalp, pulled apart several tangled strands of hair, and thought back to when she researched constantly. Often the simplest method was the right one. Returning the chair to its four legs, she opened a new tab and simply searched: *Hemp Revel Natchez Mississippi*. She clicked on the first result—*Hemp Revel from Ward 4 Natchez in 1920 Census District 51–14*.

And there he was.

There they all were.

Hemp Revel, 55, male

Negro

1865

Mississippi

Other people in household:

Minnie Revel, 42, female

Thurgood Revel, 22, male

Lacy Revel, 22, female

She leaned in closer to the screen and hovered her mouse over all the names.

Keeping the tab open, Willie went back to the census search and typed in everything she knew about Hemp, including his birth year and the other people in his household. This time, his complete census record appeared.

> *Able to read?: Yes.*
> *Able to write?: No.*
> *Home value: 600.*
> *Home owned or rented: Owned.* He owned his home.
> *Attended school: No.*
> *Father's birthplace: North Carolina.*
> *Mother's birthplace: Virginia.*

She clicked on Minnie's record. *Occupation: Schoolteacher. Mother's birthplace: Virginia. Father's birthplace: Virginia.*

Willie navigated out of the 1920 census and tried to find Hemp's record for 1880. She tried different combinations of the information she knew, typing in his name, his parents' birthplaces, but couldn't find any 1880 records for a Hemp Revel. She swiveled her chair around to look at Paloma, who was doing her homework. Family history is a paradox. The further each generation gets from the genesis, the less it's relevant, but the more, perhaps, it's needed. Paloma looked up and asked Willie, with her eyes, *What are you looking at?* Willie contemplated how best to answer.

—

The next night, Willie hung her coat on a hook and took in the crowded bar. A bartender in a short vest poured her a glass of water and smiled. The man next to her kept circling his wrist, swirling the ice in his drink like marbles, while the woman with him laughed. "All it takes is one person," Willie overheard the woman saying. The man looked annoyed. "Damn, Trish. Your family is different from mine."

Jared stepped inside and brushed rain off his blazer. He gave a low wave in her direction.

As she watched him approach, she tried rehearsing interesting things to say about herself. He seemed like the type of man who wrung positivity out of his women. A frightening prospect when you're accustomed to treating yourself in the opposite way. Celine and Nell had stopped trying to set her up, because she was always ready with a trivial excuse. She was too busy, she lived with her parents, he was too short, too white, too quiet, too dull. Jared was the first man she could remember who made her nervous.

"Sorry I'm late," he said, kissing her on the cheek and pulling out the stool next to her.

He ordered a whiskey and pushed air out between his teeth. "It's good to see you again."

She didn't know what to say, so she asked him if he had trouble parking.

"No, I interviewed someone not far from here and came early," he said. "A woman who conducts psychedelic research to see if psilocybin can help with the impact of trauma."

Jared reminded her of Seb when he spoke about his work. His eyebrows narrowed and he talked quickly, licking his lips as if he were greasing a motor. "The hardest part is that you need a formal diagnosis to participate in the trials. But the people with the worst trauma, of course, don't have a formal diagnosis. They don't even have a dentist, let alone a therapist who will formally diagnose them."

"When I read about the arguments against the Forgiveness Act, the term *mutual hallucination* keeps coming to mind. People who believe that racism doesn't exist or that slavery wasn't bad."

He looked down into his drink and nodded, pressing his lips together tightly. Willie's palms were on top of the bar, and he reached out and lifted her right hand, flipped it over, and pressed his thumb into the center, causing the blood to disperse in a multitude of directions.

"Sorry, I didn't mean to bring up slavery on the first date."

He laughed and gave her palm one final press before dropping her hand. "Hard not to these days."

She told him about her conversation with Marcus.

"How did it make you feel?" he said, sensing her earnestness.

She thought for a moment, trying not to feel embarrassed. "It made me sad. But it also made me want to find the right records. I would need to find his grandfather's parents. I assume they would have been in Mississippi, but truth be told I'm not sure."

"You should go to the Mississippi archives. I had to go there once for a story. They have an incredible collection, all on microfilm."

She nodded, her mind becoming a reporter's mind again but also drifting to the news reports of the violence in the South after the announcement of Forgiveness. One attack had left three Black women dead.

He told her more about his own family. How his dad was an electrician but now worked downtown at a bank. His mother had wanted to be a poet, he said, but instead raised six kids and scribbled lines down late at night.

"Four sisters." Jared widened his eyes in mock horror.

"I always wanted a big family. I wanted my parents to have more kids. I have a daughter. Paloma. She's ten." She searched his face for surprise or desertion, any sign of fear or retreat, but he only nodded.

"I have a niece and a nephew who are both ten. It's the best age." Jared paused for another sip of his whiskey. "Your daughter's dad, then? You two get along?"

"He's not in the picture." She forced herself to maintain eye contact. "I never wanted kids," Willie continued. "At least, it was never anything I planned on specifically. I think it's because I watched my mom approach it like a job and I wanted my actual job to be the thing I worked at, not another human being. I can't imagine my life without Paloma, but it took a long time to think of myself as a mother. Is that a strange thing to say?"

"It's not wrong to feel a certain way, especially with family. You feel what you feel and just hope to be able to make some sense of it someday."

After drinks, Jared walked her to her car. They paused in the lot and faced each other, her back against the driver's window, though she couldn't feel the chill of the glass through her jacket. "I had a nice time." She drew out the words, hoping to extend the moment.

"Me too. Really nice."

He leaned down and kissed her, long enough to allow her to

reach an arm around and cup his neck. After several seconds she pulled away and opened her car door. "Thank you again," she said.

The next day, Willie phoned the Mississippi Department of Archives and History. She was put on hold for thirteen minutes while a robotic voice apologized for the longer wait times and shortage of staff.

"This is Mary," a woman finally answered. "How can I help you?"

"I'm wondering if you have state census records or marriage records for individuals who lived in Natchez?" Willie asked, consulting her notebook, where she had written her ideas for how to track down Hemp's and Minnie's records.

"Are you local?" Mary sighed. "The records will be on microfilm, which you have to come in to view in our media room. Ordinarily our staff could help you over the phone, but we're short on hands since the Forgiveness Act passed, and we're not able to field any more requests." She spoke quickly, as if confiding in a friend about a hard day at work. "Yesterday alone we received three hundred calls looking for death certificates. But if you can come in person, it's your best bet. We won't be able to sit and help you, but we'll offer some guidance, help you get going. Ahead of coming, you should convert your ancestor's last name into Soundex code, which is the indexing system we use, because that will be how you'll find the index for any records you want to look up."

"Soundex code? What is that?" Willie asked, grabbing her pen.

Mary sighed again. "If you look up Soundex code, you'll figure it out. It's not hard. Convert the name you're searching for into Soundex code and bring it with you."

"I don't know if I can come in person," Willie explained. How could she fly to Mississippi now and leave Paloma at home after someone had put bricks through the dining room window?

"Your other option if you can't come in person is to order a death certificate. This is going to give you a lot of the information you need—it'll have the name of the deceased's parents, their spouse, and the name of the person who registered your ancestor's death. I can email you the form if you want."

"That would be great." She gave Mary her email address.

Moments after they got off the phone, her phone vibrated with a new email. Willie opened it and scanned the questions. *Date of death. Place of death. Age at death. Name of mother or parent.* She didn't know any of this information for Hemp or Minnie. She wasn't even sure Marcus could answer these questions.

Lourdes walked into the library. She placed two bowls on the coffee table, one filled with string beans, the other empty and awaiting the broken ends. Lourdes sometimes prepped her food in the library, as if imploring the rest of the family to take her work seriously. What she didn't realize was that the family already took her seriously; it was always her approval they were after. She glanced at the computer screen and sat in a chair by the window. "You knew it wasn't going to be easy," she said, understanding what Willie was doing. Lourdes snapped a string bean in half, depositing the end in the empty bowl. "Did Marcus tell you anything useful?"

Willie gave Lourdes an overview of what she learned. "Have you ever heard Dad or Marcus mention anything about Minnie's maiden name?"

Lourdes shook her head.

Willie wanted Lourdes to be as excited and invested as Jared had been, to show any force of emotion, but all her mother said, half joking, was, "Maybe you just have to go down to Mississippi."

Willie pivoted her chair so she was facing Lourdes. "Come with me," she said, surprising herself.

Chapter 15

The attacks were random. They would be no less safe in Jackson, Mississippi, than they were in Philadelphia. At least this is what they told themselves. "Plus it will be safer if we're together," Lourdes reasoned. Willie disagreed but kept quiet, glad for the company.

There would be too much discussion, too much protest, if they waited for family consensus, so Willie booked their flights without telling anyone besides Paloma. They would tell the rest of the family over Thanksgiving dinner.

"But why do you have to go now?" Paloma asked. "Mr. Jeremy is choosing the winner for the Flash Festival next week. Didn't you get the letter he sent out to parents?"

Willie had received a letter from the school but hadn't opened it. She thought it might be on the bureau in her room, buried under her notes about genealogy research, but she couldn't be sure. She also might have thrown it out.

"You call me as soon as Mr. Jeremy announces his decision," Willie assured her, "and I promise to be the loudest person in the front row on opening night if yours is selected. Which I'm sure it will be."

"Front row is reserved for crew."

"Second row, then. I'll stand the whole time either way, so it won't matter."

"Why can't you just wait and go in a few weeks so I can go with you?"

Willie shook her head. "I need to go. For both of us."

Paloma pushed on the top of her pen until a blue dot began seeping through the paper. "Bring me back a souvenir?"

"Of course," Willie said, and kissed her on the forehead. "Now show me the latest with your play."

Paloma explained to Willie that it was about when the governor, Thomas Hutchinson, made Phillis Wheatley prove she wrote her poems, because he didn't think she could write them herself. "Her owners just named her Phillis after the ship she came over on, but no one even knew who she really was. No one cared."

On Thanksgiving morning, Willie moved meticulously through the house, dusting the dressers and nightstands, wiping down the bathtubs and counters, vacuuming the living room, library, and dining room rugs. She stood in the powder room on the first floor and gazed at herself in the mirror. It was the house's most ornate bathroom, painted dark green with fine lines to make it look like leather. She stayed there for a few minutes with the door closed, thinking about the trip to Mississippi. Until the tickets were purchased, Lourdes had not fully believed Willie was serious about the trip, but when she shared flight details, her mother's mouth had opened slightly in a look of apprehension and excitement.

Marcus sat at the table, while everyone else filled in around him.

"You outdid yourself." Seb kissed Lourdes on the cheek, squeezing in at the round table in the kitchen, which had an added leaf to it. He introduced Shani, the woman he was dating, while Lourdes and Max's friends Roy and Eva transferred sweet potatoes to a serving bowl and their dog, Fee Fee, sat begging in front of Paloma, who occasionally slipped her pieces of turkey skin.

"Y'all hear about that Morehouse brother who got his check?" Roy asked.

"I read about it," Seb said, reaching for more stuffing. "Are you going to apply?"

Eva nodded. "We're going to apply with mine. You know Miss Kelly kept her records meticulous." She said the word *meticulous* with four drawn-out syllables, and Lourdes and Eva broke out in laughter.

It was raining, and the wind picked up, hurling large drops against the window. Willie tried to sound casual. "Mom and I are going down to Jackson to check out the archives next week for Pop's grandparents."

Max narrowed his eyes. "Since when?"

"A guy I'm seeing said we should go to the Mississippi Department of Archives," Willie continued, annoyed at herself for blushing. Paloma narrowed her eyes, confused at the mention of a man. "To see if there are more records on Pop's grandparents." Marcus finally looked up, candied yams halfway to his dentures.

"You don't go on dates," Max said.

Seb looked up from his plate. "Why didn't you tell me you were going? I could have gotten someone to cover for me and gone with you. It's too dangerous for you and Mom to go down there by yourselves."

"We'll be fine," Lourdes said, cutting in. "We'll be careful."

"No," Max said. "Seb's right. What do you even expect to find that you can't find here?"

"Census records, birth certificates. We need the records of Pop's great-grandparents to get the Forgiveness money. And Seb, I need you to stay to help take care of Paloma. It will get too chaotic if there's too many of us. Mom and I will be fine."

"The government has all of you running around looking like a bunch of damn chickens with their heads cut off. It's exactly what they want," Max said.

"Son." Everyone turned to look at Marcus, who held a turkey leg to his chapped lips. "Shut up."

Willie and Lourdes couldn't get seats next to each other, so she watched as her mother boarded the plane, rolling her bag behind her like she was gripping the hand of a child while her other hand held her license and boarding pass. Willie settled into an exit row next to an older gentleman clutching a folder on his lap. As he leaned over to buckle his seatbelt, a photograph fluttered to the floor. Willie fished it off the cabin floor for him, and the man nodded his appreciation. "My grandmother," he said, pointing at the photo and shrugging as if he knew why Willie was also traveling to Jackson. Why the flight was so full of hopeful faces with similar mementos.

Willie watched the airplane wing cut through clouds like a butter knife and thought about the different levels of desperation the Forgiveness Act had revealed. The desperation of wanting to claim the money out of principle. The desperation of wanting to know where you came from. The desperation of needing the money. The desperation of pretending not to care. Willie shut her eyes and had only half-dreams throughout the bumpy flight, waking up groggy and anxious as the pilot announced the beginning of their descent.

She had booked them a room at a small inn in downtown Jackson, the rear of which abutted the archives building. Packing, like the trip itself, had been hurried, and she realized while standing in line for the rental car that she hadn't brought appropriate clothing, expecting it to be cooler than it was. Lourdes fanned herself with a tourist brochure, and Willie gathered her curls on top of her head as she inched forward in line. For the first time in a long time, though, she felt purposeful about her intentions.

Lourdes and Willie climbed into their rented car and merged onto I-20. The flatness of the roads and the greenery made Willie feel disconnected, like she was both in the car and floating through the fields. Generations removed from the land and soil returning in the hopes of finding more than she could even say out loud.

While Lourdes went to check in and escape the heat, uncharacteristic for this time of year, Willie stood outside the inn for a moment, letting the sun scorch her bare shoulders. She had read that the Old Capitol Inn used to house the Young Women's Christian Association and that it had rented rooms to women moving from rural Mississippi looking for work. It had boasted the first integrated pool in all of Mississippi, and Willie thought how separate the South felt from who the Revels were—she had felt this the first time they came and she felt it again now. Philadelphia was the root of their history, the place Marcus, Max, and Lourdes liked to believe their story started. But the major flaw in that logic was that it was a lie. And the lie haunted them all, even if Willie was the only one willing to admit it. It gnawed at them, reminding them of the missing pieces, like a book you know you own but can't find. They all tried to escape the nagging feeling by being the best, by working on themselves, but the holes showed: When a cab driver asked her where she was from? Where she was *really* from? When there was that nowhere look. When there was nowhere to look beyond Philadelphia for answers.

She looked at the parking lot across the street. Only a few cars drove by, but the inn's lot was full. She nodded to a man walking past, and he took off his sunglasses and gestured in her direction. "Must be mighty proud of how easy you're standing out on this street," he said, and kept walking. Her stomach muscles clenched, and she stood a minute longer before walking back to the car and wheeling their bags inside, where she found Lourdes laughing and talking with the woman at the front desk.

"Welcome to Jackson," the woman said, handing over the keys.

Their room was small but nice. A queen bed to share behind

a skinny pair of double doors, a Juliet balcony, and a couch and armchair near the television. Wide panels resembling the spines of books hung behind the bed. *Light in August; Go Down, Moses; As I Lay Dying.*

"They couldn't have chosen a better title than *As I Lay Dying* over where we sleep?"

"Let me check my notes for a second before we walk over to the archives," Willie said, and sat down at the small desk. She had deciphered the Soundex code, as Mary suggested, and the equivalent of *Revel* was *R140*. She opened her notebook and looked at the scant bullet points she had written there:

- *Find Hemp's or Minnie's parents*
- *Find 1920 census*
- *Look up 1910 census*
- *Look up Hemp and Minnie's marriage record for Minnie's maiden name*
- *Try to find Hemp in 1880 census*

Before she left, Jared had given her advice: "Persistence," he said. "The records can be hard to read. And it will probably be crowded since the act passed, which means people will be clamoring to get on those machines. Try to use the new microfilm machines if you can: The light's better. Makes it easier to read the records." For the past few weeks Jared was a recurring character in her thoughts. His sturdy compactness. The way he was a little bit nervous around her but still direct. His eyes, which he tried to keep guarded but revealed kindness, excitement.

Lourdes read over Willie's shoulder before squeezing it. "I'm changing. Give me two minutes." Her mother seemed giddy, like a child arriving at the beach.

Willie closed her notebook, stood, and stretched. Her mother's demeanor infuriated her, because it made it seem like all of this wasn't real. Where was the urgency? The hope that they'd succeed?

The two of them walked around the block to the archives, passing by the old Standard Oil Company on their left; the Spanish-style building was now home to the State Board of Dental Examiners. On their right was the Old State Capitol and the War Memorial Building, with the words ON OUR PROUD BANNERS BREAKS THE SUNRISE LIGHT OF HONOR etched across the top.

They crossed the street to the archives and paused under the large columns. Willie questioned for a moment whether this building, so vast and imposing, could contain the answers she needed about her family.

They walked toward the doors but were stopped short by a woman fanning herself near the entrance. She jabbed the air behind her, indicating that the line, which wrapped around the western side of the building, started around the corner. Many people, Willie now noticed, held spots for older relatives whom they gestured toward, positioned on benches in the shade.

Across the street, behind a line of police officers, a crowd of fifty or so people shouted obscenities and held signs. Occasionally one of the protesters would push past a police officer and attempt to yell in the face of someone approaching the archives. The police made half an effort to restrain them. What Willie noticed about the protesters was the range of ages. There were children as young as five and six but also many older people, all intent on preventing those in line from entering the building. Everyone in line tried to ignore the protesters. Willie and Lourdes greeted the people in front of them, making casual conversation about the weather, but the protest continued to grow. As they inched forward, someone threw a glass bottle, which shattered a few feet in front of Willie and Lourdes. Willie pushed Lourdes to the inside against the wall to shield her in case another bottle was thrown. People scrambled and yelled. A few ran for their cars, fleeing the line. Finally, the officers pushed the protesters back and removed the woman who had thrown the bottle.

The bottle had been intended for an elegant-looking man about to enter the building. Wealthier Blacks—or at least those who looked like they had a little bit of money—were being targeted, and Willie saw how her mother marked them. With Lourdes's flat-ironed hair and silk trousers, her silk scarf and gold bracelets, they became personifications of the arguments people made against the Forgiveness Act. For those who opposed Forgiveness, Black people of a certain class or those who flashed signifiers of wealth represented how little Forgiveness must be needed. The existence of some wealth, of any means, of any *desire* for means, obfuscated all need for Forgiveness. Willie wished she had told Lourdes to pack more plainly. She had been so focused on what they would need to find once they got there and had been so dismissive of the fears for their safety that she'd failed to be practical.

The whole scene, when she zoomed out and looked at it objectively, was absurd. A group of white people angry that a group of Black people were in line to gain information about their ancestors. *What are you so scared of?* Willie wanted to yell into their cavernous mouths. They would say they were scared of socialism, of communism. But what they were really scared of, Willie knew, was power. Perhaps they feared the revenge that might be invoked. Deep down they carried the fear of their sins. The inherent belief of their own entitlement and power.

She wanted to write an article explaining how whatever Black families owned, they owned *despite*, not *because*. She wanted to enumerate the hypocrisies in their arguments, arguments propped up by the belief that the government had the freedom to tell people what to do, as long as those people weren't white.

Lourdes signaled to Willie that they should leave. The protesters had quieted down, but there were still many of them, and it was clear the police were not going to protect individuals in line. Willie counted fifteen people in front of them who'd enter the building before they would. "You go back to the hotel," she told Lourdes. "I'll go in."

"I don't want you standing out here."

"I'm fine. You go back. We can get dinner when I'm finished."

Once she saw that Willie had no intention of leaving, Lourdes relented.

An hour later, Willie finally made it into the archives. She was expecting the quiet of a library, but it pulsed with conversation and movement. Staff members with lanyards walked back and forth, talking to the clerks who checked visitors in at the front desk. Periodically, they came forward and led a visitor away, as if taking them into a back room to break bad news. Perhaps they were. Maybe the staff members looked so exhausted and harried because they had to let each person know that no records existed for their loved ones. They wouldn't get the Forgiveness funds; best to go home now and save their time.

She moved closer to the front of the line as people peeled away into the depths of the building. Her stomach growled, but she was too anxious to think of food and instead clenched and unclenched her fists like she was preparing for a boxing match. She'd read somewhere that transferring anxiety into a repetitive physical motion was a good technique to calm the mind. What if her dad was right and this was a fool's errand?

After twenty more minutes, she was close enough to the front to hear what questions people asked. The 1880 census records. The papers for the Plaugh plantation. Birth certificates. Death certificates. Freedmen's Bureau labor contracts. Willie saw a staff member wearing a name tag that said *Mary*—probably the same Mary with whom she'd spoken on the phone. Not that the woman would recognize her, but still she hoped to end up at her desk for a small measure of comfort or familiarity. The staff members kept having to explain to the visitors that their questions could be answered in the reading room, not at the front desk.

When Mary waved "Next," Willie walked quickly forward. The woman wore a pair of glasses around her neck, and her chair was pumped up to the highest level. She continued typing while asking how she could help.

Willie replied that she was there to research census and marriage records.

"You and everyone else, honey."

"You actually helped me on the phone the other weekend," Willie said. "I decided to come in person."

Mary finally glanced up. "You're going to go into the media reading room. Do you have ID?"

Mary took and scanned Willie's license, smiling as she handed it back. She gave Willie a small plastic card. "This is your research card. You can add money on it in the reading room for printing and copying. No pens or big bags allowed. There are lockers to your right as you enter. There's staff in the reading room who can help if you get stuck or have questions." Without waiting for Willie to comment, she waved over the next person in line.

Willie walked into a small area the size of a pantry, lined with black lockers. All the lockers were taken, to the point where visitors had flung their bags on the floor, hoping for the best. Willie took out her notebook and folded her bag into a corner.

She signed in at the desk in the reading room and was directed to the microfilm readers, which were in the back, in a dark room with two rows of desks topped with the machines. She stood off to the side, getting her bearings. Some people were sitting unnaturally close to their screens, as if they were trying to climb inside the records. Most of the machines were taken, and if they weren't, there were people searching in the cabinets, trying to hurry back to claim one. A staff member wearing a white polo shirt and a lanyard weaved through helping people, as if giving crumbs to mice in a maze. His name tag read *Ollie*.

"Excuse me?" Willie asked him. "Where do I look up records if I already have the Soundex code?"

Ollie forced a smile and sighed, perhaps anticipating her own future weariness. "There are binders, there, on that table behind my desk," he said, pointing. "Find the relevant one based on which records you're looking up—census, death, what have you. And then find the roll number associated with your Soundex code. Once you have that, you're going to find it in one of these black filing cabinets, and you'll take it over to a machine there. If you're looking up a census record, you'll get the roll with the census card first, and then that will tell you what line and sheet number you can find the full record on. I can help you feed it in if you're nervous, but there are also instructions on the machine. Put money on your card if you want to print anything. When you're finished, put the roll back in the box, and put the box in that bin over there. Whatever you do, don't put it back in the filing cabinet. You wouldn't believe the way people return these rolls, and if they're not in the right spot, they're as good as lost. I'll be around if you have questions. My shift doesn't end for another two hours. Good luck." He patted her on the back, causing her to tip slightly forward.

Willie put money on her card then located the roll for the 1920 census and found the correct microfilm for Adams County. She waited behind an older couple who were starting to pack up, then took their machine. When she sat down, she fed the tail of the microfilm through the rollers and between the glass plates, then around the core of the uptake reel. She inserted the end of the film into the hole, turning it a couple of times to make sure the film caught, and then she adjusted the lever.

Eventually, she found the right census card—the Soundex code was in the corner—and there she saw the year of the census, and Hemp's and Minnie's names. She realized she had gone against Jared's advice, winding up at an older machine. Willie cranked the film through the halo of light until she got to the right sheet and line numbers. And there it was, harder to read because of the cursive and the poor light, yet humbling in its authenticity:

> *Hemp Revel, 55, male, Negro*
> *Other people in household:*
> *Minnie Revel, 42, female*
> *Thurgood Revel, 22, male*
> *Lacy Revel, 22, female*

She ran her fingerprints over the image of Hemp's name and printed out a copy. Then she repeated it all again for the 1910 census, trying to glean any other information.

As she was scrolling, Lourdes appeared next to her.

"I couldn't stay in the room and the line went down. How are you doing?" Lourdes leaned down and looked at the records. Willie felt glad to have the company. If nothing else, it confirmed she wasn't crazy for caring and trying. Her mother didn't waste energy on frivolous pursuits, and so despite this not being Lourdes's history, despite her mother seeming too calm, it confirmed for Willie that it still mattered. She continued to scroll, the old faded brown paper and original cursive passing by like the pages of a book. Alphabetically by first name she went: F, G, H. And there he was again:

> *Hemp Revel, Negro, male, 45, farmer, MS, NC, VA*
> *Minnie Revel, Negro, female, 32, wife, teacher, MS, VA, VA*
> *Thurgood Revel, Negro, male, 12, son, MS, MS, MS*

Joe Revel, Negro, male, 9, son, MS, MS, MS
Rose Revel, Negro, female, 8, daughter, MS, MS, MS

"Thurgood," Lourdes said. "That's Marcus's dad. The other two must have been Marcus's aunt and uncle."

Joe and Rose. They hadn't appeared in the 1920 census. "Why wouldn't they have been living with their parents in the 1920 census, too, if they were younger than Marcus's dad?"

"They could have gone to work on another farm. Maybe Hemp and Minnie sent them to school." Her voice trailed off. Willie copied everything down in her notebook and drew a circle and a question mark around Joe and Rose's names.

Willie needed to find Hemp in the 1880 census. She knew from her research that a family appeared in different enumeration districts and sheets on the 1880 census and that she had to use the 1880 Soundex to find him. But when she searched through the census cards for 1880, there was no Hemp Revel.

She flagged Ollie down. His breath smelled like licorice, and the lingering heat from it made her think of Jared, even though Ollie was much older. Willie asked him what to do if she couldn't find a person using Soundex.

"You can try searching the county roll line by line," he said, then shook his head and muttered, "I'm glad this passed, but the people who need the money the most are the ones who aren't here." He warned her that she'd have to give up the machine soon because there were so many people waiting, then moved on to help an older woman across the room.

He was right, of course. She was fortunate enough to be able to book a flight, pay for a hotel. Almost a month since Forgiveness had passed and only ten thousand families across the country had been issued money. She read that a congressional committee was weighing whether genetic testing could be used to prove enslaved ancestry, but the conversations were stuck in an endless loop of bureaucratic purgatory, held up by senators who insisted that people needed to show individual names, not percentages, to claim the money.

"What now?" Lourdes asked.

Something in her face must have struck a chord of pity in Ollie as he walked by. "We open at eight," he said quietly. "Get here on the dot and you have pretty much free rein until ten. People like to eat their good ol' Southern breakfast first, and the protesters probably won't be here yet either."

Outside, a few protesters still gathered across the street, but most of the crowd had by now dwindled. It wasn't yet dark, but a few streetlights were already turning on and the parking lot surrounding the building was empty. Back at the hotel, Willie phoned Paloma.

"I went to Dave & Buster's with Uncle Seb."

"On a Monday? Why?"

"She wants to know why we went on a Monday." Willie could hear Paloma asking Seb. "He says we're expanding our consciousness by breaking out of routine."

Willie rolled her eyes. "Any word on the play?"

"Not yet. Any word on my souvenir?"

—

As she and Lourdes walked into Saltine, an oyster bar not far from the inn, Willie recalled a memory of the last trip she had taken alone with her mother. Lourdes had purchased tickets to the New York Philharmonic. Willie remembered the look of peace and contentment on Lourdes's face while the music played, and as they walked back to the hotel, it was as though a curtain dropped on the happiness and tenderness in her eyes. Lourdes drank too much at the hotel bar, and she kept repeating that she wasn't ready to go home. "We're only going up to our room," Willie kept saying, as she placed a hand around her mother's shoulders in case she fell. Willie remembered it clearly, and probably always would, because it so disturbed her to hear her mother say she didn't want to go home. It made Willie feel helpless— where do you go if you don't want to go home, if home has become too oppressive or empty or any of the other reasons her mother kept saying she didn't want to go back? It was one of the only times she saw her mother's doubt beneath the studied composure.

Now the restaurant felt especially loud after a day spent inside the archives. Not that many tables were full, but the music and the voices amplified like a few wolves mimicking a whole pack. She and Lourdes ordered smoked-catfish deviled eggs, a salad, and oysters.

"I know this may not be the easiest thing for you," Willie said once the food arrived, "coming down here and digging up Dad's history when you know so little about your own."

Lourdes laughed and sipped her wine. "I gave up wanting to

know who my people were a long time ago. Knowing a name is not the same as knowing a person."

Willie knew her mother simply didn't have space in her to care whether her people came from Georgia or Mississippi or Haiti. Not because she didn't want to know, but because she couldn't justify that type of wanting. Wanting to know your parents, your grandparents, was natural. Wanting to understand your place in America and your place before America carried with it a more primal type of longing. Feeling like you didn't need to know carried its own set of privileges.

"Look." Lourdes set down her fork and used her napkin to wipe her mouth, even though she had taken only a few bites of food. "I don't want you driving yourself crazy over this search."

Willie looked up, surprised. "You don't think we're actually going to get this money, do you?"

"Your dad told me about the business, about the retirement account. We talked about selling the house to cover some of the debts."

"The debts from the business? We don't need to sell the house for that."

"There's more you don't know about. There's so much we owe from all of Max's medical bills. We've been trying to pay them off for years, and now, with the problems in the business, it's just too much."

"How much do we owe on his bills?"

"We're going to take care of it. And you and Paloma will be okay."

"Selling the house?" Willie repeated, unsure if she had heard correctly. The house, she thought, was the point. She and her mother had their safe conversations, which they never strayed too far from. And now she was reminded of how much depth existed beyond the safety, and how much love—for Max, for Willie, for Seb, for Paloma—so that selling the house became just one more option in a litany of options to continue moving forward.

"It's paid off. It will give us a cushion and some time to figure out what we want to do, what your father wants to do with the business."

"But we can't sell the house." A grotesque panic filled her.

"Well, we can. That was the point of owning a house like that to begin with."

"I thought the point was to pass it down."

"The point is to preserve what we worked so hard to build."

"And we're preserving it by selling the house?" Willie knew she sounded desperate. "The Forgiveness Act means something to me, especially after seeing those records today. It's hard to explain. But I am going to make sure we get this money. Trust me."

"As much as I would love to believe this bill just happened to come at the perfect time to help us, it doesn't work that way. Life doesn't work that way."

The waitress cleared their plates and asked if they wanted dessert. Willie and Lourdes stared at her a moment, trying not to cry at the banality of the question. Instead, they ordered more wine, pretending they weren't in Jackson searching for anything except a brief reprieve.

Rather than sit in their room after dinner, Willie and Lourdes walked to a bar near the inn. The lights were low and the bar was crowded. Christmas lights around the televisions gave the illusion of laughing fireflies. A large stage and a lonely microphone were positioned in the right-hand corner. It was dirty, grungy, yet somehow serene, not trying to be anything it wasn't, the patrons not wanting to be anywhere other than where they were. The northerners you could spot from a mile away, and Willie prepared herself for stares, cold shoulders, but no one even looked at them. All she got was a smile from the bartender, a skinny woman with thin red hair. "What can I get you?"

"Two white wines please."

"Actually," Lourdes interjected, "vodka martini for me. Extra dirty."

They turned away from the bar like coconspirators without a plan. "Nice scarf," a woman said, nodding to Lourdes. She sat with her elbows on the bar, two empty bottles in front of her. "You ladies are mighty dressed up for Martin's."

Lourdes smiled sweetly. "Don't let the scarf fool you. I grew up working the tobacco fields every summer in Virginia."

"What brings you two down here?"

"My daughter is researching her family."

The woman laughed knowingly but not unkindly.

"What was it like going to Virginia every summer?" Willie asked after the woman had moved on to a different conversation.

"Taught me how to take care of myself. There was this man I used to see in the store where I shopped on the way back to my aunt's house. He would come up behind me and touch my waist. I hated it so much. He would hold my waist just hard enough so I couldn't turn or move. So I just stood there. One day I had enough. I taped tacks around my knee, and when he grabbed me,

I spun around and kneed him so hard he screamed. The Solomons wanted me to experience other parts of the family, and they trusted I would figure out how to make it. Paloma's going to be okay, you know? She can handle it."

Willie looked up, surprised. It felt like an accusation but, truthfully, she was grateful to be reassured. "What kind of woman can't tell her daughter anything about her father?"

"'Tell her the truth. It's all she wants. The truth is enough."

Chapter 16

Willie woke up at six-thirty, leaving a note on the nightstand for Lourdes to meet her at the archives. She took her breakfast from the buffet out to a stone ledge, where she watched the sunrise and waited for the building to open. While her heart raced at the thought of them having to sell the house, she was also resigned to this fate, if that was what you could call it, because it released her in some ways from responsibility.

As security unlocked the doors, Lourdes joined Willie in line. A few people filed in alongside them. In the reading room, Ollie seemed pleased to see them.

"Could you help me find a marriage license?" Willie asked him. "I think it would have been around 1895."

"Let's look at the index."

They scrolled.

"There," Willie said, pointing. "It's there. There he is." Hemp Revel. They noted the location of the record. Hemp Revel married to Minnie Barrow.

"Barrow," Willie said, repeating the name out loud.

I hereby certify that on the ninth day of May in the year of our Lord one thousand eight hundred and ninety-four in Natchez of Adams County, I the undersigned, Joseph B. Statton, did join in the holy bonds of matrimony according to the laws of this State Hemp Revel of the county of Adams state of Mississippi and Minnie Barrow of the county of Adams state of Mississippi.

Without speaking, Ollie pulled out the 1880 Soundex sheet and copied down the code for Barrow: *B600*.

"The Barrows," Ollie repeated, like he was working out a math problem. "They were well-known slaveowners in Natchez. The family just made their papers available to people who need them for the Forgiveness money."

Ollie looked back and forth between Willie and Lourdes as he spoke, his hands working the microfilm into the reader. He adjusted the lever and stood back, letting Willie flip through the census cards. As she flipped through looking for *M* to find Minnie Barrow, she passed *H*, scrolling so fast she almost missed it. *There.* Hemp Barrow.

She turned the lever back. Hemp Barrow? Could he have been a Barrow before he was a Revel?

She vaguely heard Ollie say to Lourdes, "Amazing, isn't it.

When you find your people like this." Lourdes smiled politely.
Willie copied the enumeration district and sheet number so she
could locate Hemp in the county census roll.

She walked quickly to the filing cabinet, found the right roll,
and loaded it into the machine, scrolling through until she found it.

> *Lou Barrow, White, male, 70, NC, England, England*
> *Williams, Negro, male, 42, boarder, day laborer, MS, MS, MS*
> *Jim Benbow, Negro, male, 22, boarder, day laborer, MS, MS, MS*
> *Hemp Barrow, Negro, male, 14, grandson, MS, VA, NC*

Lourdes leaned over Willie's shoulder as Ollie reappeared
next to them.

She tried to organize her thoughts. *Minnie Barrow. Hemp Barrow. Lou Barrow. Hemp was Lou Barrow's grandson?*

"You said the Barrows were prominent slaveowners in
Natchez?" Willie asked, turning back to Ollie.

"Fairly prominent. They owned slaves and kept diaries—
many owners did back then. There's a whole manuscript collection: estate papers, correspondence. They're at the foundation in
Natchez." If Hemp was listed as Lou's grandson, and if he was in
fact the same Hemp who was her great-great-grandfather, then
his father must have been a Barrow. Which meant she would
need to find Hemp's mother to get the papers they needed to
apply for the money.

"And those records are available only in Natchez?" Lourdes
asked.

Ollie nodded. "Afraid so. But you'll find, soon enough, all
roads lead to Natchez."

Willie didn't know what she had been expecting—certainly not a clean history; there was no such thing. But was it possible she'd hoped to learn more about her family's past while avoiding the realities of it? There were only a few ways for her ancestor to have given birth to a slaveowner's child. She felt an acute ache for the woman whose name she didn't even yet know.

By the time they left the archives, it was decided that Willie and Lourdes would drive the two hours to Natchez to look through the Barrow papers.

"Ask for Dee. Tell her Ollie Winters sent you."

Back at the lockers, Willie saw she had several missed calls from Max. She showed her phone to Lourdes. They walked quickly back to the hotel, wanting to get somewhere quieter, and dialed him from their room.

"Where have you been?" Max said when he answered, his voice hoarse. "Seb's been arrested. I called you four times."

Lourdes pulled out the desk chair and sat down, finally unwrapping the scarf from her neck and folding it neatly on top of the desk.

"What happened?"

"He was at a protest. The cops are claiming he got into a fight and that he hit several people."

"Is there bail? Just pay it," Lourdes said. "Pay whatever it is."

"They haven't said yet."

"Call Graves and see if he can help us."

"I did. He says he can't help."

"I'm coming home."

"Mom—"

"I said I'm going home."

Lourdes hung up, and there wasn't much more to say. They waited for another call from Max to say Seb had been released, but by midnight nothing came.

The next morning Lourdes rose and dressed early. She turned to Willie on her way out of the room, her hand resting severely on top of her suitcase. "I know this isn't the life you imagined for yourself. But it's a good life."

It was a strange thing to say and a stranger time to say it, but Willie repeated, "It is a good life," like she was trying it on for size.

After checking out of the inn, Willie propped her phone in the drink holder so she could easily see the directions to Natchez. Seventy miles along the Old Natchez Trace, she called to make a reservation at a hotel in Natchez, and then phoned home to check on Paloma, who told her Seb hadn't come home last night.

"He probably slept at his own place because he had to work late," Willie lied.

"Are you sure everything's okay?" Paloma asked her.

"Everything's fine. I have to go. Have a good day at school, okay?"

"Mr. Jeremy is announcing the winning plays today," Paloma reminded her. "I guess I'll call you when I hear."

She hung up, and found a station on the radio to distract her from her guilt.

Senator Abbott: *Well, it's not uncommon, right? We see this frequently, where the logistics have not been completely hashed out. I would have liked to see the committee from the study spend more time outlining the logistics. We should have tested this with a small group of African Americans to see if it was feasible. In drafting this bill, Democrats should have planned better for this outcome. I think if you ask many Senate Republicans why they opposed the Forgiveness Act, it wasn't because we didn't think it was necessary— although that was a convenient narrative. It's because we're pragmatic.*

Host: *Dr. Wiley, you were more skeptical of the Forgiveness Act before it passed. In the past you have advocated for baby bonds or universal basic income. Dr. Jones, you were a proponent of the Forgiveness Act. You both have been studying income inequality and the racial wealth gap for almost two decades. Dr. Jones, are you still optimistic about the Forgiveness Act?*

Dr. Jones: *Look, here's the problem: This interview, along with media coverage of the Forgiveness Act in general, misses the point. It's not about the poor implementation, the fact that millions of Black families are feeling duped out of money they not only need but deserve from their country. It's the fact that no one is talking about forgiveness. Ultimately, that's what this plan is about. It's about the United States of America looking into the eyes of the ancestors of human beings forced to pick this country's most profitable crops, into the eyes of human beings alive today who did not, have not, and will not get equal treatment under a rule of law that claims every man is created equal. It's about the country asking those people to forgive its transgressions. The founders of this country made* *it so Black people lost our heritage. Our families were torn apart. Part of what makes this country great is the vast melting pot of cultures: of people who still celebrate being Irish, or Polish, or Italian. It is the coalescence of the individual expressions of those cultures that makes us feel alive and special in America. It is our greatest marketing tactic. But Black Americans were robbed of that. Celebrating where in America we came from is the best we can do. Black Americans are the most patriotic individuals in this country because it is the only home we've ever known. But what about when your home takes advantage of you for centuries? Beats you and whips you and holds your throat to the fire. But you love it anyway. And one day, the day you dreamed would come, your home asks you to forgive it. Will you forgive? Of course you will want to. And then you discover the question of forgiveness was posed to shut you up so it could continue getting what it wanted.*

I think the Forgiveness Act offers us an opportunity here to see what was really lost and to give America the chance to make it right. To make it right by offering to help African Americans discover their heritage rather than saying, "This proof doesn't work and you're denied the funds." I think if America continues looking the other way and pretending the status quo is the best it can do, this country may never be able to heal its wounds. How can you be a competitive nation if you're too embarrassed to acknowledge your past? People like Dr. Wiley here want to say it's not about the money. But it is about the money. People are hurting where this money will make a difference today. And the salt on the wound when people try to claim these funds and are denied is that the money isn't even close to what is really deserved. You took away our history, denied us homes, and mortgages, and the vote, and equal

service, jailed us, killed us, blamed us. And yet—we would still find
it in our hearts to forgive, because this is the only home we know.

On the Trace, loblolly and longleaf pine trees arched overhead. One mile contained fields peppered with cows, while the
next was full of cypress swamps and ravines. Traffic was light on
the two-lane road draped in the changing colors of leaves, and
she passed a few cyclists intent on their destinations. Every now
and then, a National Park Service marker appeared, placed there
for scenic purposes, some relic to a time gone by. After Lourdes
left, Willie had packed quickly, with a new resolve to ensure the
trip bore fruit. When she thought about it, there were few goals
in her life she had succeeded in achieving. She had vision, and
then the vision was always derailed. This time would be different,
she reasoned. This time, for her family, she would succeed.

Her phone vibrated in the cup holder, and she smiled when
she saw it was Jared. "How did you know I needed a distraction?"

Jared laughed. "Because I need one too."

They hadn't had sex yet, but they had that fragile intimacy
that comes with anticipated pleasure.

"I'm driving to Natchez," she said. "It turns out that my great-
great-grandfather is listed in the census connected to a slaveowner whose family made their papers available. A guy who
worked at the archives told me I could find more there, his will
and diary."

"I'm a little jealous."

Jared had traveled to Kentucky to research his own family.
"Still no luck?"

He sighed heavily. "As a journalist I should be used to this feeling, energized by it even. But my sisters and I hit a wall. The 1890 census was burned; we can't find anything in the 1880 census with the names we know of. I am currently standing outside my office, watching protesters walk by, trying to keep myself from joining them. The city is charged right now. People protesting the act, people protesting the fact that they can't qualify."

They were both silent for a while. Willie glanced down at her phone to make sure she hadn't lost the connection, but the call time ticked upward, and it was nice, realizing they were comfortable enough with each other to allow for seconds of silence on the phone.

"Well, drive safe and be careful down there."

They hung up, and she had to go to the bathroom. She saw a sign for the Mount Locust Inn and Plantation Information Center and pulled off the Trace, parking the car in the nearly empty lot, set back in a clearing in the woods. For a moment she hesitated, wondering if it was safe to stop in such a deserted area. *Black men they put in jail,* Willie thought, thinking of her brother, *and Black women they attack.*

There were two other cars in the lot—the sound of the birds and the trees made it hard for her to imagine anything bad happening. In Philadelphia, people often stared straight ahead rather than make eye contact with a stranger. They kept to themselves, their group of friends, but here, people seemed to crave connection and wanted to help. In many ways she felt safer here than in her own city.

A small pink outpost housing the information center stood next to the bathroom. The inn sat off to the left at the top of a hill, a small wooden cabin with bright-blue shutters. She went to the bathroom and then wandered up to the cabin, stopping to read the informational signs posted along the way.

Mount Locust remains as the only one of more than 50 inns that existed between 1785 and 1830 along the 500 mile Old Trace. It has been restored to its 1810 appearance, the time when travel on this historic road reached its peak.

In an era when women were typically shunned from business, Paulina proved to be extraordinary. Despite losing two husbands and raising 11 children, seven with William and four with James, Paulina kept Mount Locust bustling. Sometime after 1810, James was gone, leaving her and the children to raise the family and run the farm and inn, which provided a comfortable living for the family. By the mid-1820s the steamboat and other roads all but brought an end to the Natchez Trace. After 1825 the inn no longer catered to travelers but instead to Natchez residents who sought the rural solitude of Mount Locust. During her life, Paulina oversaw a small corn farm that became a thriving cotton plantation. Paulina Chamberlain died in 1849 at the age of 80. The Civil War (1861–1865) brought an end to the plantation system and Mount Locust began a slow decline. In a testimony to her spirit and the lasting impression she made on her family, her descendants still refer to her as "Grandma Polly."

The doors to the house were open, and without walking up the porch steps, Willie could see that it was a basic restaged cabin, like one she'd seen as a kid while touring colonial towns in Pennsylvania: The wooden rocking chairs and wide wooden farm tables. A small kitchen. A quilt hanging from the wall. She walked through the cabin and felt a film of uneasiness. The small beds tousled to look as though children recently slept in them.

Out back there was a well and an open grassy area the size of a soccer field. A wooden sign with yellow writing marked the area: SLAVE CEMETERY.

Another placard, like the one about Grandma Polly, was placed there.

A small number of families were forced to endure the bondage of slavery at Mount Locust. The 1820 census lists 26 enslaved people at Mount Locust, and by the middle of the 19th century, the number had reached 51. In 1834 the average prices for enslaved men and women who worked in the cotton fields were $800 and $600 respectively. Archeologists believe 12 to 16 slave cabins once stood on the property, with four to five people occupying each dwelling. On the west side of Mount Locust, a cemetery holds the remains of 43 enslaved workers.

"Eight hundred dollars," Willie said aloud.

The cemetery for people who helped run Mount Locust was pushed to the periphery, as if they were a nuisance to the beauty of the place, gnats needing to be swatted away so people could focus on the wonder of Grandma Polly. The significance wasn't lost on her, nor was the proximity—that someone buried here might very well be related to Hemp, related to her.

On her way back to the car, she saw two tourists. The man carried a large camera around his neck and was studying a map, and the woman standing next to him said in awe, "I just love old houses."

By the time Willie pulled off the Trace and into downtown Natchez, a downpour battered the windshield. She could faintly make out the Mississippi River, like a gray sheet of ice hemming the city in its place. She parked under the portico at the hotel lot, where groups of people stood about smoking cigarettes, leaning against their motorcycles, drinking wine in rocking chairs. As she climbed out of her car, it became clear there was a power outage.

Inside, the front-desk staff checked people in by jotting down names and rooms in a notebook. No one seemed particularly concerned or bothered by the creeping darkness or the lack of an electrical hum. Willie got her key and was told to try Little Easy or Smoot's Grocery to get something to eat.

A little girl standing with her parents kept taking lollipops out of the jar on the center table and throwing them on the floor. At first the mother was embarrassed, picking them up and reprimanding her daughter, but after the third time the mother gave up, laughing and smiling at the woman behind the front desk. Their son stood off to the side, ignoring his father's pleas for help with the bags. Willie studied the couple. A white man who worked for the hotel kneeled in front of the little girl, whose cheeks and eyes were splotchy from crying. He picked up a lollipop from the floor and handed it to her. Willie looked at the little girl, now enjoying the lollipop she had just dumped on the floor, blissfully unaware of how in a different life, with different skin, she might have received a backhand or worse. She watched the girl and her mother, knowing Paloma was disappointed that Willie wasn't the type of mother who was ardently devoted to her daughter. She was like a pelican who swooped down periodically and then was just as quickly gone. Willie tried to reassure herself that she was chasing ghosts for her daughter as much as for herself, but was this true? Paloma's future felt as abstract and tenuous as her own.

In a rocking chair under the portico, she waited out the rain next to strangers, making up stories about why they were there. By the time the power was restored, it was nearly six P.M. Seb answered the phone when she called home. "Hang on," he told her, while he changed rooms to avoid Paloma overhearing their conversation.

"I was standing there, and I don't know what came over me," he said. "There was this white woman standing across the street with sunglasses pushing her hair back, and she was bobbing a sign up and down: MOVE ON ALREADY. That's what the sign said. MOVE ON ALREADY. And she and I made eye contact and she's looking at me, moving this sign up and down, and I lost it. I started running toward her side of the street. I wasn't going to do anything, Wil. I only wanted to see her. Look her in the face and ask her what harm we were doing to her. But a cop slammed me down in the middle of the street. His club hit me and it felt like my ribs were glass, I swear to God. He dragged me to a police van and tased me."

She was sorry, but she was sick of being sorry. "Are you going to press charges?"

"Against who? The cop? Waste of time." He sounded so angry that Willie closed her eyes.

"I started doing my own research," Seb said.

"What do you mean?"

"I started researching Mom's family. I thought it could be an insurance policy, in case you can't find what we need. And I thought it could be a nice thing for Mom."

"How did you even know where to start?"

"I didn't. I tried to find an adoption record with the Solomons, but there was nothing. I asked Pop if he knew anything, and he said Mrs. Solomon's sister had gone to church with Mom's biological mother in Macon and that's how they came to adopt her. But it was off the books, and Mrs. Solomon's sister is no longer living." He paused. "Do the best you can for us. That will have to be enough."

She told him about driving to Natchez and about finding Hemp and Minnie's marriage license. "I found the family who I think owned our great-great-grandparents."

"Good," he said.

He went and found Paloma, who got on the phone and asked her when she was coming home. Willie's return ticket was in three days, but she was willing to pay the $250 change fee if it took longer to find what she needed.

Paloma sighed. "Mr. Jeremy chose my play. It'll be performed opening night of the Flash Festival."

Willie thought of the little girl enjoying the lollipop. "I knew he would. I'm so proud of you."

When there was a break in the rain, Willie walked the path along the river. On the bluffs she took in the expansiveness of the Mississippi, lights from Louisiana shining neatly on the other side of the bridge like pieces on a board game. The scene was stunning, but it was colder here by the water. By the time she walked into Smoot's Grocery, her arms were covered in goosebumps and her feet were damp. Her eyes adjusted to the darkness—bodies moved around her or posted up at tables outside.

"Don't worry," the person standing next to her at the bar said. "You're safe here. At least I think you are. I've been here four days by myself, and as far as I can tell, the most ominous thing has been the amount of gravy served in the morning." She held out her hand. "I'm Ashley."

They shook hands, gripped their drinks, and turned to the stage, where candles were being lit as a jazz quartet warmed up.

"Four days?" Willie repeated. "Where are you from?"

"Kansas City. It's part social experiment, part I really need the fucking money. Cheers." Ashley's head tipped back, and a small nose ring in her left nostril glinted like a speck of gold dust. Willie learned that Ashley, recently separated from her husband and with a son left behind in the care of her father, was a painter and a paralegal. Unlike Willie, she was there on the currency of family lore. As Ashley spoke, Willie thought about the peeling layers of desperation. Willie wanted the money too, badly, but in a way that braided together need and relevance. It made her feel relevant to be there, looking at her great-great-grandparents' records for a worthy cause, one that wasn't fanciful but that made her feel full. She hated feeling like she had lost herself for her family, and yet she needed that feeling of loss. She realized now that it gave her purpose. She girded herself for Ashley to laugh or grow bored as she explained her father's business, how she had ended up working there for longer than expected, how her parents were thinking of selling their house because of his medical bills, and how she couldn't stomach working for a man like Hank Lasure. But Ashley simply listened, letting Willie continue unabated, and when Willie was finished, Ashley tipped back her beer again and said, "I'm glad I met you."

Chapter 17

Again Paloma had dreamed she was standing on a stage surrounded by people, though she couldn't see their faces. They were yelling insults at her, telling her to leave, she was a fake. She was somehow both Phillis and herself, of this time and a place beyond it.

If she hadn't had that dream, if Willie had been home, if her grandmother was there, she probably wouldn't have said yes to the Chasers. One of the girls had passed her a note in math class, and she wanted so badly to fit in, to feel normal, that she'd said yes. She didn't want to be the kind of girl who had weird dreams at night and then hid out in Mr. Jeremy's classroom. She filled in the bubble next to *yes* and passed the note back. Then she stared out the window and worried about what she had just gotten herself into.

It was a well-known fact that twice a week during recess, five girls snuck under the chain-link fence and ran around the campus as fast as they could. At first the teachers were furious. But soon it became cute how the girls pumped their legs and worked up a sweat over the idea of breaking the rules. They were cunning, but they weren't bad, their amber waves and blond ponytails swishing behind them. To receive a lunchtime invitation from the Chasers became a badge of honor.

Paloma stood watching the girls gather by the fence, stashing their backpacks under the oak tree and tightening their laces. The girls represented a type of comfortable Paloma could only watch from afar. She strode across the soccer field, feeling the air prickle her hands through her gloves and slightly pierce the down lining of her coat. The sun danced and followed her like a spotlight. The grass bent beneath her footsteps.

The girls nodded at her when she reached them at the fence, and she was struck by how much older than her they seemed, as though they were Olympic athletes instead of fifth graders. One girl applied a fresh coat of gloss to her lips and then, one by one, they slipped through the fence, where a small hole had been cut. Paloma wondered if the girls cut the hole themselves or if an animal accidentally caused the first break and the girls merely seized the opportunity, making it larger and larger until they could easily fit through.

The girl with the longest hair took off running. She was the leader, and the other girls broke into a sprint, trying to catch her.

Paloma still had her backpack on. She tightened the straps around her stomach and took off, inhaling gulps of air through her nose like she did when she raced Seb up the driveway. She caught up to each girl, passing one, and then another, and then another. She passed the leader of the group, catching a whiff of her shampoo as she glided past. Paloma rounded the corner. She didn't care that the air lifted her hair into an airborne crown. She didn't listen to the shouts of "Hey!" or "Wait up!" She just ran, and it felt good. She ran and ran and ran. She ran straight into Mr. Wallace, whose stomach propelled her backward when she hit it at full speed. Seeing the collision and the look on Mr. Wallace's face, the other girls turned and ran back the way they had come.

Paloma tried turning to do the same, but he gripped her elbow from behind. "Oh no you don't," Mr. Wallace said. "To the office."

Paloma went to Mr. Wallace's office, the first girl to get in trouble for running. "You cannot, under any circumstances, run around outside unsupervised," Mr. Wallace told her. "Do you understand?"

"Yes, but it wasn't just me! I was . . . I wanted . . ." He waited, but as she fumbled, she understood. She understood there were different rules when it came to someone who looked like her in a school like that.

Mr. Wallace leaned across the passenger-side window to explain to Paloma's uncle how she had been caught breaking the rules of recess. Seb laughed, and Paloma could tell by the sound of his voice that something was wrong. Her grandfather had stayed on the phone for hours on Tuesday night, with the door to the sunroom closed, and Paloma knew then that *something* had happened, only she wasn't sure what.

"Was she in danger?" Seb asked.

Mr. Wallace—used to parents who apologized profusely, asking what they could do to make it better—looked confused. "Excuse me?"

"Was she in danger?" Seb repeated.

"She could have been, which is why we don't let the children play beyond the fence unsupervised."

Seb laughed again. "If I were you, I'd spend more time finding out why my niece wanted to break the rules in the first place. Especially since it's not like her, now, is it?" He winked at Paloma and gestured for her to get in the car. Mr. Wallace stepped back, confused.

Seb rolled the window up and asked if she wanted to get pizza.

"Sure," she said.

His shirt was untucked, and he gripped the steering wheel so tightly it was like his knuckles could break through the skin and steer the car themselves. "Is everything okay, Uncle Seb?"

He stared straight ahead.

In the pizza shop, he told her to get an extra slice. While he paid, she stood outside the store, eating a pepperoni, bouncing from side to side to keep warm. She bounced so hard that one of her slices slid off her plate and landed on the hood of the police car beside her.

Seb came barreling out of the shop, grabbed her elbow, and pulled her into the middle of the sidewalk, causing her to drop the other slice.

"What is wrong with you?" he hissed. "Pay attention to what you're doing."

The cop laughed and said, "It's alright. Car could use a wash anyway." But Seb refused to look at him and pulled Paloma to his car, the tomato sauce bleeding into the cracks of the sidewalk behind them.

It was the first time he'd ever yelled at her.

Years later, when people asked, she always described her childhood as a happy one. There was laughter and there were homemade meals; warm embraces and freshly made beds; pool parties and music. There was a house her family felt at home in. And once you know the feeling of home and those who have made it, it builds up inside you like grains of sand. And some part of you always defines yourself the way you defined yourself when you were home—curious, a risk-taker. But if someone had asked Paloma that question in the weeks following the passing of the Forgiveness Act, she couldn't have answered so persuasively. And there was some persuasion at work—there had to be. For childhoods can be both happy and sad. Over the next few weeks, everything she thought she knew about her family would be turned inside out. Before, she had been the center of their world. Now she was an afterthought. An embarrassing reminder of how little they knew about their past, about the history they were at once running from and hoping to uncover. The Forgiveness Act was supposed to be a good thing—this is what her mother had told her—but so far it had seemed to wreak only havoc and confusion. She was scared to go out on errands with her family, scared to play alone in the yard in case that car was out front watching the house again, scared even to go to school, not because her teachers or classmates were mean but because they looked at her curiously, wondering if the Revels had gotten the money. "Are you rich yet?" Olivia asked her once.

"The money won't make us rich," Paloma said.

"Because you're already rich."

"No, we're not."

"My mom says it's a lot of money."

Could it be that she missed the days when the only thing that made her different was the fact of her existence?

Chapter 18

Natchez was a town of fifteen thousand, but in many ways it felt more alive, more vibrant, than downtown Jackson. Voices in the hallway woke her, and by seven the path along the river was peppered with pedestrians.

Willie agreed to meet Ashley for a small breakfast. After they went their separate ways, Willie walked the short distance to the Historic Natchez Foundation, arriving at a brick building not unlike the one that housed MRA. A large magnolia tree near the entrance added to its residential ambience, as did the people milling about out front, overflowing from the lobby onto the sidewalk. People in groups of twos and threes held folders and talked in hushed voices. A little girl sat with her back against the tree, balancing a drink in the grass. A policeman stationed near the entrance watched two protesters who held cardboard signs: FOR-

GIVE & 4GET and WE OWE NOTHING! The signs were written in black
Sharpie, and the people holding them seemed restless, like they
were tailgating at a game that wouldn't start for several more
hours.

Inside, the foundation was compact. Cubicles and towers of
binders and books competed for floor space. As soon as Willie
entered, a man appeared, short and eager to help. She asked for
Dee, as Ollie had suggested, and the man led her to a slightly
larger room on the other side of the wall. It was lined with book-
shelves and had a long mahogany table in the middle.

Dee looked to be in her late sixties or early seventies, with
short gray hair and burgundy lips. Her face was unwrinkled—
a dark complexion made smooth from the sun rather than weath-
ered. She said hello to people as she moved through the room,
gripping the shoulder of one woman in a red shawl and then pat-
ting it reassuringly.

"Ollie told me he was sending a persistent young lady my
way," she said to Willie after her colleague introduced them. "I
have never seen the foundation this crowded, and it's a blessing."

The foundation had a more casual air than the archives, with
only one computer at what appeared to be Dee's desk and people
leafing gingerly through folders. Desperation lingered, but it was
a familiar desperation, one that Dee calmed with a touch on the
shoulder.

"Ollie told me the foundation recently acquired some papers
from the Barrow plantation. Could I see those?" Willie asked,
pulling out her notebook.

"You can find most of the conveyance records in this room,"
Dee said, pointing to shelves along the wall. "Conveyance records

are going to give you everything. Anything of value transferred between people. Could be timber, mules, a gift of some kind. This bottom row here," she said, pointing to another bookshelf, "contains personal papers, diaries, letters, that sort of thing, from the Barrows. Take your time, take notes. And take pictures." She winked at Willie and placed a hand on her arm. "Good luck. If you need anything, I'll be at this desk here."

Willie found a spot at the table and spread out her notebook, feeling more at ease than she had at the archives. Although Dee said she'd be at her desk, every time Willie looked up, she was talking to someone, helping them carry books to the photo-copier, or laughing in the hallway. Willie found her presence com-forting.

Willie thumbed through an indirect-index real estate convey-ance book labeled *Ra–Ri*, moving quickly and passing page after page of typed certificates. She was on autopilot, working me-thodically until she found it.

Filed: 4 October 1925
Date of Deed: 5 November 1907
*Grantor: **James and Sarah Barrow**, sale of five acres @ $15*
*Grantee: **Hemp Revel, Emeline Barrow** at ½*

Willie turned the page, hoping for some sort of explanation. There was none, only another record:

Filed: 4 October 1940
Date of Deed: 30 January 1908
*Grantor: **James and Sarah Barrow**, sale of 20 acres @ $60*

Grantee: **Hemp Revel**

Description of Land: Township 19, Range 10, Section 20

Willie wrote everything down, noting the conveyance-book record in her notebook. She underlined *James and Sarah Barrow* and turned the page, but the next record was for someone else. She flipped back to the first conveyance. Emeline Barrow? Who was that, and why would she have bought the land with Hemp? Maybe a sister? A wife before Minnie? Willie wrote a question mark next to the name in her notebook and circled it. She could think of only a few reasons why someone buying land with Hemp would have the same last name as the person selling it to them. Either she had been white or she had been owned.

"Oh, I recognize that look," Dee said, walking over and moving her index finger right to left like a metronome.

"I'm not sure I found anything that's useful."

"Everything is useful depending on how you look at it," Dee replied, leaning over Willie's shoulder.

"My grandfather told me his grandfather was a landowner. I can't believe the original record is sitting here like this." As she grazed her fingers over the words, Willie felt she could almost feel Hemp's heart, his ambition. "I wish my grandfather could see this."

Dee nodded. "You'd be surprised at the records you can find in local courthouses. All the records we have at the foundation were moved here from the courthouse for safekeeping. Adams County has extremely thorough records. Courthouses were everything back then. Pain, joy, hope. People congregated there. Courthouse records are a map of people's lives and the major events that marked them. See Pat over there?" Dee nodded to the woman in the red shawl whom she had greeted when Willie first walked in. "The other day she found a record showing her grandmother borrowing money on a mule. Things we don't think are worth recording today meant a lot back then."

Willie listened politely, her mind on unanswered questions.

"Where are you from?" Dee asked.

"Is it that obvious?"

"We've had a few out-of-towners. But, you know, a lot of people can't just pick up and fly to a local courthouse or the archives, so I've been on the phone. Doing what I can to help folks get the records they need. There's always a catch in government, isn't there? An olive branch with an ultimatum. But I'm thankful to be able to help. My mom's side of the family is from Natchez, my dad's is from Greenville. I always thought I'd break out of small-town living, but I love it here. I love introducing people to this place. We have our demons, but we're not afraid to talk about them." The opposite of the Revels.

Dee handed Willie a folder, and Willie noticed that her nails were painted the same burgundy as her lips. "This might be an interesting place to look," Dee said. "The red marker on the tab here means that it's correspondence relating to property— including slaves. A lot of people come here with an idea in their mind about what slavery meant, but it's so much more brutal and complicated than you can imagine. White folks thought of their houses in Natchez as their suburban villas, and they wanted their slaves to be an extension of what they thought of as their own fine manors." Dee's gaze intensified. "It was a different kind of brutality here than across the bridge in Louisiana, where slaves were working large plantations in grueling conditions with the hot sun beating down. But two miles up Devereux Drive, you have what was one of the largest slave markets in the country. You know, given the nature of slavery in Natchez, it had one of the highest rates of miscegenation compared to any other Mississippi community. So sometimes you would have slaveowners grant manumission—you know, free their slaves, their offspring." She backed away and stood up straight. "I'm talking too much. Look through this folder and be careful, because they're all the original documents."

Dee wandered away, and Willie began leafing through the papers, which were as delicate as moth's wings. She lifted them up slowly with her fingertips, as if picking through glass.

There were so many papers associated with the Barrows in one folder alone that after two hours she had barely made it halfway through. She had a hard time being ruthless: Each page, written in scrupulous cursive, proved hard to look away from, so she found herself reading nearly every word on every page.

A TRUE and perfect Inventory of the Goods, Chattels and personal ESTATE of Fountain Barrow late of Adams County, deceased, made by us whose names are hereunto subscribed, the 27th day of September A.D. 1816

Negro
Peter $250
Bill $300
Benjamin $700
Baby and 4 children $1300

It was night when Willie left the foundation, having found no proof of Hemp's mother or any other mention of Minnie and having made it through only one folder—there were at least ten more. "Be patient," Dee said as Willie was leaving. "It may take a while. But when it clicks, it clicks, and information will start tumbling into place. You already have a lot more to go on than most people."

One of those people was Jared, who explained over the phone that his family had only found more dead ends. He sounded despondent, and Willie wasn't sure what to say to comfort him. They each understood that there was little to say and platitudes wouldn't help. Instead, they enjoyed the comfort of breath on the other end of the line, and they made plans to see each other once Willie returned. She phoned Nell, whose family had already submitted their completed application. Nell's happiness had been tempered by the fact that one night after work, as she was walking to her car, three boys hurled a glass bottle at her, and she now had stitches along the length of her forehead that would leave a scar.

"Thank God you're okay," Willie lamented.

"Those bastards are lucky I didn't run them over with my car. How are you? How is it down there?"

Willie hesitated to say she was enjoying it. That she wished she wasn't there because she had to be, that she had been smart enough to come without a law. Nell waited for Willie to tell her something horrible, some grotesque violence she had encountered in the South. The Forgiveness Act had brought out the worst in people, but it had also, somehow, brought out the best. What you encountered maybe was the luck of the draw.

Willie told Nell about Seb. "Jesus, Wil. Is he okay?"

"I think so. Mom went home because of it. And she wants to sell the house to help pay off some of Dad's medical bills."

Nell was adamant. "You can't sell that house."

Willie spent the next morning working relentlessly, combing through more of the Barrow records. She got a paper cut and sat sucking at her index finger, rolling her neck right and left, back and forth, trying to relieve the tension rocketing toward the base of her skull. She worked quietly, by herself, praying for guidance. Around noon she found several more land-transfer records between Lou and Bennet Barrow, but nothing else concrete showing who Hemp's mother might have been or why James and Sarah Barrow would have sold Hemp so much land. Nothing explaining who Emeline Barrow was or why she had purchased the land with Hemp. There weren't any records about Hemp himself, and she was forced to circle around his existence through other people, through the Barrows. It felt like diving underwater to find a lost earring, groping in the dark, only to come up for air and go back under again.

When Willie was ready to call it quits for the day, still empty-handed, Dee approached and placed a flyer triumphantly on the table in front of her. "Come to this," she said.

Willie read aloud, her voice hoarse and scratchy from lack of sleep: "*Ancestral Libation. Come take part in a divine tradition and find guidance from your ancestors as you embark on the great work of unearthing their stories.* Dee, there's a bubble bath with my name on it." Willie pushed the flyer back toward Dee and closed her notebook. "I'm too tired. But thank you."

Dee shook her head. "It wasn't a question. You're searching for something. And you're not going to find it by sitting in here sifting through old papers."

"Should the woman who works at the Historic Natchez Foundation be saying that?" Willie joked.

"Honey, at my age, I can say whatever I want."

Willie stood, towering at least six inches over Dee, who didn't move. "Fine," Willie said, throwing up her hands in surrender. "Okay."

She phoned Jared on the way, driving slowly down the main road next to the river. "This woman Dee has me going to a voodoo ceremony to connect with my ancestors."

"Send my regards," he snickered. "See if you can find mine while you're at it."

When Willie arrived at the church, ten or so women stood near the entrance, talking and laughing. Dee's face grew warm and welcoming at the sight of Willie.

"You came," she said, walking over and grasping Willie's hands between her own.

Willie returned the smile. "You didn't give me much choice, did you?"

The woman with the red shawl, Pat, was also there. Willie smiled at her and nodded, and the woman waved back.

The group descended the stairs to the basement and sat in folding chairs, facing a small altar covered with plants and candles. The basement smelled like a mix of wet wood and potpourri, and Willie inhaled, reminded of the bowls of potpourri Lourdes placed throughout the living room and downstairs bathroom.

Dee stood at the front of the room, lighting the candles, while the other women introduced themselves. They were all older, in their seventies or eighties, and Willie wondered why Dee had chosen to invite her. There had been plenty of other people milling about the foundation whom Dee could have asked.

Dee quieted the group and held up a small potted plant. Willie watched the buttons of her cotton shirt move up and down with her breath in the dim light.

"We are here," Dee said, "to acknowledge we come from greatness. To honor the divinity within all of us. To create a bridge of transition between those who came before us and those who are yet to come. Ashe." At the end of every sentence, she poured a little water into the soil of the plant. "In honor of all that is and ever will be. Ashe."

Dee held the plant at arm's length. "Join me in shouting out the names of your ancestors, living and passed on, who have brought you to this place and who will guide you on this journey. Who sustain you. After each name, please seal it with *Ashe,* meaning *let it be so.*"

Willie glanced at the other women to see what they would do. It was silent for a moment, and then the other women spoke. Softly at first, and then louder, names rolling off their tongues like beads hitting the floor.

Pat closed her eyes and raised her arms. "Mona," she said, "my grandmother. Ashe. Hanna, my great-grandmother. Ashe. Aunt Bernyce. Ashe."

Dee gave Willie a nod.

"Marcus," Willie said quietly, "my grandfather. Ashe. Max, my father. Ashe. Lourdes, my mother. Ashe. Paloma. Ashe. Seb. Ashe."

The room grew louder, filling with names. Dee poured water into the soil as names from the other women poured out. Willie raised her voice. "Hemp. Ashe. Minnie. Ashe. Thurgood. Ashe. Emeline. Ashe." With each name she spoke, she felt a part of her spirit lift, freed. The names rooted her to a place beyond the physical space she occupied in that church basement or at 512 Lewaro. They grounded her firmly in a place slightly beyond her own comprehension. Saying the names aloud, acknowledging in front of other people that Hemp and Minnie and Thurgood were hers, even if all she knew were their names, broke a part of her open. She had run out of names of her own, but Willie closed her eyes, listening, as the women shouted. Eventually the room grew silent. Willie opened her eyes, blinking to readjust to the darkness. Dee had come to sit next to her, and she reached for Willie's hand as the candle flames on the altar swayed as if by lingering breath.

"Ashe," Dee said. "Let it be so."

Knowing that the foundation had extended its hours because of Forgiveness, Willie showed up as soon as it opened, planning to comb through the Barrow papers. She'd pushed her flight from Jackson back. A delivery man standing in the rear of his truck sorting packages watched her as she crossed the street. She held his gaze, looked away, and then glanced back to see if he was still staring. She knew what he was thinking: *That she had no right going to the foundation to try and claim this money.*

Do the same thing at the same time for three days and suddenly it's a routine. Dee greeted her eagerly each morning, sometimes helping her sift through papers. Still, Willie couldn't find the names of Hemp's parents or any other way to prove she was a descendant of slaves.

She turned to a leather-bound book with deep lines etched into the cover and a leather string holding it closed. She looked at Dee. "Can I open this?"

Dee nodded, miming fingers untying laces. "Gently."

The name *Bennet H. Barrow* was carved into the front. There was a handwritten prayer on the first page:

> *Oh Lord, I thank You that the earth is Yours and everything in it. I pray that we will all turn from our wicked ways and return to the true and living God. We declare the coming of revival in our Land in Jesus' Name. Lord, may You awaken each of us that has fallen asleep that we may worship You in spirit and truth. I pray that our desires will be godly desires and that we will seek the kingdom of God and His righteousness. Amen.*
> *Psalm 24:1, Matthew 6:33*

"Bennet Barrow was the last slaveholder in the family," Dee said, stepping forward and pointing at the diary. "His son inherited the plantation just as slavery was abolished."

Willie picked through the first couple of pages.

There were several letters, a few from before the war.

Lou,

I know you got to my house nigger, Alice. Don't ask how I know.

—B

Lou,

What is it about my negro wenches you can't keep your hands off of? You choose the bright ones, they are almost too white for slavery. But you take them so young they are out of work for much longer to heal. Mightn't you take an older one next time?

—B

Willie turned quickly, nearly ripping one of the thin pages in half. She felt dirty, reading this filth by men who performed such unspeakable acts. The worst part, though, was that they weren't unspeakable. They were so common as to be commemorated on paper. She pulled out a yellow sheet. **Inventory and Appraisement: Estate of Bennet Barrow, Deceased.**

Inventory and appraisement of the personal property belonging to the Estate of Bennet Barrow, late of Adams County, MS, taken this 12th day of December 1864

Cash on hand 16.75
100 Bus. Corn 100
8 pork hogs 1000 lbs. 80
1 bull 10
1 cow & half 10
3 heifers 30
1 gray stallion 100
1 Bay Horse 50
1 spinning wheel 1.50

1 shot gun 1

1 bed stead & furniture

6 cottage chairs 4.50

1 tin safe & tables 2

7 head geese 2.80

2 Bee Hives 2

6000 lbs. seed cotton

Prices of a partial list of slaves:

1 negro woman Hetty 450

1 negro woman Alice 400

1 negro woman Charlotte 800

1 negro man Malone 1600

1 negro man Shadrach 800

1 negro baby Emeline 200

1 negro child Betsy 450

1 negro child Pleasant 100

Last Will and Testament of Bennet Barrow deceased I Bennet Barrow of the county of Adams in the state of Mississippi do make and ordain this to be my Last Will and Testament. After the payments of my debts, I dispose of my property in the following manner.

I give and bequeath to my son Strickland Barrow the land I gave him in the State of North Carolina, and also the sum of one dollar.

I give and bequeath to my son James Barrow the remainder of the plantations in Natchez and Louisiana.

Item 3rd I give and bequeath to my daughter Jane Neece and the legal heirs of her body the negro woman Charlotte and her children now in her possession.

Item 4th I give my daughter Patience twelve hundred dollars.

It is my will that all my property both real and personal be sold as soon as the law will permit and the above bequests paid and the re-mainder if any of the proceeds arising from the sale of my Estate be divided equally between the heirs of my son . . .

Willie moved stiffly, absorbing Dee's gaze, her body growing warm, wishing she was alone or at home instead of in a room filled with strangers.

James,
As you know, Alice's offspring are my own kin. It is my Will
and desire that I leave Hemp and Emeline a small allotment
of land and a cow each. When the time is right, I also wish
you to sell them what land you think fair. As you well know,
I have claimed him as my grandson as that is a more respectable position to take than what I truly am, as you may know
from your father. Hemp is a bright mulatto and in other
circumstances could make something of himself, I believe.
                                                        —Lou

Willie felt rigid and sick. She took a deep breath and contin-ued flipping through the pages, her palms slick as though from a fever.

The entire picture came into focus for her. Hemp was Lou's son. Lou had raped Bennet Barrow's slaves, fathering Hemp and Emeline and who knows how many other children. Hemp's mother's name was Alice. Of course. Of course Hemp hadn't talked to Marcus about his past. How could he? Some things were in your blood without your having to say them. Willie had been naïve. Naïve and conceited, asking around about who the Revels were, without being prepared to care. She, however far removed, was a product of Lou Barrow's women. The part that survived despite the destruction, despite the tearing down of souls.

Where did Minnie fit in all of this? Who were her parents? Willie couldn't muster the fortitude right now to dive back under for more information.

Willie started taking pictures of the documents. She would need to submit all of the documentation to tell the story of how Hemp was related to Marcus and how Alice had Hemp. She stopped to examine a small square photo. On the back, written in pencil, were the words *Wedding celebration;* the front showed a group of people sitting around on upturned buckets, two of them—the couple, maybe—embracing. There was a small blur in the foreground, what could have been either smoke or a child running. There was no name on the photo, nothing indicating who they might be. But Willie stared at it, wondering if she could see herself in the faces.

"You wouldn't have any correspondence between Black family members, right?" Willie asked Dee. "Any letters from the children Lou Barrow would have fathered with his family's slaves?" She sounded hurried and frantic, but any embarrassment she might have felt had been replaced with urgency and, yes, that desperation again. There was no way to keep your dignity intact while searching for clues about the people who made you, she thought. The very act itself required looking foolish. It was why no one in her family had tried very hard beforehand.

Dee shook her head. "What we have is in those folders, so it's possible. But without going through it all I would have no way of knowing if what you're looking for is there. It's not likely, though."

One name kept circling in Willie's mind as she tried to fall asleep that night.

The next morning, she went to the foundation and searched only the records for Emeline Barrow. Dee pointed her toward an obituary in the *Natchez Daily*.

Emeline Barrow, investigative journalist who launched the weekly newspaper The Daily Wage, *died in her sleep at the age of 42. Emmie Barrow was born a slave on the Barrow Plantation in Natchez, Mississippi, shortly before the Civil War. She ginned cotton with her mother until her mother died, shortly after giving birth to Emeline's brother, Hemp Barrow. Her mother is believed to have been raped by her master's brother. Emmie Barrow left Mississippi to attend Fisk University. She returned home, buying land with her brother with money the family saved from selling cotton and milk. On her way home from college, she was raped by three white men aboard the train. When Barrow tried to get help from the conductor, the conductor threw her off the train, accusing her of disturbing the peace. Barrow wrote an article for the* Free Speech and Headlight *and then went on to start her own newspaper focused on women's rights. The Daily Wage ran for ten years, reaching a circulation of*

some twenty thousand readers, most of them African American.
She remained close to her brother, who later changed his name to
distance himself from the Barrow family.

The text framing Emmie Barrow's face looked like an enlarged halo. Emmie Barrow wore her hair pinned into a bun on the top of her head. She looked stern but on the verge of a smile, like she had a secret she couldn't wait for the other person to find out, even though it wouldn't come from her. A lace collar was clasped underneath her chin. Willie gazed at her and felt both energized and saddened. So maybe there was a reason she had been so dogged about what she wanted? Would she have fought harder if she had known about Emmie?

Willie stayed for several hours, reading old articles written by Emmie Barrow for *The Daily Wage*. That night, she pulled the covers up to her chin and thought about how the answers to her questions lay with the most successful woman in her family. She closed her eyes and allowed herself a handful of silent tears, which rolled down her cheekbones like rain, coating the pillow so that she felt glued to the cotton.

Chapter 19

Paloma was convinced Willie thought of herself as inter-changeable with anyone in the family, as though any Revel could step in and play the vaguely defined role of "Paloma's mother."

A couple of days after Lourdes got back from Mississippi, Paloma heard her grandparents fighting in the kitchen. She kept pretending she needed a soda, then chips, then more ice for her soda, so that she could pick up enough snatches of their conversation to deduce it had something to do with Willie and Max's work and the house and money. "With what money?" Lourdes repeated several times. Her grandfather had locked himself in the sun-room for the majority of time Lourdes had been away. Now he paced wildly back and forth. Paloma sat on the stairs listening, and after a few moments she heard Lourdes comforting Max. "I don't want you working with him, but I trust you. . . ." When she thought of her grandmother, Paloma imagined a beacon on top of a lighthouse, a light guiding the object of her attention to safety. First the object had been Lourdes herself, and then it became Max, then Seb and Willie, and finally Paloma.

Her grandmother's world consisted of the house. It was the one thing she could always control. For many hours of the day, with Max and Willie at work and Paloma at school, it was just Lourdes in the house. From the moment she woke, it cradled her, reminding her that every sacrifice was worth it. The cool marble of the kitchen countertops against her palm as she waited for coffee to brew. When she opened the back door and walked down the slate steps to her garden, there was only the most beautiful side of nature to greet her. Hummingbirds and ladybugs and finches in the summer. An expanse of snow in the winter, magnifying their yard. It was her own little kingdom. And then Paloma and Lourdes alone in the beauty on the days when Lourdes picked her up from school. The house helped each of them become themselves.

Paloma found her grandmother crying in the laundry room. She hadn't meant to startle her, but the basket tipped off the dryer, spilling clean towels all over the floor.

"Honey, you scared me." Her grandmother's voice was angry, but then her tone quickly changed. "Come on," she said. "Take a ride with me."

Paloma wanted to apologize when she saw Lourdes crying in the towels, but she wasn't sure what she was apologizing for. In the car, Lourdes hummed, which made Paloma wonder if maybe she had simply caught her grandmother at a bad time; maybe it was the exact moment lint flew into her eye and she hadn't been crying at all.

The car traveled down Germantown Avenue, farther than normal. The cobblestone road and trolley tracks remained, but the tenor changed. White faces became brown ones. Mothers became men. Stone twins with red shutters morphed into concrete two-stories with narrow windows. They pulled in front of a store with a black awning and gold lettering pasted across its windows. Her grandmother looked around and blinked her eyes, like she had been sleepwalking and woken up to find herself in the neighbors' yard. But they were there now. She got out of the car and Paloma followed. "Come on, hold my hand," Lourdes said.

Lourdes clutched a small cloth bag like the one Max's shoes came in. Paloma had seen her grandfather shine his shoes in his sunroom plenty of times, replacing them one by one to the cloth sacks and tightening the drawstrings. Lourdes held the black drawstring now and placed the bag on the counter.

Few pleasantries. There was no respectful greeting or small talk. A woman sat on a high stool at the other end of the glass counter, punching numbers into a calculator, and a man near the register gave them a mildly amused look. A light pulsed in the corner. Paloma could barely see over the top of the counter, eye level with a stack of black business cards: *Powell's Jewelers*, they said. Lourdes took out a watch from the bag and placed it on the counter. Paloma had played with that watch while sitting in her grandmother's lap, asking her if the time it told was the same as time everywhere. "Time doesn't play favorites," her grandmother had said. "Unlike me." And then she tickled Paloma, dangling her upside down on the couch. That watch—gone. The green hummingbird brooch her grandmother wore every day—gone. Earrings, bracelets, Christmas gifts from Max. The gold quill brooch that Lourdes had lent her after the incident in Miss Jacobs's class. Paloma could hear them making soft clangs on the glass. When she saw the gold quill broach, Paloma lunged for it. "No, not this. Please." Lourdes looked down and nodded. "Put it in your pocket." Paloma caught glimpses of the jewelry from beneath the counter like she was trapped underwater. The woman on the high stool barely paid attention to Lourdes or Paloma, but as they were leaving, the man smiled, revealing two missing teeth in the back of his mouth. He offered Paloma a red lollipop, but Lourdes kneed Paloma out the door.

Her grandmother was the type of person who believed if you arrived on time, you were already five minutes late. One needed time to get settled, to catch up with friends, and if you didn't allow for the padding of life's inevitabilities, you were at best foolish, at worst lazy. From what Paloma could glean of the situation, Lourdes realized the Revels were late. And what did *late* mean? What did *comfort* mean? Freedom to buy what you wanted at the grocery store, to host parties with a full spread, to buy new clothes, to plan, to execute. Paloma didn't know the particulars—Lourdes shared a lot with her but not that. The Revels' comfort had always ebbed and flowed with the business, but after Mississippi her grandmother seemed less content to ride the waves.

Chapter 20

The ancient Greeks called it *nostos*. A gallant homecoming.
Those left at home content themselves with routine, but for
the hero, the homecoming is always part of the point. A
thunderstrike of pride at the anticipated reactions; the thunderstrike turning to a cloud of disappointment as the homecoming
inevitably falls short. Some stretch to make it meet their expectations. Others pacify themselves knowing what they have seen is
for their eyes alone. Willie was pacified once she realized no one
saw her as the hero she'd hoped to be.

"What do you expect them to say?" Lourdes said while transferring a loaf of bread from the oven to a cutting board. What *did*
she expect? She thought she'd get questions—about Lou Barrow
or the letters or Emmie. But all she got were the muted reactions

of "That's something" or "Hmm." Or from Marcus: a blank stare and the hint of a smile.

Maybe it was because they already knew how the story ended. Willie wanted the name of the Barrow family, the discovery, the confirmation, to mean something, but as she read the ledger out loud, pointed to the census records, she slowly understood the power of history is that it works in reverse. The magic had lost its luster for Max and Marcus, because it would be of little help—they had already figured out how to define themselves without knowing who they came from. But perhaps it could still mean something for the rest of them—herself, Seb, Paloma.

"That son of a bitch," Seb said after reading the Barrows' letters, which Willie happily showed him when they were out to dinner with Paloma the night after she got back. His anger was a welcome revelation. The letters were somewhere they could put it all; all the emotion and angst stored up, waiting to explode, finally with reason. When she told Max and Marcus and Lourdes about Emmie Barrow, they had been appreciative but not awed. Now she laid out copies of Emmie Barrow's obituary and articles from *The Daily Wage* and pulled Paloma in closer.

Paloma's eyes scanned the pages. "Is this my souvenir?"

Willie pointed to Emmie's picture. "This is your great-great-great-aunt. She was a writer like you. She started her own newspaper in Mississippi."

Paloma examined the pages. As if remembering an unpleasant task, she looked up at Willie and asked, "And what about my dad's side of the family? How will I know about them?"

Willie inhaled sharply and looked at Seb.

"The truth is I know very little about your dad," Willie replied, turning back to Paloma. "We met only twice. He said he wasn't ready to be a father. We never spoke again after that."

Paloma's expression made her look older than she was, conveying somehow both concern and disappointment. "So, you don't know who he is?"

"I can tell you his first name and where he lived the last time I saw him. That's the best I can do."

Paloma looked back down at her paper. "What's his name?"

"Arman."

"Where did he live?"

Willie pictured herself standing in the filthy room with the black curtains. "He lived in an apartment downtown."

Paloma nodded and picked up Emmie Barrow's obituary, examining her face until the waitress brought their food.

Later, Willie scanned the photocopies, uploaded them, wrote in the required explanations underneath each document about what it meant and why it mattered, and submitted her application for Forgiveness. Seb did the same, and they watched as their status slid to *Pending*. Max and Marcus complicated things. She tried submitting applications on their behalf, but the system rejected them. "I'll walk you through how to do it," she told them. Willie brought her computer to Marcus and sat with him as he created an account. She felt his palm lightly grip her shoulder when he finally submitted the documentation. Max tapped the papers on his desk and handed her the signed Soteria contract. "If you get the check, then I'll submit mine." Their total pending compensation was $875,000.

—

The night of Paloma's play Lourdes stood across from Willie in the kitchen, her ears naked of her special-occasion pearls.

"This was the point of the house. Selling it and not having to lose everything means it served its purpose." Lourdes kept repeating versions of this around the house as if trying to convince herself it was true, her eyes unyielding and alert.

Willie looked out over the backyard, where her old yellow swing gently swayed back and forth. Her heart shuttered. First Hemp and now them. Maybe it was a family curse to lose the homes they loved the most.

They took separate cars to Paloma's play. Willie and Jared in one. Max, Seb, and Lourdes in another. Willie placed her hand on the back of Jared's neck as he drove, feeling the rope of his muscles tighten. "We signed the contract with Soteria," she told him, trying to take his mind off the lawsuit: His family was one of thousands suing the House Appropriations Committee because the plantation owners with the necessary records refused to release them to the public. They had tried to pick up where they left off and the relationship was taking slowly, like a jumped engine. Neither of them had anticipated how much energy the Forgiveness Act would take out of them. But while Willie was slowly being replenished, Jared shut down, burrowing into his work and trying not to be jaded by Willie's pending application.

"Hank's company wants to demolish a few houses near the processing facility to enlarge it before we start work," Willie continued. "Something feels off about it."

Jared shook his head. "Why would they need to demolish houses?"

"I don't know. The facility is already up to code. We ran a hauling job there years ago when it was first being built. Probably why Max feels some weird loyalty to the place."

"How are you feeling about working with Hank?"

"Have you ever seen your parents scared?" she replied, and he sighed and glanced at her before saying he understood. What she didn't say was that it no longer mattered what she felt, and that her acceptance of this could be seen as either a failing or a reckoning. The extent of the shift surprised even her. As if by learning her history she undid the trivial things that couldn't define her.

The auditorium was already full when they arrived, but Paloma had reserved seats for them. They made their way to the left wing, looking as if they were expecting to meet the cast of a Broadway show.

Willie spotted Paloma at the edge of the stage. She watched as her daughter tucked a pen behind her ear and pointed eagerly to a piece of paper, giving notes to two cast members. Paloma turned, saw Willie, and waved reluctantly. Then she quickly disappeared behind the curtain.

Willie sat down between Jared and Lourdes, scanning the room. Mr. Jeremy stood in the wings with a clipboard. A few mothers hovered in a semicircle near the exit, gossiping. Willie was happy to have kept an appropriate enough distance that she wouldn't be expected to join them. The lights flickered twice, signaling everyone to take their seats. Willie looked at the stage, which was designed to resemble a mansion. Large columns were positioned in each corner. Green curtains made of crimped construction paper hung in the middle of one wall. The students had painted portraits of the former governor of Massachusetts, Thomas Hutchinson, his wife, and their five children, in varying degrees of leisure: Hutchinson with a gun, hunting; Hutchinson and his wife, Margaret, sitting in a chair gazing out a window; Hutchinson with his wife and children sitting on a sofa. The portraits were surprisingly detailed and professional. Willie glanced at Jared and raised an eyebrow, impressed. He squeezed her hand as the lights dimmed.

Paloma, who it turned out was playing Phillis Wheatley, stepped onstage wearing a white petticoat and bonnet. She walked to the center, illuminated by a single spotlight, and began to sing.

> *Little drops of water,*
> *Little grains of sand,*
> *Make the mighty ocean*
> *And the pleasant land*

"Do you know my name? They say they want me to prove I wrote the poems. But can they prove to me what my name was? Who I was before they took me and named me? Phillis: a pleasant name for a terrifying journey. Prove to them I'm capable of poetry? For what else could I possibly be made? On the other side of this door my judges await. Steel yourself, Phillis: Proof will take more than knowledge."

Then she sang again, before stepping into the audience and asking people along the aisles, "Do you know my name? Do you

know my name?" until she made her way to the exit of the auditorium.

The lights came up. Moms reached for purses propped against
their chairs. Dads stretched their legs. The rest of the audience
stirred as Willie held her breath and stayed rigid in her chair.

"You sure she's only in fifth grade?" Jared whispered.

As in art, as in life, the first act prepared everyone for the second. It moved quickly. Children pretending to be old men formed
a semicircle around Paloma and lobbed questions at her, trying to
get her to prove she had written the poems. Twenty minutes later
the play ended, and Willie moved slowly through the aisles, not
wanting to talk to anyone for fear of bursting into tears. While
Jared was in the bathroom, Willie stood in the hallway, pretending to appraise a student's rendering of a tulip. Mr. Jeremy approached her, his fedora tipped back, revealing his forehead. "Ms.
Revel?" he said, touching her elbow. She turned to face him. "I
just want to say how talented I think Paloma is. I really had to
fight the powers that be to get this play performed"—his eyes
gestured toward Fern Jacobs, who was lingering behind them at
the entrance to the auditorium—"but I wanted you to know I
fought for this because I think she has real potential. I'd love to set
up a time to discuss Paloma's options with you. There are programs we can enroll her in. I sent you a letter a few months ago,
but I never got a response."

Willie nodded, forcing a smile. "I can't thank you enough for
giving her a home here."

"I'm so proud of you," Willie told Paloma when she approached, and pulled her forcefully into a hug.

"Mom," Paloma whined, squirming away but smiling.

—

The next day Lourdes made fish sticks and garlic potatoes for Paloma's celebratory lunch. They all raised glasses of lemonade. "Here's to our future playwright." Paloma stood and took a bow as she laughed and nudged Willie, telling her it was time to go. The cast and crew were having a party to celebrate the play.

Back home, Lourdes tried to convince Willie, Seb, and Max that selling the house was the right thing to do.

Max tried to avoid having the opinion he knew was the right one. The contract with Hank was signed, he said, though they hadn't started working for Soteria. One contract, he knew, was not enough to bet the business on.

"We can't sell the house," Seb said before breaking into a persistent fit of coughing, which had more or less lingered since his arrest.

"What if the business goes under?" Lourdes asked.

"We won't let that happen," Max said softly, looking at Willie.

Willie's mind kept returning to Hemp refusing to leave Natchez and the little good it did him.

She didn't know how to ease into it, so Willie told Paloma about the house while out for a walk after her party. "We're selling the house," she blurted, taking a sip from her water bottle and looking over at Paloma.

Her daughter nodded. "Yeah, I know. I mean, I figured that was happening."

Paloma stopped to pet a stranger's dog that had tangled its

leash around her legs. Afterward they walked on in silence, the wintry air biting any skin that was exposed. "I can leave Walton," Paloma continued, her voice serious. "You can take me out of Walton and sell the things in my room. That will give us money, maybe enough to keep the house?"

Willie wished she could take her daughter up on the offer. Nothing more than a simple bargain. "I wish it were that easy." She watched an eagle circle wide overhead, then land on the top of a tree, drawing in its wings like a blanket wrapped tightly around itself.

"How did this happen?" Paloma asked. She had a stern look on her face, the one she used when she didn't want to cry. How did it happen? Willie asked herself this often. The answer was that Max's strengths were also his weaknesses, and his ambition put them on the road to success but also ran them off it.

Willie pushed her hands deep into her pockets. "The banks wouldn't lend your great-grandpa money to buy a house. Did you know that? They wouldn't give him a mortgage. And then your grandpa worked very hard to build a company that made enough money so we could afford our home. Everyone faces rough times at one point or another. Some people don't have any-thing to fall back on when it happens, and some people do. Our cushion is medium. We can sell the house and we'll be okay."

They stopped short of a red covered bridge and watched the water. Paloma picked up a few stones and tried to skip them, but they crashed into the creek and sank.

"You and Pop Pop work all the time. I don't get it."

Willie put her arm around Paloma's shoulder, and the two of

them stood looking out at the brown water, the orange tails of a few fish motoring by.

"Try to think of it as a new adventure. You and me, living alone." Willie sounded like Lourdes, trying to convince herself it was true. But standing by the creek's edge with her daughter, she chose optimism. Despite the ways family hurts you, you stay because they're yours. Max belittled her, was at times misogynistic, but had come to depend on and appreciate her. Lourdes infuriated her with her demands, but her demands were the avenues through which her love traveled. Willie was frustrated with her family but also proud and grateful. In the end, if you were lucky, family was all you had.

Willie and Paloma walked across the covered bridge, and Paloma stopped to pet another dog, this time a golden retriever, its tail kicking up dust in the dirt. The dog sat in front of a stone marker that explained how the Wissahickon Valley Park once belonged to the Lenni-Lenape. Willie looked at Paloma petting the dog urgently, that stern look on her face to keep herself from crying.

Chapter 21

Why would Soteria need to tear down those houses? She drove to the material-processing facility and parked behind a large white Soteria truck stopped just beyond the metal gates. Workers loaded construction debris into the back of the vehicle, oblivious to Willie standing there watching. This facility, she knew from reading documents on the job requirements, was supposed to have a tightly controlled process for any trash entering the space, since it was reserved for recycling. She peered through the metal grates and took pictures of heaps of trash and debris.

MRA had not yet been granted access to the facility. When she drove up to the entrance, she tried explaining to the guard that she was a subcontractor.

"Can I see your pass?"

"I don't have one yet," Willie said. "But I can show you a copy of the contract."

He stepped away and radioed someone elsewhere in the plant. A few moments later a skinny man in a navy suit approached her car, wearing a forced smile. "We can't let you in today," he told her sympathetically. "All guests have to be cleared beforehand. But let me talk to Hank and see if we can't expedite a pass for you in the next week. Why exactly did you need to come in?"

Willie made up an excuse about needing to see where her guys would be working.

"Right," the man said. "I'll be in touch."

"I think you should look into this," she said, calling Jared and explaining what she saw. "I took pictures." She was grateful he didn't laugh; it would have been easy to dismiss her curiosity for the boredom of a failed journalist.

They began work on the job—both Max and Willie were given limited clearance to the facility. Max rarely went, but every day Willie drove down and walked through the areas where she was permitted, taking more pictures, striking up conversations with Soteria employees.

A few weeks later, Jared called to tell her that together with Clean Water PHL, an environmental nonprofit in Fishtown, he'd found that illegal disposal of the debris and illegal dumping created a risk of arsenic, lead, and asbestos leaching into the groundwater. He had interviews scheduled with several Soteria employees who were willing to talk anonymously. Soteria would likely lose the contract and probably also the ability to control a plant in the future. Hank had been getting tax write-offs for the facility. He never planned on recycling—just on hiding it long enough to get the pub-

lic dollars and then getting out of management of the facility before anything could be pinned on him or Soteria. Willie reasoned
that Hank probably would have tried to blame the illegal dumping on his subcontractors, including MRA. "My editor wants this
published within the week," Jared told her.

Before Jared's article was published, Willie began preparing a
formal bid for MRA to take over the facility, so that when it became public, they would be prepared. She wanted to wait until
the details were worked out, but when Max saw her working late
and asked what she was doing, she explained what happened.

"It means the city will sue Soteria. If they accept my bid, we'll
inherit the contract instead."

Max stared at her for so long that she thought he was upset
with her for ruining a relationship she didn't know about. "You
would have been a damn good journalist," he said finally.

There was enough money in the pipeline to keep the business
going, so, if they could keep chipping away at Max's medical bills,
whether to sell the house was up to them. *Real inheritance. Our
people don't get that kind of thing every day.*

When people toured 512 Lewaro Street, Willie went on long
drives after dropping Paloma off at school. She didn't tell anyone
where she was going. When Jared asked how her day was, she
told him, "Busy," or "Nothing special." If Max wondered where
she went during the day, he never asked. Her office sat untouched,
as though she had merely stepped out for a meeting. Now that
she had gotten them control of the facility, she needed to figure

out what it was she really wanted. If they got the money from Forgiveness, would she stay?

On her first drive, she ended up down the shore. An hour and a half down the Atlantic City Expressway; no traffic because it was a Tuesday. She took off her shoes and walked barefoot to the water's edge, moving back slowly out of reach as soon as the tide came in. The sand felt rough and soothing, grinding underneath her toes with no water to give it traction. She preferred it this way—the tactile and fleeting nature of it. She took out a blanket and spread it over the sand, sitting on top until the sky turned gray. She watched the waves, the soft folding and tucking of foam. She had ceased yearning for the unattainable. There was no one to blame. At this point, she had tried to stop thinking about the Forgiveness money in terms of tangible funds—it had been over three months since she'd submitted the application. She still wanted the Revels to get the money, of course, but her future didn't, it couldn't, depend on it. Maybe she would begin pitching articles again; she imagined starting her own magazine if they did get the money. She needed to find the grooves in the path, the clues, like she would in a story. She walked to the boardwalk, wondering how the owners of the stores decided to stay open: A T-shirt store was closed, but the souvenir shop next to it was open. A clerk leaned over the glass counter, looking out at the water. Willie stopped in a café and purchased a cup of coffee and a blueberry muffin. She sat on a bench near the café's entrance and stared at the ocean, breaking off pieces of the muffin and licking crumbs off her fingers, tasting the salt from both the topping and the air.

One morning, she asked Celine and Nell to take off from work and go to the beach with her.

"So, what are you going to do with the money?" Willie asked Nell, drawing one knee and then the other up to her chin.

Nell smoothed the blanket over the sand. Across her forehead was a thin, dark scar from the bottle, giving her face a new look of severity.

"Am I not supposed to ask that?"

"You can ask it. It feels anticlimactic. I'm going to pay for a better doctor for Mom, and I decided I'm going to apply for medical school."

Willie told them about getting control of the facility for MRA.

"That means you're going to stay?" Celine asked.

Willie looked at her, confused. "I mean," Celine said, looking at her watch, "it's Wednesday afternoon and you're not at work. Are you going to keep working there?"

"For a while I was so scared of the regret I'd feel in the future. It's like it stopped even being about writing stories or what it would be like to *be* a journalist and was more about what I would think of myself in the future, could I live with not achieving this one thing I thought I wanted."

"Of course you can live with it," Nell said. "The point is you think you shouldn't have to."

"I *thought* I shouldn't have to. We're all living some version of our lives for our parents. What we think they want; what we think they don't want. Maybe you have to realize that before you can live the life *you* want."

"What do you want?" Nell asked.

"I want to be happy even if nothing changes."

They sat shoulder to shoulder, staring out at the water, until the cold sent them home.

Many, many times, Willie imagined how the conversation might go if she ran into Arman on the street. When she was nine months pregnant: *She's real. It's not too late for you to change your mind.* When Paloma was a baby: *This is your daughter. She's beautiful, isn't she?* When Paloma was five: *She needs her father, but I wasn't sure how to tell you now that it's been so long.* Now: *I should have insisted you be part of her life.* She wouldn't even admit to herself where she was driving to until she pulled up in front of Arman's building—or the building that used to be his.

As she parked, the hosts on NPR were trying to guess at what the president would say when she came on for a press conference, a thing that always annoyed her. Why not just play music if they didn't know how to fill the time, Willie thought, or admit they had no idea like everyone else.

She watched the entrance to Arman's building as the president began speaking.

This is an important time for our nation. We are coming together now to ask for forgiveness from a group we have wronged for far too long. But it is not simply enough to ask for forgiveness. We must— all of us—mean it with all of our hearts and acknowledge that the way we seek forgiveness is just as important as the why.

I understand that the past few months have been difficult for many Americans. Families have come forward seeking to claim the funds they are rightly due, and far too many have been denied. The road to forgiveness is not a straight and narrow path but a long and winding journey. We wish there was a simpler way. We wish we could hand out funds to everyone who requests them. But to maintain order we must put in place checks and balances. We appreciate America's patience as we work to understand how to implement these checks and balances.

It is imperative to ensure that new legislation is viewed as living and breathing. Which is why the executive branch of government must be ready to adapt when the new legislation we enact is not functioning as intended. Such is the case with the Forgiveness Act. Effective immediately, the United States government will offer genealogy grants to every American who has identified as African American on the census for the past ten years and who is at least eighteen years of age. A genealogy grant in the sum of two thousand dollars will be issued to pay for the excavation of individual historical records, distributed by family.

The purpose of this grant is to ask the Black Americans of our nation once again for forgiveness. One of the most heinous effects of slavery is that it has made the process of proving ancestral heritage extremely difficult. This was not given enough weight when the Forgiveness Act first passed. This grant is an effort at good faith.

In addition to grants, we will also hire five thousand people immediately to help process Forgiveness Act applications. We will no longer require official government records to approve each application but will instead attempt to adapt to the nuance of unique situa-

tions. By offering jobs to thousands of Americans, we will have the ability to read through the applications and deduce whether unofficial records, such as family Bibles or photographs, prove eligibility. These updates are to show the American people, and the world, that when the United States government commits wrongs, we hold ourselves accountable. Even if it comes four hundred years too late.

With love and compassion, we will move this great nation forward.

Willie watched a man get out of a gray Honda Accord, and she knew without him having to turn around that it was Arman. His hair was the same. The way he held his wrist at a nervous, agitated angle. She should get out and yell to him. Show him a picture of Paloma. Give him a chance, another one. Instead, she started the car and drove away, with the idea of resubmitting the Revels' application given the president's new announcement, in the hopes that submitting it again would increase the chances of how quickly it was reviewed.

Back home the front door of 512 Lewaro was open; the family touring the house was in the backyard. She walked quickly up to her room, refusing to admit she was sneaking into her own house.

On her way upstairs, she heard a man—the husband, she assumed—tell the realtor that he built model airplanes in his spare time, and she hated the image that came to mind, of winged structures hanging from a ceiling, spinning uselessly in the basement.

She put her keys on her dresser and her purse on the floor. She raked her hands through her curls, trying to ignore the tangles, yanking anyway. It felt like the room was closing in on her. They could keep the house—as long as she could get the application submitted again, if the government could approve the documents and issue the checks before anyone put an offer in.

Willie suddenly heard a rustling in Paloma's room. She found a girl sitting at her daughter's desk. The girl didn't hear Willie approach behind her. She continued looking through the papers, stopping every now and then to peer out of the window.

"Can I help you?" Willie asked loudly.

The girl spun around quickly, dropping a notebook. "I—" She stopped and stood.

"Tami?" Willie recognized her as a girl from Paloma's grade.

"I'm sorry," she said, squatting to pick up the notebook and returning it to the desk. "I . . . I stayed home sick from school and everyone said Paloma's play was so good and I've never been inside her house. We walked through her room, and I just wanted to feel what it was like."

Willie narrowed her eyes, fighting the urge to grab the girl by the arm and drag her out of the house. "Feel like what is like?"

"To be good at something."

Willie tried to relax her face. "Why don't you go find your parents?" She nodded toward the window. "They're probably looking for you."

Tami sprinted out of the room.

Willie sat down at Paloma's desk and opened the notebook Tami had been holding. Paloma's handwriting was etched neatly in the margin: *Phillis never had a home, not really, so how can I be upset about losing mine?*

Chapter 22

Tami approached Paloma in the library. "I saw your room," she said. Paloma hated when people spoke loudly in the library, as if whatever they had to say was more important than what anyone was reading, which could never be true.

Paloma narrowed her eyes. "I'm sorry?"

"I saw your room." Tami looked left and right. "My family is thinking of buying your house."

Can only one person feel an earthquake? Paloma had sick visions. Tami in her room playing dress-up or acting out a marriage between plastic Barbies.

"Don't worry," Tami said. "I don't think we're going to get it. My mom likes new construction."

Paloma's face grew hot. She looked back down at her book.

"We really shouldn't talk in here," she said, and stared at the pages until she felt Tami leaving.

Sometimes she wondered what it would be like to live alone with Willie. She imagined worse food and empty silences. Nights filled with Willie in her own room, contemplating alternate realities, and Paloma in hers, creating them.

Chapter 23

The check arrived one hot afternoon in June, nearly five months after Willie resubmitted their application. She had finally moved on from waiting for the money and was sitting in the library after work when Lourdes presented her with an envelope stamped in the corner with a sky-blue seal.

In fact there wasn't one check, but two, one made out to Willie and one for Seb for $87,500 each.

"I don't think they sent a personal apology," Lourdes said, as Willie peered inside the envelope, dumping it upside down, confused by the lower amount. There wasn't an apology but there was a letter, explaining how the remaining $87,500 for Willie and $87,500 for Seb was being kept in a trust. *A method,* the letter explained, *implemented to prevent inflation.*

Willie put the checks on the desk, and she and Lourdes stared down at them like they were fabric swatches for new curtains. "Well," Lourdes said, "Marcus called and said he got his too. You did it."

Willie looked down at the checks again and felt the way she should have felt when a lab had spit out the origins of her DNA. There was significance and ownership and names and sacrifices, a point and a weight to it that until now had been unaccounted for. Yes, the money helped.

Until then, Max and Willie had gone back to work, Lourdes had picked up several odd jobs at the library. Ultimately, they had been unable to sell the house when the time came to choose among the offers. It was Lourdes who looked around the table at her family and then quietly picked up the papers with offers written on them and tossed them in the trash.

It was as if the Forgiveness Act had been a flash flood, sweeping up the country in the momentum of change until there was nothing left to grasp ahold of or to save. A lot of families continued to have pending applications, hanging in a state of uncertainty where they were forced to carry on as they otherwise would have. Once it became clear there was not going to be an immediate windfall for millions of families, the mobs grew tired and found another cause to focus on.

She tucked the checks back into the envelope. Willie looked up at Lourdes. "We should have a party."

Cars lined the driveway and spilled into the street. Seb stood at the grill, flipping hamburgers and toasting buns. Lourdes and Max scoured the garden, picking more tomatoes to add to the already robust salad. Willie, taking in the bounty they had brought inside, gazed at the spheres of tomatoes that had once lent the vines their purpose; the five eggplants striking as large teardrops. She remembered when the garden used to be her favorite hiding spot, pretending to hide but secretly hoping to be found. She inhaled deeply. Each season the soil offered itself up as a clean slate with the promise of all that was possible: the potential, if the seeds were planted just right and given enough diligence and attention, to feed, to nourish, to sustain. But as much promise as it held, there was also the not-unlikely chance of disappointment, of a natural event beyond your control destroying all your careful planning.

Willie looked out at the pool and watched as Paloma and Jared took turns dunking a basketball, twisting and swirling in the air, each of them eager and sun-drenched. The doorbell brought her back. She ran to answer it and gazed up the driveway, her eyes taking in what, for now, was still theirs.

Lourdes appeared next to her. "Who lives here?" she asked.

Epilogue

The front yard of the Revel home in Natchez, Mississippi, on the edge of town, near the school. It is June, and the air from the Mississippi River is warm and fragrant.

The stage is bordered by a white picket fence, and shrubs not quite two feet tall appear to the R and L, creating a feeling of comfort and safety. A garden can be seen to the R in the front yard. Upstage there is a small white house with faded porch steps. A small well is situated to the L with a red bucket next to it, the rope languishing, limp in the shade.

It's early in the morning. HEMP REVEL stands on his porch and gazes out in front of him, one hand on his hip while the other holds a pipe between his lips. MINNIE REVEL and a young boy, their grandson, come out and stand beside him. People begin to gather behind the fence. Three, four, five, six. A small crowd stands and waits for HEMP REVEL to speak.

Paloma placed the pages aside, put on her slippers, threw on a sweatshirt, and walked into the kitchen for a glass of water.

She sat down at her desk and opened her computer. Her desk was nestled into a corner next to their green velvet couch, facing a black-and-white framed photo of herself with Willie, Max, Lourdes, Seb, and Marcus—the last photo she took with her great-grandfather. She kissed two fingers and placed them on top of the photo, like she always did before beginning to write.

Because she still didn't know what to say in her speech, she pressed the space bar and watched the cursor dance across the screen.

She leaned back, placing her feet up on the desk, and reflected on the defining moments of her life.

The night she performed her first play.

The day her mom picked her up early from school to watch the president sign the Forgiveness Act.

The day in sixth grade when she and her mom moved out of 512 Lewaro and into their own two-bedroom apartment a few minutes away.

The day she got into Juilliard.

Paloma had spent evenings digging in the backyard of Lewaro Street, looking for talismans she had buried over the years. A drama-mask key chain, a white marble, a gold heart previously attached to a necklace from a Wheaties box. Those were the things she could find. Somewhere in the yard at 512 Lewaro there remained a black pen with her initials, more marbles, a sofa from a dollhouse, and a pair of wings. Maybe she would look for them again the next time she went home.

Her phone rang and she greeted the raspy voice of her publicist.

"Are you done?"

Paloma caught a glimpse of herself in the mirror and stuck out her tongue at her own reflection. "Working on it."

"Look. They called and asked me how many seats you want to reserve."

"How many seats?"

"I thought you only get two tickets but turns out they're giving you more." Janine started whispering as if someone could overhear her, but Paloma heard Janine's chihuahua barking in the background, which meant Janine was home alone in her apartment, probably wearing sweatpants. "I think this means you're going to win. I mean, they didn't say that. They can't say that. But, you know."

Paloma was sitting there trying to write a speech, so she must have considered the possibility of winning. But hearing Janine, she realized it had only been a wish, like a stage before a play. Paloma dug out old coffee grounds from under her fingernails.

"Let me think about it and get back to you."

Janine sighed. "Let me know how many tickets by the end of the day. And, Paloma? Finish the goddamn speech. We know you're not good off the cuff."

—

When she first moved to New York, she was sitting alone at a bar, and the woman next to her kept staring. Eventually Paloma gave in and stared back.

"I knew it was you!" The woman pointed. "Paloma Revel, right? We went to Walton together. Sia Dorn."

They talked for hours and became the friends they never were at school. Now Paloma waited for Sia to answer the phone, tapping her fingernails impatiently on the linoleum.

"Why are you calling me so early?" Sia said, yawning on the other end of the line.

"What if they find out I'm a fraud?"

Sia sighed. Paloma listened to her drink some water.

"The only thing they're going to find out is how brilliant you are. Trust me."

"Will you come to the ceremony?"

"I'm offended you're even asking."

Paloma smiled. "Thank you. Go back to sleep. We'll talk later."

Paloma looked out the window. The same bar that a few hours ago had thrown people out onto the sidewalk was now subdued. A busboy sprayed the pavement down with a hose. Paloma left the apartment, hoping she could write better at the coffee shop in her nook by the window. It was a Friday, and the restaurants and stores were peppered with tourists and young workers. The sun cast a halo of weekend promise. She lifted her eyebrows, shrugging her sunglasses over her eyes, and hitched her bag higher up her shoulder.

Two white women walked toward her, blocking the sidewalk. It was a game she played, to see if they would make space. As often happened, neither moved, instead expecting her to step into the dirt where dog shit lined the base of a tree, but she never did, which meant she ended up standing face-to-face with one of the women like they were preparing to box each other, until eventually the woman stood behind her friend before continuing on. "Unbelievable," she could hear one of them saying. "So rude."

She nodded to Ryan when she got to the coffee shop. "Make it a double, okay?" He gave her a thumbs-up, and she walked over to her table and put her bag down in the center to save her spot. People were dotted throughout the café—stragglers reading books; a few tourists examining maps; stressed young professionals typing hurriedly, as if the harder they hit the keys, the sooner their bosses would stop bothering them. She swiped a discarded *New York Times Magazine* from the table next to her and sat down. The cover was a profile of Maurice Dunbar, the entrepreneur who a week ago was named the richest man in the United States. She flipped to the story and read the pull quote in the center of the page: *I wouldn't have succeeded without the comfort of knowing I could fail.* He was who he was because of the Forgiveness Act, just like her. And she wondered, like she often did: Would they have become themselves anyway? Was it destiny or just the crude calculation of dollars and cents that landed them on their paths? She had no college loans and could focus on the play that had now gotten her nominated for an Obie.

Paloma called Willie, waiting impatiently as she found a quiet spot away from the job site. "It turns out I get extra tickets for the awards ceremony. They asked me to tell them how many people I want to invite."

Willie squealed excitedly. "This means you're going to win. I knew it."

"We don't know that."

"They only tell you to invite more people if they know you're going to win."

When she met Kevin for dinner, their favorite bartender was pouring him a shot of sake and leaning over to whisper something into his ear. Paloma placed her hand on the middle of his back, and he swiveled around, slowly, to encircle her waist without breaking eye contact with the bartender.

They were still tender from their fight a few days ago, tiptoeing along the edges of their affection. "Not all of us had fancy teachers to pave our way!" he screamed at her from across the apartment, slamming his palm against the wall so that the little dish with their keys rattled.

"Why do you always do that? Don't compare our journeys," she said. "Everyone is on their own grind." She bit into an apple then and knew it infuriated him. Her faux casualness. They say girls marry their fathers, but what if you didn't grow up with one? What type of person do you end up with then? She was eighteen by the time she finally asked Willie for her father's address. With Jared in their lives, the issue was less urgent, even offensive. For all intents and purposes, Jared was her dad. He was there every morning and every night. His sister took Paloma to her first concert. His people became her people. There was a dull nagging, but the relentless drive to know who her father was had subsided.

Paloma drove by her father's supposed apartment once. She waited half an hour but didn't see anyone walking out of the building who looked like her. She started the car, turned on Tracy Chapman, and drove off. Two days later she moved to New York.

She and Kevin sat down in a corner booth now and she unwrapped her chopsticks, rubbing them together as if starting a fire. The waiter brought over rolls: salmon and avocado, eel, and shrimp tempura.

"You wrote your speech?"

"Yup," she lied, piling wasabi on top of the avocado and balancing ginger slices on top of that.

"There's nothing to prove, you know. Especially if you win, but even if you don't. You made it. Just have fun."

She laughed and moved her index finger to grip the roll and bring it to her mouth. "That's what you don't understand," she said. "There's always something to prove."

The day of the ceremony, Willie, Jared, and Lourdes stood in Paloma's small kitchen, pouring themselves coffee. Kevin sat on the couch, his feet crossed on top of the coffee table, Max asleep next to him. Sia sat on the window ledge, holding a cigarette out the window.

"I don't think I want to go," Paloma announced.

"That's your introversion talking," Kevin said, turning on the television.

"Have some water." Willie walked to the faucet and filled Paloma a glass.

They piled into a black SUV and rode into Manhattan. As they arrived, Jared whispered into her ear, "I will take care of your mother and grandparents. You have fun, okay?" He gave her a kiss on the cheek as they climbed out of the car. She checked her phone, and there was a text from Mr. Jeremy, whom she had also invited to the ceremony. *We're here!! Thank you again for the opportunity. Go give 'em hell.* She typed back quickly, *Thank you for making this all possible.* Seb too had texted her, a series of exclamation points at which she smiled, knowing he would have loved to be there but was traveling.

Paloma was the underdog, and most critics viewed her nomination as nothing but a courtesy to acknowledge the potential of her future work.

"You look stunning!" Janine appeared and gripped her elbow. "I'll show you where your seats are." Janine understood Paloma's anxiety, appreciated it even. And while other publicists would be forcing their clients to mingle and sip champagne, Janine handed her a glass of red wine and got her settled into the fourth row without any pressuring or cajoling. She preferred to let Paloma's work speak for itself.

The lights dimmed and the music started. Paloma tried to breathe deeply, focusing on the rise and fall of her chest. And then it was her turn, and they were listing the nominees for the playwriting award.

She went to reach for Kevin's hand, then thought better of it, tucking her fingers between her thighs instead and glancing at Sia.

The announcer opened the envelope, slower than Paloma would have thought possible. She paused and Paloma's palms filled with sweat. She waited to hear anyone's name but her own, but when she heard hers, her mouth opened and her first instinct was to look at Willie, who was nodding, ignoring the tears running down her face. Paloma pretended to know what to do next and walked to the stage, gripping the award when it was handed to her. She had never written her speech. She hadn't needed to.

"The first play I ever produced was about a woman who had to prove she was capable of her own poetry. Who had her identity stripped from her. I'm standing here today because of my mom. Because my family always believed I was capable—my grandparents, my uncle. I love you. And I'm here because of one teacher—Mr. Jeremy—who taught me to know my space even if the space I was in was never built to know me. To every child wondering if they're worthy of following their dreams: You are all the proof you need."

Before she walked off the stage, she stared out into the audience, finding Willie once again and thanking the faces that weren't there.

Author's Note

The world looked very different in October 2019, when I first started writing this book, than it did when I finished. I had recently written a piece for *The Atlantic* about the racial wealth gap in America and was thinking about what a federal reparations policy might actually look like. Some of those questions, I felt, could best be answered—or at least explored—through fiction. Then, while writing the first draft, Breonna Taylor, George Floyd, and Ahmaud Arbery were murdered, and the United States, once again, underwent some semblance of a racial reckoning. I have intentionally left the present time frame in the book ambiguous. While the country paid attention to the murders of Breonna Taylor, George Floyd, and Ahmaud Arbery, there were many more who were killed when the country wasn't watching. By declining to pin the events in this book to a specific year, I want to acknowledge the prevalence of these events in our country's history and try to push back against what they mean for providing a "justification" around the conversation of reparations.

As the disclaimer states in the beginning, the events and the characters are fictional; however, there are real-life influences throughout the book. Willie's reflection on Lukács and Dostoevsky when she first enters college is from a book titled *Mimetic Lives: Tolstoy, Dostoevsky, and Character in the Novel* by Chloë Kitzinger. The Jamaican proverbs that come back to her are from Zora Neale Hurston's *Tell My Horse*. Much of the genealogy information and archival documents, including the questions in the genealogy workshop, come from *Finding a Place Called Home* by Dee Parmer Woodtor. Some of the information Willie reads while researching at the Historic Natchez Foundation comes from the Historic Natchez Foundation, Betty Shields McGehee Collection, Box II, "Journal of Dr. Walter R. Wade, Rosswood Plantation, Mississippi, Years 1855 to 1862." *From Here to Equality* by William A. Darity Jr. and A. Kirsten Mullen was an invaluable resource in thinking through the practical details and implications of Johnson's reparations policy. I visited the Mount Locust Inn while researching for the book, and certain language is taken from actual descriptions about the property written by the National Park Service. Certain excerpts from the Barrow papers are real; however, the letters between Bennet and Lou are fictional. Willie's ancestor Emmie Barrow is inspired by Ida B. Wells. The conversation Willie has with Celine and Nell on the beach is inspired by a conversation from James Baldwin's novel *Another*

Country. Willie's reference to "Lou Barrow's women" is inspired by Gayl Jones's incredibly powerful book *Corregidora.* Finally, the song that Paloma sings at the beginning of her play is from a Works Progress Administration slave narrative transcript that I read while researching this book.

Acknowledgments

I am indebted to too many people to name. My incredible agent, Stephanie Delman, for understanding my vision and helping me see it through. Khalid and the entire Trellis family for helping to bring my first book into the world. My editor, Chelcee, for believing in Willie and the Revels and for our many meetings and plotting sessions. Your advice and patience made this book better. Sydney and the Ballantine team for your care, energy, and attention. The staff at the Mississippi Department of Archives and the Historic Natchez Foundation—thank you for being so thoughtful and for walking me through Willie's journey as though she were a real person and not someone from my imagination. The trip was a spiritual journey I will never forget. Thank you to my early readers, especially my mom, but also William Thompson, Dr. William A. Darity, Larissa, and Laura. I am incredibly grateful for

Dee Parmer Woodtor's book *Finding a Place Called Home*. To Zach, always my first reader, for your encouragement and faith every step of the way. To my grandfather, for your stories and sense of humor. Endless gratitude for those who inspired me who are no longer here: Elizabeth Parker, Marjorie Cheeks, and Lenny Parker.

ABOUT THE AUTHOR

MAURA CHEEKS has published writing in *The New York Times*, *The Atlantic*, *The Paris Review*, and *Tin House*, among others. In 2019 she was awarded a masthead reporting residency with *The Atlantic*, where she produced the feature-length article that would later inspire the idea for her book. *Acts of Forgiveness* is her first novel.

Twitter: @mauracheeks

ABOUT THE TYPE

This book was set in Dante, a typeface designed by Giovanni Mardersteig (1892–1977). Conceived as a private type for the Officina Bodoni in Verona, Italy, Dante was originally cut only for hand composition by Charles Malin, the famous Parisian punch cutter, between 1946 and 1952. Its first use was in an edition of Boccaccio's *Trattatello in laude di Dante* that appeared in 1954. The Monotype Corporation's version of Dante followed in 1957. Though modeled on the Aldine type used for Pietro Cardinal Bembo's treatise *De Aetna* in 1495, Dante is a thoroughly modern interpretation of that venerable face.